BREAKING WORLD

THE LAST SANCTUARY: BOOK FOUR

KYLA STONE

Printed in the United States of America

Cover design by Deranged Doctor Designs

Book formatting by Vellum

First Printed in 2018

ISBN 978-1-945410-18-5

Paper Moon Press

Atlanta, Georgia

www.PaperMoonPress.com

 Created with Vellum

ALSO BY KYLA STONE

To Caleb and Ella, may you always fight for what is right, even when it requires risk and sacrifice.

1

AMELIA

Amelia Black lay belly-down against the hard, snow-packed dirt, dressed in camouflage tactical gear, a semi-automatic rifle in both gloved hands. She peered through the scope of a weapon she had no intention of firing.

Most of the time, you didn't know death was coming until it was already looming over you—a shadowy demon of howling fear. She felt that fear now, cold and sharp as a knife. Not for herself—for her mother.

Yesterday, a team had chosen the best location for the ambush— just after a steep bend, where the road carved deeply into the hills. Amelia, Gabriel, Micah, Willow, Silas, and two dozen New Patriots took the high ground. They were hidden among the trees and boulders along the steep hills bordering either side of the two-lane road leading off the highway.

They were surrounded by old forest, towering oaks interspersed with bristling pines and barren maple, birch, and hemlock trees. The underbrush was thick and tangled, sheathed with thorns.

Amelia sheltered beneath two pine trees. She couldn't see any of their people on the opposite hill, but she knew they were hiding there —waiting, ready. They had rubbed Georgia clay and dirt on their clothes and faces and covered themselves with dead leaves, twigs, and pine boughs.

Melting snow clung to the uneven ground in dirty patches. The air was bitterly cold. The sky was a brooding iron-gray, forecasting another snowstorm.

A dark sense of foreboding crept over her. Though it was Christmas morning, this was not a day that promised hope.

Two days ago, New Patriots scouts had sighted the Headhunters skirting the northern Atlanta suburbs on their way to the Sanctuary. Celeste, Finn, and Benjie remained at the compound, but everyone else insisted on joining the rescue mission.

She wasn't a skilled enough shooter to take part in the ambush. But she'd refused to remain at the New Patriots' compound, useless.

This was her mother. This was the rescue she'd traded her own freedom for.

She'd agreed to infiltrate the Sanctuary and offer herself to their scientists so they could formulate a cure from her blood. She was the only known survivor of the deadly pandemic known as the Hydra virus, which had wiped out most of the world's population.

Once the scientists formulated a cure, she was supposed to somehow steal it, escape the Sanctuary, and give it to the New Patriots.

The Sanctuary might offer salvation—or be crawling with the surviving members of the Unity Coalition. The powerful, corrupt government officials had secretly released the Hydra virus as a bioweapon against their own country. Declan Black, her father, had designed and implemented the entire thing...

She couldn't let herself fall down that rabbit hole. She had to focus on the now. First, they had to rescue her mother.

"Targets sighted," said a voice in her earpiece. "Two miles out."

Beside her, Gabriel Ramos Rivera said, "Copy that."

Amelia pushed a strand of her short white-blonde hair behind her ear. She breathed in the cold air through her mask, trying not to shiver. The adrenaline had faded after two hours spent stiff and unmoving, but the warning sent ice spiking through her veins. "The Headhunters are coming."

A vicious biker gang of thugs and criminals, the Headhunters had attacked them at Sweet Creek Farm after Harmony, the leader of Sweet Creek Farm, had betrayed them. The Headhunters had attempted to kidnap Amelia, Celeste, and Nadira to sell as "resources." They had succeeded in stealing Amelia's mother. Their friend Nadira had been killed in the battle.

Her stomach knotted at the haunting memory. But now the tables were turned. They were the ones setting the trap.

Still, there were too many questions, too many unknowns. Was her mother alive? Would they get her back safely? Would anyone she cared about get hurt in the process?

Gabriel shifted next to her. His breath came in shallow puffs of white steam. She could feel the tension in his body, a coiled spring ready to snap. His broad shoulder bumped into hers. Her stomach fluttered—from nerves, but also something else.

"How are you feeling?" His black hair curled over the collar of his uniform, one stray lock falling across his forehead, which furrowed in concentration. He adjusted his gaze from the scope of his rifle to glance at her. Those dark, smoldering eyes pierced her with both pain and longing.

Gabriel. The handsome, enigmatic Puerto Rican boy who'd both betrayed and saved her. More than once on both counts.

"I want it to be over." She meant more than just this moment, more than the ambush. She was tired of running, scavenging, of fighting for their lives, never knowing what dangers the next minutes, hours, and days would bring. She was exhausted to the marrow of her bones.

Gabriel nodded as though he understood all the things she hadn't said. "It will be. We'll finish this, I promise."

Before she could reply, she heard them. The low, spitting growl of motorcycle engines approached rapidly. Heart hammering in her throat, she kept her gaze on the road, waiting for the men who'd stolen her mother and killed Nadira.

The Headhunters rounded the bend with the roar of dozens of motorcycles. She recognized the furred animal pelts rippling from their shoulders like capes: dogs, wolves, leopards, tigers. The men wore menacing weapons strapped to their backs, waists, and thighs. They rode in formation: two dozen bikes up front, a dozen more riding on either side of a transport truck, even more taking up the rear.

Her breath caught. She scanned the bikers; no female riders or passengers. Her mother must be locked inside the transport truck.

Her mind barely had a chance to register the Headhunters' presence when the voice in her earpiece—Captain Cleo Reaver—spoke again. "Detonate now!"

The road in front of the lead Headhunters exploded. Chunks of asphalt sprayed the air in a cloud of fire and smoke. Six motorcycles were caught in the blast, the bikes and their riders instantly shattered. Two more bikes burst into flames, their owners lighting up like matchsticks.

Another slammed on his brakes, but it was too late. He careened into the steep cliff-face and smashed against a car-sized boulder.

Another explosion rocked the rear of the convoy. Five more Headhunters gone in a fiery blink. The explosives Gabriel and Micah had carefully planted in potholes yesterday had paid off.

The Headhunters were still dozens strong, immense and hulking in their animal pelts—like beasts themselves, animalistic killers, hardly even human. Even knowing it was intentional, the pelts still had the desired effect. As instinctive as breathing, an equally primal fear shot through her, the terror of prey in the face of a predator.

The surviving bikers slammed their brakes, leapt from their bikes, and knelt behind them, using the motorcycles as shields. They swung their weapons from their backs and aimed into the hills on either side of the road.

"Duck!" Gabriel hissed.

A volley of automatic fire peppered the air. Bark spit from the pine trees next to her, raining pine needles down on her head. They both rolled and ducked behind a boulder a few feet to their right. Rocks and twigs dug into Amelia's belly and thighs. She barely felt them.

"Come fight us like men!" shouted a Headhunter.

A chill ran through her. She knew that voice. Cerberus, the fierce leader of the Headhunters. The man who had killed Nadira.

She and Gabriel exchanged wary, uneasy glances. They'd both hoped he was dead from the gunshot wound Gabriel had inflicted back at Sweet Creek Farm.

Amelia dared to peer over the boulder. Cerberus stood tall behind his bike, shoulders back, legs splayed, not even crouching. Two of his men stood on either side of him, their machine guns leveled, sighting the trees, searching for prey.

Cerberus cut a formidable figure. He was tall and barrel-chested, with brown hair shorn close to his skull and a beard stubbling his solid jaw. Most of his body was covered in protective gear, but she recalled the blue digital tattoos squirming like snakes across his thick, bulging arms and neck. She remembered his eyes, cunning blue-gray, as cold and soulless as that of the wolf whose striking white pelt draped across his broad shoulders, all the way down to the tops of his shiny black boots.

"Why do you cower like curs?" Cerberus shouted into the silence.

"Let me take this scumbag out!" Amelia's brother, Silas, snarled into her earpiece. He was somewhere a few dozen yards to the right of her and Gabriel, half-buried in a rut between the roots of a giant red oak. "I have a clean shot."

"Wait for the signal," snapped Cleo Reaver, a New Patriot and the daughter of the New Patriot commander, General Reaver, who'd put her in charge of the mission. "Activate smoke bombs now."

Amelia grabbed the spherical object on the ground next to her and pressed her thumb to the biometric scanner. The scanner identified her thumbprint as a pre-approved user and activated, blinking once. The New Patriots had programmed it to detonate in five seconds.

She half-raised herself and lobbed the bomb at the transport truck. Next to her, Gabriel did the same. The rest of their team hurled two dozen smoke bombs at the Headhunters.

"What the hell!" one of the Headhunters shouted, shooting at the bomb as it landed a few feet from him. The sphere clicked open with a faint hiss. Smoke poured out from all sides, filling the air with dense gray smoke.

"Snipers, activate now," Cleo said into Amelia's earpiece.

From above, their tactical team could still see clearly enough to shoot. But the disoriented Headhunters, who could barely make out their hands in front of their faces, wouldn't be able to tell the direction or location of the shooters, keeping their own people as safe as possible.

"Remember, not a single bullet better hit that truck," Gabriel growled.

He aimed carefully and took a shot. A Headhunter in a German Shepherd pelt dropped to the ground with a shriek. Two more fell to the right, each taken out by Silas and Willow. Amelia couldn't see what was happening on the other side of the truck, but by the sporadic gunshots and the cries of the Headhunters, the plan seemed to be working.

Cerberus shouted something. Several Headhunters crouched and staggered through the smoke toward the transport truck. While four men did something to the truck's rear doors, two provided cover, shooting wildly into the trees.

Amelia ducked again, dropping the rifle and covering her head with her hands. Bullets chewed through the air, striking trees and smashing into the hillside behind them. A pulse blast hit a large maple branch. It thudded to the ground with a sizzling crash.

Gabriel lifted his head, aimed, and cursed. "They're too close to the truck. I can't risk a shot."

"What are they doing?" she asked.

Gabriel cursed again.

Amelia lifted her head, risking a glance. The Headhunters were dragging people out of the truck—their hands bound and cuffed behind them—and forcing the prisoners in front of themselves. They were using the prisoners as human shields.

Fear speared through her, icing her veins. "Tell them to stop shooting!" she gasped. "Stop shooting!"

"Cease fire!" Cleo commanded. Her voice was tinged not with disgust or rage, but reluctant admiration. "Those filthy scumbags outmaneuvered us."

No one fired as the smoke slowly dissipated. A dozen Headhunters held prisoners—mostly women and children—while the others crowded in close to the truck, weapons pointed toward the woods. They had figured out what their attackers wanted.

"We have more hostages inside the truck," Cerberus announced loudly. He pressed a woman against his chest with one hand. With the other, he held a gun to her head. "Now, I think this is what we call a stand-off. So why don't you put down your guns and show yourselves, and we can talk turkey like real men. That is, if you have the balls to face us."

Her friend, Willow Bahaghari, let out a stream of curses into Amelia's earpiece. Willow was short and solid but fearless, fierce and unrelenting as a bulldog. Amelia always felt better knowing Willow had her back.

"I'll show him what real balls look like," Willow snarled.

Amelia might have laughed. But she recognized the long, curly auburn hair of the woman gripped in Cerberus's meaty fingers—the perfect, ramrod-straight posture, the elegant profile and high cheekbones. Even now, every inch dignified and graceful.

Elise Black was alive—and Cerberus's human shield.

Amelia froze.

"I see her," Gabriel said softly. "Target sighted. She's with the leader—the white wolf."

"Don't shoot," Silas said. "Target not clear. Not even close."

The cold wind blew more of the smoke away. Soon, they would lose their advantage. Her whole body went numb. Icy tears stung her eyes. They were so close. Yet everything could still slip away between their fingers. Cerberus could still kill her mother in the space of a heartbeat.

She took a breath. "Gabriel."

He turned to her, a questioning look in his dark eyes. She swallowed. She knew what she was asking.

Gabriel gave a short jerk of his head, his jaw set. He clicked off his comm. "I'll get her. I'll bring her back to you."

She should tell him no, that it was too dangerous. But the words wouldn't form in her mouth. She hated the part of herself willing to trade Gabriel's life for her mother's, but she didn't stop herself, didn't stop him. She needed her mother. "Be careful."

He nodded once, and then he was gone.

2

GABRIEL

Gabriel Ramos Rivera left Amelia tucked safely behind a boulder. He clicked his comm back on. "Silas, are you with me?"

"Already moving," Silas said.

"I'll provide cover," Willow said, her voice calm and steady.

"Me too," Gabriel's brother, Micah, said into his earpiece.

"What the hell do you think you're doing?" Cleo snarled. "I haven't approved—"

"Apologies, cupcake," Silas said sweetly. "Let's continue this nagging session at a later date, shall we?"

Cleo sputtered. Willow laughed.

Gabriel ignored them all. They had less than two minutes before the smoke dissipated. He had to act before then. "I'm going in. Cover me."

He moved swiftly but silently through the trees, his rifle high and ready, careful not to trip on a root or stumble over a jutting rock. He made his way parallel to the road until he reached the still burning motorcycles destroyed in the explosion. The biker who'd smashed into the boulder lay crumpled on the side of the road, dead.

Gabriel reached down, unhooked the cheetah pelt strapped around the dead man's neck, and pulled it free of the body. He draped it around his own shoulders and hurried back toward the transport truck, the milling Headhunters, and the smoke.

He was betting everything on the New Patriots maintaining the ceasefire. Otherwise, he'd just painted a giant target on his back.

The smoke shifted and swirled around him in a thick, eddying soup. He blinked his stinging eyes. Everything was a dingy gray, every shape more than a foot away dark and indistinct.

The truck loomed in front of him in the haze like a monstrous beast. He turned to the right, resisting the urge to flail his arms.

Fear and adrenaline pumped through him. He might die here, on this road, surrounded by Headhunters and this bitter, choking smoke.

But his sense of purpose was stronger than his fear. He would save Amelia's mother. He knew he could do it. It would never pay back the wrong he'd done to Amelia, the betrayal that had almost cost her life, but it was something.

And he could take his revenge for Nadira's death. Nadira, who'd been kind and sweet and gentle, the only one to offer him grace and forgiveness when he—a murderer and terrorist—had least deserved it.

He didn't have the time to reach into his pocket and feel the square of pale blue cloth, part of Nadira's head scarf. He knew it was there.

In the battle at Sweet Creek Farm, Nadira had leapt in front of Cerberus's gun. She had taken the bullet meant for Gabriel. She had sacrificed her life for his, offering him a redemption he'd believed was beyond his grasp.

Nadira had given him a new life, a new purpose. The least he could do was kill her murderer.

Gabriel skirted carefully around the truck, passing within inches of several Headhunters. His pulse thundered in his ears. If they even glanced at him...but their eyes were on the hills, their panic causing tunnel vision, blinding them to the enemy in their midst.

He moved among them, unseen, unnoticed.

Several men cursed, aiming wildly at nothing. A skinny Headhunter in a coyote pelt leaned against the truck, clutching his leg as blood gushed between his fingers. The women being used as human shields whimpered and cried softly.

A Headhunter in a bristling black bear pelt held a child to his chest. A girl, tiny, not more than five. Gabriel glimpsed wide, panicky blue eyes and stringy blonde hair before a swirl of smoke rose between them.

Bile churned in his gut. An image of the little girl in a yellow bathrobe flashed through his mind, her black hair flung around her delicate face like a halo, blood seeping from a hole in her chest. The girl from the heaving, burning deck of the *Grand Voyager*. The child who'd died because of Gabriel's actions, his single-minded determination to win at any cost—even innocent lives.

He forced himself to turn away from the blonde girl. Helping her now would only doom Elise Black and the other hostages. He wasn't abandoning her; continuing with his mission was his best shot at saving them all.

A few Headhunters let loose a volley of automatic fire into the hills.

"I'm out!" someone cried.

"I'm low, too," a man in a leopard pelt said.

"Save your ammo!" Cerberus hissed. "Don't shoot at ghosts!"

Gabriel turned toward the voice and caught sight of the wolf pelt a few yards away, a dazzling streak of white in a haze of gray. He smiled as he stepped over another Headhunter's body and inched closer to Cerberus's exposed back.

He was about to show Cerberus just how deadly a ghost could be.

He let his rifle drop against his shoulder strap and slipped his pulse gun out of its holster. He pressed it against the side of Cerberus's skull. "Long time, no see, asshole."

Cerberus barely flinched, but his lips curled back in a snarl of rage, revealing his canines sharpened like fangs. He was caught in a trap, and he knew it.

"Nobody move!" Cleo shouted from behind a massive tree just up the hill. "We outnumber you ten to one." Which was an outright lie, but the Headhunters didn't know it.

"Come out, little girl, so we can blow your head off," said a burly Headhunter to Cerberus's right. "Every single one of you. Are you gonna shoot these innocent women and children to get to us?"

"We don't have to." Cleo's cool, confident voice cut through the chilly air. A gust of wind dissipated more of the smoke. "From my count, your automatic weapons are nearly empty. While you're busy attempting to reload and hold on to your hostages at the same time, we'll pick you off, one by one. Besides, we have a gun trained on your leader. Make a move, and he goes. Then so do each of you."

Silas materialized out of nowhere, his semi-automatic pointed at the burly black Headhunter directly to Gabriel's right—likely Cerberus's righthand man.

"We'll take some of the hostages with us," the Headhunter growled. He wore a panther pelt and silver hooks in his ears. His skull was thick and angular, his nose blunt, his eyes dull and deadly.

"We only care about one," Cleo said, the shrug evident in her voice. She wasn't bluffing, either. Cleo might be on Gabriel's side, but she was cold as a mountain glacier.

Gabriel shoved the barrel of the gun against Cerberus's head. "Let Elise go."

"You kill me, and my men will open fire on you, consequences be damned," Cerberus said.

Now Gabriel shrugged. It was a calculated risk. But he had seen the way the Headhunters obeyed Cerberus's every word back at Sweet Creek Farm. He was their alpha. His men wouldn't risk his life if they didn't have to. "I'm willing to take that chance."

"Just let me go," Elise said in a trembling voice. Gabriel dared not take his gaze off Cerberus, not even for a second. Elise was only a glimmer of pale face and dark hair out of the corner of his eye. "They'll have mercy if you let me go."

Cerberus let out a bark of laughter.

"Did they hurt you?" Gabriel asked her.

"No," Elise said. "Not in the way you're thinking."

"We're traders," Cerberus said darkly. "We never damage the merchandise. Well, almost never."

Gabriel's heart jolted as he sensed movement. He had no time to react. The burly Headhunter in the panther pelt moved swiftly, his gun lifting toward Gabriel.

Silas pulled the trigger. The Headhunter lurched, blood spraying from the bullet that entered the back of his skull and exited somewhere in the vicinity of his shattered left eye socket. Blood splattered Gabriel, Cerberus, and Elise.

Gabriel didn't flinch. He didn't even blink. He couldn't afford to. "Thanks," he said to Silas.

Silas smirked as he wiped a spray of blood from his lean face. He was tall and wiry, his short brown hair spiked off his forehead, his gray eyes glinting with amusement. "Anytime."

Behind Gabriel, a second Headhunter fired. The bullet whizzed past his cheek. One of their people further up the hill shot once.

Gabriel heard rather than saw the body crumple. The hostage screamed, though she was unhurt.

"Guess a girl can shoot after all," Willow quipped from behind a pine tree ten yards up the hill. She stepped out into the open, a semi-automatic half as large as herself grasped in both hands. "Well enough to take out a few filthy mouth-breathers, anyway."

Silas spun around to level his gun at the Headhunters behind him. "Looks like you just lost."

"Surrender now, Cerberus," Gabriel said.

Cerberus sighed and dropped his gun. "Stand down."

One by one, his men lowered their machine guns, grumbling in protest but obeying. The hostages staggered forward, crying with relief. The little girl with the blonde hair dashed into the waiting arms of an older woman—likely her mother.

"Drop the weapons and kick them aside. Lose your handguns and knives, too," Gabriel ordered. "And release your hostages."

Cerberus dropped his gun and lifted both hands, palms out. Elise Black stumbled away from Cerberus, clutching her neck and gasping.

"Mother!" Amelia sprinted down the hill, her arms already opening wide. Amelia and her mother clutched each other. Elise burst into sobs. Amelia put her arm around her mother's shoulder and whispered soothingly into her ear.

Gabriel's chest filled with warmth as they embraced. He watched as Amelia pulled her mother out of the road and back up toward the safety of the hill. "You're okay now," she said over and over. "You're okay."

Cleo strode down the hill, her rifle leveled at Cerberus. One of her trusted soldiers, a well-built black guy named Jamal Carter, came down with her. He was in his mid-twenties, with a full beard and a bevy of piercings in his lip, nose, and ears. In spite of the hardware, he was quiet and laid back—until it was time to fight. He knew his way around guns, and he didn't hesitate to shoot to kill.

Cerberus eyed the patch on Cleo's arm, a closed fist raised in the air against a field of blood-red. "Before you shoot me, I have a proposition your leaders would very much like to hear."

Cleo cocked her brows. The scarred left side of her face was smooth, the burned skin stretching from below her left eye across her cheek and jawline to the side of her neck. "I'm listening."

"You know who we are, just like I know who you are. We're traders and service providers. We collect valuable resources—items, people, information—and exchange those resources in fair trade to surrounding communities for services rendered."

"You're monsters!" Willow strode down the hill. She was a Filipina firecracker, short and thick but incredibly strong, and a gifted fighter. She huffed her bangs out of her dark eyes and glared fiercely up at Cerberus. "Thieves and murderers."

"Only when we have to be," Cerberus said evenly. "Our mercenary skills are in high demand in communities all over Georgia and beyond. Don't mistake business for anything but what it is, girl." He lifted a hand and rubbed his right shoulder, right about where a scar from his bullet wound would be. The bullet wound Gabriel gave him after he murdered Nadira. "At least, until certain members of your group made things personal."

"I'm just sorry I missed," Gabriel said, fresh rage filling him. "Lucky thing I have another chance to get it right. It's time to put you in the ground."

"Wait." Cleo lifted one hand. "What do you think you have, trader?"

Cerberus straightened his broad shoulders, the white wolf pelt rippling in the cold breeze. Digital tattoos slithered over his neck and the back of his hands. "Information."

"Speak now or forever hold your peace. I don't play games."

Cerberus tilted his head as he studied her. "Let me speak with your leader, girl. This is a subject for men to handle."

Cleo patted the gun holster at her hip. She wore a knife sheath at her other hip and strapped around her right thigh. Her eyes blazed. "I *am* the leader, you misogynistic bastard."

Cleo was smaller and younger than Cerberus, but she held her own without flinching. Her hair was shaved to her skull on both sides of her head, with a knot of purple braids on top that tumbled down her back nearly to her waist. She was Indian, with rich brown skin, cunning eyes, and a vicious smile.

Cerberus frowned in displeasure. He and the Headhunters liked the old ways, he'd said at Sweet Creek Farm, back when women knew their place. "The leader of your Patriots, then."

Her smile widened. She glanced at Gabriel, amused. "Oh, you mean General Reaver."

"Yes, him. He'll want to know this information, I assure you."

Cleo lifted one shoulder in an insolent shrug. "Well, I'm afraid *she* is busy right now. And if it's up to me, which it is, I'd rather just kill you all right now. So if you have something to say that might save your worthless hides, I advise you say it."

Cerberus's face purpled with anger. But he maintained control. Which was unfortunate. Gabriel was tired of this back and forth. Anger ate at him. His hands trembled with rage. It was time for justice for Nadira, for all of them. It was time to kill this jerkwad. His finger tightened on the trigger.

Cerberus seemed to sense Gabriel's movement. He set his jaw. "So be it. I know what you want. We've heard the whispers in the surviving communities we trade with. Your people been searching for certain high-powered weapons."

A shadow crossed Cleo's face. She bit her lip, frowning. Her sharp gaze darted to Gabriel, then back to Cerberus. "I'm listening."

"The Settlement. It's southeast of here. They have an armada of airjets—"

Cleo spat on the road. "We know the Undergrounders. They're too well-fortified to take anything by force. They're not interested in playing ball, but they keep to themselves. They aren't a threat or a resource. They're nothing. So, if that's all you've got—"

Cerberus licked his lips. "We know where a Phantom is."

Cleo stiffened. Gabriel had no idea what Cerberus was talking about, but Cleo clearly did. She was startled, but she quickly regained her footing. "You have a Phantom."

"We know where one is located. Rogue soldiers took it from Robins Air Force Base before being ambushed themselves. We found it and hid it with a transponder and GPS locator."

"And you're claiming you can get it for us?"

"Keep us hostage, if you must, while you verify it. You can go get it tomorrow. And I can offer more. I have fifty skilled fighters right here. I can summon two hundred more within the week."

Cleo's eyes narrowed. "And how do I know you'll stand by your word?"

Cerberus spread his hands. "Like I said, trust but verify. We're businessmen. We're traders. It's what we do. We have services to offer you, resources to trade. This is business. More, it's the future. Someone in your position should think long and hard before throwing away something so valuable for a bit of revenge."

A second conversation was happening between Cleo and Cerberus, a negotiation Gabriel wasn't privy to. He knew the words but couldn't discern the underlying meaning. The hairs prickled on the back of his neck.

"We've asked you before," Cleo said.

Cerberus smiled, flashing white teeth. "Let's just say the circumstances have changed."

"Permission to engage," Gabriel hissed between gritted teeth. "Why are we wasting our time—"

Cleo held up a hand, silencing him. She kept her eyes on the Headhunter. Her lip curled in distaste. "You will have to release your...resources."

Cerberus flipped his palms skyward. His gaze flitted up the hill to Amelia, who stood with her arms wrapped around her mother, consoling her. "I'm sure we can negotiate mutually beneficial terms."

"What the hell is he still talking for?" Willow stalked across the road and jabbed her gun in a Headhunter's face. She glanced back at Gabriel, her features contorted in fury. "We don't need *her* permission. It's time to end this."

"Stop, Willow," Cleo ordered. "Or we'll be forced to make you."

Cleo gave a signal to the New Patriots standing at the tree line. Four of them shifted positions. The New Patriots weren't just aiming at the Headhunters. They were aiming at Willow and Silas, too.

Anger surged through Gabriel. "What the hell are you doing?"

"Your men need to stand the hell down," Cleo said calmly.

"Not until we've finished our business." Willow was right. They didn't need Cleo's permission to do anything.

He refocused his attention on Cerberus, the man who'd murdered an innocent girl. Who had tried to kidnap Amelia and stole Elise. He was evil. And without courts or police or a government, the only justice was the justice they enacted themselves. "Control *your* men. Get their guns away from my people."

"Don't do this, Gabriel," Cleo warned.

But Gabriel didn't listen. "This is for Nadira. Be grateful yours will be a quick death instead of the one you deserve—"

Cleo lunged forward in a single, swift movement. Something cold and metallic touched the side of Gabriel's head. "Do not pull that trigger."

Dread knotted his gut. "Or what?"

"Or I will do whatever I have to do to stop you. Don't make me order Jamal to take out Willow." Cleo spoke with a cool indifference that sent a spear of certain fear through his heart. She would do it as easily as she had branded Willow with her cigar. To a girl like Cleo, the ends justified any means.

Gabriel knew that. He'd believed he could keep the situation under control.

He was wrong.

"Lower your guns," Jamal said.

"Listen to him," Gabriel said through gritted teeth.

Silas spat colorful obscenities and hurled his gun at Cleo's feet. She didn't flinch. "There's been a change of plans," Cleo said loudly so that everyone could hear. "We all have a common enemy. So, let's put this little squabble behind us and look to the future—the only thing that matters. We don't have to like each other—" she glanced pointedly at Cerberus and Gabriel. "Hell, I hate most of you. It doesn't matter. If you want to live, if you want your kids to live, then we must work together."

Cleo reached over, seized Gabriel's gun, and wrenched it out of his hands. With her rifle to his temple, he had no choice. He let go. "Why are you doing this?"

Cleo ignored him and turned to the Headhunters. "Gentlemen, welcome to the New Patriots."

3

MICAH

M icah Ramos Rivera hadn't seen his brother so angry in a long time. Maybe since the *Grand Voyager*. That was five months ago; it felt like five years.

"What the hell is going on?" Gabriel snarled.

"I have something to show you," Cleo said, nonplussed. She puffed a circle of smoke from her cigar. It drifted between them in the cold air. "Then we'll talk."

They had just returned to the New Patriots compound. The Fort Cohutta Detention and Rehabilitation Center was a self-sufficient, previously abandoned prison tucked halfway up Wildwood Mountain at the base of the Blue Ridge Mountains.

Cerberus and around forty of his Headhunters were already sequestered in the quarantine barracks to ensure none were infected. A handful of Headhunters had declined to join the New Patriots; Cerberus sent them back to their own headquarters to send more Headhunter reinforcements. For what, exactly, was still unclear.

Micah didn't trust them. Neither did Gabriel. Not after what happened at Sweet Creek Farm. Not after Nadira.

Now, Micah and Gabriel strolled between several barracks, following Cleo and her right-hand man, Jamal Carter, as they entered the large, warehouse-like training center on the far side of the compound.

The whole place stank of stale sweat and bleach. Several people in sweatpants and T-shirts sparred on a moldy-looking mat. Others lined up at a virtual target practice module or jogged on the VR treadmills. A massive, bare-chested man fought a shimmering holographic assailant in the simulation combat ring. Still more lifted ancient dumbbells, sweating and groaning on bench presses, power racks, and smith machines.

There were over two hundred men and women, some of them heavily tattooed, all of them tough, muscular, and battle-scarred. Many wore camouflage fatigues without name tags or unit patches. Everyone watched Micah and Gabriel with closed, suspicious expressions.

"In here." Cleo made a hard left, pressed her right palm and eye to a biometric and retina security scanner, then yanked open a steel-reinforced door. Harsh fluorescent lighting flickered as they stepped inside.

There were racks and racks of weapons. Shelves of ammunition. More racks bristling with mobile artillery, huge machine guns, rifles, pistols, hand grenades, and grenade launchers.

Micah swallowed hard. "What is this for?"

Jamal crossed his arms and lounged against a tall, metal gun safe. "Protection."

Cleo cocked her head, appraising them frankly. "We have a right to defend ourselves."

Gabriel's jaw pulsed. "All this for defense. Why do I not believe you?"

Cleo tapped ash impatiently from her cigar and took a long pull.

"Why do you think the Sanctuary contracted the Pyros to burn Atlanta and obliterate every other gang?"

"They're clearing it of dead bodies, infection, and violence to make the city livable again for the survivors." Even as he found himself doubting the words, Micah repeated what the leader of the Pyros, Tobias Moruga, had told them.

Moruga had hunted them through the burning ruins of Atlanta after Silas had accidentally killed Moruga's thirteen-year-old son. Moruga was a thug, a gang leader, and a violent criminal. He'd had his own reasons for distorting the truth.

Cleo snorted. "How adorably naive of you. That may be one small part of it. The other, larger motive? To destroy any potential rivals before they gain the strength to fight back or threaten the Sanctuary."

Micah adjusted his glasses and stared at the rows and rows of guns. So much firepower, capable of so much destruction, so many lives lost. The puzzle pieces were slowly clicking into place, and not in a good way.

"Sooner or later, they'll come after us, just like they've come after everyone else." Cleo waved her hand through the smoke wafting from her cigar. "The Sanctuary is the *enemy*. They'd sooner destroy us than let us in. They don't *want* to let us in. Even if they had miles and miles of uneaten crops and thousands of empty mansions. They'll never give a damn thing to us."

Understanding struck him like a punch to the gut. "Not unless you take it by force," Micah said quietly.

Cleo's expression hardened, but she said nothing. She stared at them with her shrewd, cunning gaze, as if impatiently waiting for them to figure it out on their own.

"That's why you offered an alliance to the Headhunters," Micah said. "You're recruiting an army."

Gabriel swept his arm toward the weapons arsenal, the training arena outside the heavy steel door. "You're planning an attack. You want to take the Sanctuary for yourselves."

It was true. Micah could see it in the coldness of her eyes, in Jamal's grim smile. And Gabriel knew it too. His brother knew better than anyone the kind of people the New Patriots were, what they stood for, what they wanted.

They might not have released the Hydra virus, but they'd bombed dozens of government buildings. They'd hijacked the *Grand Voyager*, willing to risk innocent lives, even children. Now they were aligning themselves with known criminals and killers.

But that was the problem with the New Patriots: they saw every elite as the enemy. And they were willing to do anything to destroy that enemy. Anything.

There was a thin line between freedom fighters and terrorists, between soldiers and murderers.

Gabriel's expression was stony, his jaw clenched, his eyes dark and ferocious. He took a step toward Cleo, towering over her. "I have the right to know what I'm sacrificing my revenge for. Tell me. I'm one of you."

Jamal darted forward, about to come between them, but Cleo lifted a hand, stopping him. She raised her chin, her eyes challenging. "Are you really?"

"I'm one of you," Gabriel said again, studiously avoiding Micah's gaze.

Micah knew—he hoped, he believed—his brother was lying, ingratiating himself with these people to keep them all safe.

But Gabriel was so believable. Too believable.

Micah tried to read his brother's face. What if it wasn't an act? What if Gabriel was sliding back into his old self?

Gabriel had been full of bitterness and hate and rage. He had aimed a gun at his own brother. He had attacked a cruise ship and killed innocent people. Could Gabriel shed one identity for another as easily as a snake shed its skin?

He shook the thought from his mind. He hated doubting Gabriel, hating the tense, uneasy sense of disquiet settling in his gut. He'd just gotten his brother back. He couldn't stand the idea of losing him again.

He had to trust Gabriel. He had to have faith.

Gabriel loomed over Cleo, his fists clenched. "If you're planning an attack, I'm one hundred percent on board."

Cleo stepped closer, until her scarred face was inches from Gabriel's. Her eyes were cold and hard. "We aren't waiting around for them to find and destroy us. When the time is right, we're going to take the Sanctuary by force and make it ours."

4

AMELIA

A melia sat on the small cot in the isolation block of the barracks at the east end of the Patriots' compound, in the same place they'd waited out quarantine when they'd arrived only a week ago. It was a revamped prison cell—a narrow rectangle of concrete floor, a toilet, sink, and mirror, a cot with a mattress and a few blankets.

The room smelled damp and slightly moldy. But Amelia didn't care. She was too filled with barely contained elation—she finally had her mother back.

Her mother huddled on the cot beside her. Though Amelia had brought her a thick, auto-warm cable-knit sweater, she was still shivering. Her mother was thin and haggard, her elbows knobby, her collarbone painfully sharp beneath her skin. Her cheekbones, always high and sweeping, were hollowed, almost cadaverous.

"I missed you so much," Amelia whispered, her throat dry. She wanted to cling to her mother like a little girl—like she never had, even when she *was* a little girl—and never let go. But that wasn't her family's way.

Her mother's narrow shoulders were curved inward, her shoulder blades sharp as wings. "I thought about you every minute of every day."

"Did they—what was it like?" Amelia didn't want to ask a question her mother wasn't ready to answer. She knew too well what it was like to live through trauma, how it felt like you would shatter into pieces if you spoke the words aloud.

Her mother shook her head. "I was scared all the time. But they never laid a hand on me. Cerberus saw to that.

"Don't get me wrong. They're misogynist pigs willing to buy and sell anything, including women and children, but they live by their own distorted sort of code. They think women belong in the home as nurturers and homemakers, wives and mothers. They believe men are their protectors, their masters." She brushed her tangled auburn curls back from her face. "It's too complicated and backward. It's over. It's done. I never want to think about them again."

Amelia bit her lip. The Headhunters weren't going anywhere, but at least her mother wasn't their prisoner now. Amelia didn't want to leave her mother in this place, surrounded by enemies, but she didn't have a choice. At least Gabriel, Willow, and Celeste would be here, keeping an eye on things.

She glanced at her Smartflex. "I have to go soon."

Her mother flinched. "I know. I just...I want to keep you safe."

"This is about more than keeping me safe," Amelia said. "This is bigger than me. It has to be."

"Of course. You are the cure. You are the future. I know you have to go in there...but you must stay safe." Her mother stroked her cheek, her elegant brow furrowing. "If you can't come back for us, it doesn't matter. Stay inside the Sanctuary. Do you understand?"

Amelia blinked. Surely her mother meant something else. Surely, she wasn't saying what it sounded like she was saying. "But what about you and—"

Her mother gave a sharp shake of her head, her curls tumbling around her shoulders. "Everything I've done for the last eighteen years is for you. If it would keep you safe, I'd go back with the Headhunters. Your safety is all that matters."

Her stomach twisted. She could barely get the words out. "That would mean leaving you and everyone else behind."

"It would be worth it. Don't worry about me."

Amelia swallowed. "The others—"

"No one loves you like I do," her mother said without hesitation. "You are a million times more important than any of them."

Amelia leaned back against the cement wall. The chill leached the warmth from her body. She felt the cold all the way to her bones. The thought of abandoning the people she'd come to love as her family—Micah, Benjie, Willow, Finn, Gabriel, even Celeste—it was unthinkable. "You would have left Jericho?"

Grief flashed across her mother's face—deep and real and wrenching. Amelia saw it then, what she'd suspected all these months. Her mother had loved Jericho. Maybe she never would have admitted it, or maybe if Jericho had lived, they would have ended up together. The death of what might have been was evident in the sorrow and regret etched in every line of her mother's face.

Jericho had been a great man: practical and efficient, strong and courageous, an ex-soldier who chose to stay and protect them when he could have fled and survived on his own.

In Atlanta, Jericho had taken the punishment meted out by the Pyros' leader, Tobias Moruga, after Silas accidentally shot and killed the man's son. Jericho had claimed the blame. And Moruga had shot Jericho in the head like he was nothing more than a dog.

Amelia closed her eyes against her own grief, against the horrifying images that still plagued her nightmares.

"Jericho would say the same thing," her mother said firmly. "He was pragmatic to a fault. All he ever did was protect us—protect you."

"He wouldn't be sitting here telling me to save myself and abandon my friends," Amelia snapped. She took a breath, struggling to stay calm. She shouldn't be angry—her mother was just trying to protect her, just like she always had, even when Amelia hadn't realized it.

"Jericho protected all of us. We were his responsibility, his people —" Amelia nearly choked on the words, but forced her way through. "He didn't separate the elites from the rest. He didn't make some people more important than others. He could have left all of us and survived on his own. But he didn't. Every single one of us is alive because of him. "He didn't abandon anyone. Not even you. He was leading us through Atlanta to ambush the Headhunters before they reached the Sanctuary. That's why we were in Atlanta—to rescue you."

"You're right. He was a good man." Her mother dropped her gaze to the floor. She wiped daintily at a tear slipping down her cheek. "We will all miss him. But that doesn't change the facts. Your safety is all that matters."

"Mine? Or mine and Silas's?"

"Of course," her mother said, but not with true feeling behind it.

"He's your son, too."

"I'm aware," her mother said too sharply.

Amelia recalled her conversation with Silas back in the Pyro's prison on that endless night. How Silas confessed he didn't believe their mother loved him. How Amelia had tried to protest, but the truth was there, undeniable.

"You don't act like it."

Her mother's full lips contorted. She kept her gaze on the floor, refusing to meet Amelia's eyes. Her hand fluttered to the hollow of her throat. "Of course I love him. He's my son. I'm his mother."

Amelia said nothing, allowing the silence to thrum with tension. Before all this, she would have dropped the subject, tried to smooth over the strain with charm or demure acquiescence.

Not anymore. The truth was more important.

"He's so much like his father." Her mother spoke so softly Amelia had to lean forward to hear her. "I've tried, but..."

"Try harder." Amelia grasped her mother's hand. "He's not his father. He makes his own choices just like the rest of us. He's not lost yet."

"He's not like you, Amelia—"

"I don't care," Amelia said firmly. "We have to be better than we were, better than we are. All of us. He needs you."

"I'll try," her mother said.

"We don't get second chances and do-overs in this world."

"I know." Her mother shifted uneasily on the cot. Her gaze drifted to the charm bracelet hanging from Amelia's neck. Something shifted behind her eyes. She stiffened.

"What is it?"

"Your father," her mother said dully.

Amelia's stomach twisted into tighter knots. "What?"

Her mother pulled away from her, both hands hovering at the hollow of her throat. "What if he's there? What if he's in the Sanctuary?"

"Then I'll face him," Amelia said with more conviction than she felt.

"If the Coalition is there, they might kill you just for being his daughter. Just to cover their tracks."

Before the world collapsed, Declan Black had been the infamous founder and CEO of BioGen Technologies as well as the chairman of the Unity Coalition, a conglomerate of powerful biotech, communications, and defense corporations more powerful—and corrupt—than even the government. They were the true power, the ones behind the checkpoints, increased surveillance, and the ID-tracking Vitalichip bill.

Amelia's mother believed that there was no way Declan Black acted alone. That the Coalition was also behind the bioweapon, releasing it as an act of bioterrorism in a calculated attempt to pass their rights-reducing, citizen-tracking Safe and Secure Act.

But their plans had backfired. The virus, meant to kill a hundred thousand people culled from the disposable poor, had mutated instead. It underwent reassortment, recombining with the virulent bat-flu to create the highly contagious Hydra supervirus.

"Amelia, this is so incredibly dangerous." Her mother stared at her, her beautiful face stretched taut, her eyes glassy with fear. "What if it's not worth it?"

Amelia thought of everyone she loved, of everyone she might be able to save. "It is, Mother. Even if the worst happens. It's worth it."

5

MICAH

"There are innocent people behind those walls," Micah said to Cleo, reining in his own anger. He felt sick. "Women and children. You can't hurt them."

Once, Gabriel would have grabbed Micah's arm and pulled him back, embarrassed by his moralizing. He would have lectured Micah, forced him to shut up. But Micah wasn't shutting up anymore. And Gabriel didn't try to stop him.

"I don't know why gender makes a difference in matters of innocence," Cleo said coolly, "but those people ceased to be innocent the day they closed the gates and refused to open them. And why the hell are you even here? You're not one of us."

Micah refused to be intimidated. "Not for the pleasant company, that's for sure."

Gabriel took a step back. His fists unflexed, his hands hanging loosely at his sides. He still wouldn't look at Micah. "My brother is smart and level-headed. You should at least consider what he has to say."

"As far as I'm concerned, every single one of you except for

Miracle Girl and you, soldier boy," Cleo thumped Gabriel's chest with her finger, "are consuming our food and sleeping in our beds and contributing nothing. You're parasites. And as such, your opinion means jack-squat to me."

The armory closed in around him, all those gleaming weapons, all the death and destruction and horror they were capable of wrecking upon the remaining survivors. Micah's gut roiled.

Jamal let out a bark of laughter.

The muscle in Gabriel's jaw jumped. "Did your mother teach you to treat people this way?"

"She taught me how to rip my enemy's throat out with my teeth." Cleo flashed a savage smile. "And that's exactly what I'm planning to do. Anyone who can't stomach that is welcome to leave."

"What about Amelia's cure?" Micah asked.

"We're months from an assault," Cleo said. "She'll be in and out long before that. With the cure, we can increase our recruits tenfold. We can scavenge for supplies in dangerous, plague-ridden areas. We can trade for the weapons we need."

She turned to Micah, her lip curling. "Whatever moral high ground you think you have, you're wrong. We don't turn away anyone who's not infected. We take in women and children and the elderly. We've made a safe place for families. Don't you dare judge us for wanting to keep what we have, for wanting to make a safe place for others, too, instead of allowing the elites in the Sanctuary to take what's good and destroy everything else."

"How many people can you house?" Gabriel asked.

"Less than two thousand, and we're gaining new recruits every day," Jamal said.

"So you can't hole up here forever." Gabriel's voice lost some of its edge. She was winning him over.

"At the rate we're taking people in, not even six months." Cleo blew out a ring of white smoke and watched it drift. "We need more space. We have a power source with the wind turbines, solar panels, and hydropower from the river, plenty of generators, irrigation systems, and farming equipment. We have livestock, food, medical supplies, crop, and seed stock to grow real food. But not enough for the number of people we've taken in.

"We're running out of time, but we've been unable to act without enough fighters, enough weapons. The right type of weapons."

Gabriel folded his arms and studied her intently. "That's what Cerberus was talking about. The Phantom."

"Do you have any clue what we're up against?" Cleo hefted an RBG cannon off one of the shelves and slung it over her shoulder. It looked enormous in the small space—sleek, menacing, and deadly. "The Sanctuary is surrounded on all sides by a thirty-foot electrified plasma wall. The ramparts are manned by huge cannons that make this beast look like a squirt gun. The missiles take out incoming aircraft before they get anywhere close. They're powered by internal hydrogen fuel cells, so there's no way to cut their power externally. And nighthawks—the military-grade drones—patrol the grounds within a five-mile radius. They shoot to kill and don't bother asking questions."

Micah nervously shoved his glasses up the bridge of his nose with his thumb. "Then how do we even get Amelia inside?"

"There's a single main entrance and a single road. If you follow that road and do not deviate to either side—"

"—because the entire area is booby-trapped with mines," Jamal interjected.

"—then a whole battalion of soldiers will interrogate you. If they deem you worthy of further inspection, they'll put you in the containment center, the quarantine tents outside the Sanctuary. If you're not an elite or don't happen to have a critical skill set, they'll turn you away without a second thought."

Dread gnawed at Micah's stomach. "That doesn't answer my question."

"Her name," Gabriel said heavily. "Amelia was on the newsfeeds all the time with her father, Declan Black. Everyone knows her. Who she is will get her in."

"Hopefully, they'll let you in with her," Cleo said to Micah, a wry grin twisting her mouth. "Though we have no way to ensure that happens."

Micah ran his finger over the barrel of a semi-automatic rifle. Infiltrating the Sanctuary appeared more and more difficult with every passing second. "That's a lot to ride on a hope."

She shrugged. "We don't have a choice now, do we?"

"I should go with them." Gabriel glanced at Micah, his expression tense. "It's too dangerous."

Cleo flashed that savage smile that made the hairs on Micah's neck stand on end. The smile pasted on her face when she stood beside Tobias Moruga and watched Jericho die. The smile that made her look capable of anything.

"You agreed to remain behind, remember?" Cleo said. "I have need of you. That weapon Cerberus mentioned—the Phantom—it can take out those Sanctuary cannons. While Amelia's team infiltrates the Sanctuary, we're going to get it."

Cleo replaced the grenade launcher on the shelf. She moved down the rows of weapons, then squatted and pulled a black box from a bottom shelf. She pressed her thumb to the biometric scanner, waited for the click, then lifted the lid. She pulled out a thin silver circle. She handed it to Micah. "The Sanctuary will just confiscate any weapons we give you. But our inside people will help you once you get within the walls.

These are communication devices disguised as old-fashioned dimes.

"The Sanctuary monitors digital and radio-wave output. But these use out-of-date frequencies, so our communications should stay under the radar if we keep it to a minimum. The range is one hundred miles, so we should be good."

"Who's your inside man?" Gabriel asked. "How do you know he can be trusted?"

Cleo smiled. A real smile, one that lit up her eyes and brightened her face, that made her look like an entirely different person. "Because he's my brother."

"How did your brother get inside the Sanctuary?" Micah asked, surprised.

"He's a tech genius and a hacker," Cleo said proudly as she handed the silver comm to Micah. "We crafted a new identity before the mandatory chip IDs. He's been working in mid-level government surveillance for three years now. When it all went down, he managed to get inside the Sanctuary from the beginning. A few more of our spies made it inside as well. You'll have the help you need."

"The Headhunters can't be trusted." Micah tried one last time. But he could tell by the expressions on Gabriel and Cleo's faces that they'd already decided. And Gabriel, so intent on justice for Nadira, was just going along with it. Micah smothered his welling frustration. "They're human traffickers, criminals, and killers."

"We know what they are," Jamal said.

Cleo tapped ash from her cigar. "They're a necessary evil."

"Evil is never necessary," Micah shot back. Her words might seem to make sense, but she was dead wrong. Violence only begets more violence, death more death. He had seen plenty of evil in the months they'd struggled to survive in the ravaged ruins of post-Hydra America. He wanted no part of it.

"An eye for an eye, right?" Cleo said. "That's what your Bible teaches."

"No," Micah said. "An eye for an eye, and the world goes blind."

"Whatever." Cleo gave an insolent shrug. Her eyes narrowed as she turned toward the armory door. "Hate me all you want to. I don't care. If we don't get into the Sanctuary first, the Sanctuary will kill us all, or else the virus will. We don't have a choice. Everyone out here, we're all on the same side. We have to be—or we all die."

6

AMELIA

The next morning, General Reaver and Colonel Reid prepped Amelia, Silas, and Micah with final instructions. The New Patriots leaders left to tend to other tasks, while Cleo led them to the front gates of the compound.

The day was cold, forty-three degrees according to Amelia's SmartFlex, but the sun was out, and there was no wind. Amelia was dressed in black thermopants, leather boots, two thick sweaters, and a scarf, along with the usual mask and gloves. She wore a hunting knife strapped to her hip, but no other weapon. Silas and Micah were dressed similarly, their packs filled with supplies and food.

The rest of the group arrived at the gates to say their goodbyes. Celeste still limped slightly. Finn's arm was bandaged and cradled in a sling. Her mother remained in quarantine. Benjie was sniffling, fighting back tears. Gabriel stood off to the side, his hands balled into fists at his sides, his face carved in stone.

Willow strode in restless circles, trampling the brown, wilted grass beneath her boots, her expression twisted in an indignant scowl. She wasn't thrilled about being left behind.

Amelia's heart constricted. She hadn't spent a day apart from these people in months. She couldn't bear the thought of saying good-bye, even for a little while.

In the apocalypse, every goodbye could be the last.

Cleo seized her arm and pulled her aside. "Here is my advice," she said even though Amelia hadn't asked for it. "If you are among wolves—"

"Let me guess. I should act like a wolf."

Cleo cocked her head, staring at Amelia like some exotic prey she'd never tasted before, and would love to try. "It depends," she said slowly, "on what you want."

Amelia folded her arms over her chest. "If this is a riddle, you should just give me the answer. I don't have the time or the patience for games."

"If you want to blend in, then yes. Be a wolf." Cleo smiled her predatory smile, a white slash of teeth. "But if you want to catch a wolf, it is unwise to act like one. It is far better to be the sheep."

"Thanks," Amelia said politely.

To their right, Willow rolled her eyes. "Everybody, listen to the sociopathic philosopher."

Amelia touched Willow's shoulder. "I wish you could come with us. But you're keeping Benjie safe. We'll need you soon enough."

Willow grunted in frustration. She gripped the handle of her hunting knife at her hip and blew her unruly bangs out of her eyes. "I can help you."

"I know you can." It was true. Willow was better prepared than Amelia was. But the more people they tried to bring into the Sanctuary, the more conspicuous they became. "I'd trade places with you if I could," she said with a wry smile.

Willow just sighed. "Don't let Silas get himself killed, okay?"

"I promise." Amelia wished with all her heart that it was a promise she could keep. "I'll convince them to let us all in. I still believe the Sanctuary is our best chance. For Benjie. For all of us. Okay?"

Willow nodded as eight-year-old Benjie ran up to Amelia and threw his arms around her. He buried his head in her stomach. "Don't go, Miss Amelia!"

She hugged him tightly, her chest filling with warmth—and a fierce love. She tilted his chin up and gazed into his big, beautiful brown eyes. She ran her hands through the black hair that stuck up all over his head, no matter how often he brushed it. He wasn't her brother by blood; he was her brother by choice.

"I'll be back before you know it." She glanced up at Finn, who'd come up beside Willow, cradling his numb, useless right arm. He was nineteen and huge, a towering giant at 6'6". He was intimidating and imposing—until you got to know him.

Finn gave her his usual lopsided grin, revealing the gap in his slightly crooked teeth. His walnut-brown skin crinkled around his eyes and dimpled his cheeks. He and Willow were particularly close, but Amelia appreciated his goofy jokes and big heart, especially now.

She smiled back, pushing down the emotions churning just below the surface. For Benjie, for all of them, she'd hide her fear.

Benjie's lower lip trembled. "Why do you have to go?"

She squatted in front of him, searching for the right words. "Sometimes, we have to go and do a brave thing, Benjie. This is my brave thing."

"Can I do a brave thing?"

"Of course." She leaned in and whispered in his ear. "I have a mission for you, Sir Benjie. As a sworn knight, it is your duty to watch and protect your sister Willow and Mister Finn. Mister Finn most of all, because he tends to get into mischief. When I return, I'll bestow your reward. Can you do that for me?"

Benjie nodded eagerly, tears forgotten, and thrust out his hand. "Secret handshake?"

After she'd managed the convoluted series of hand movements Benjie had taught her, she hugged him again before saying her good-byes to Finn and Celeste.

With regular showers and access to basic hygiene, Celeste was flourishing. Her eyes were bright, her flawless skin a rich brown, her crimson coils vibrant in the sunlight. She hugged Amelia. Amelia hugged her back.

Celeste pulled away and fingered a ragged chunk of her short hair. "Maybe they can do something about *this* in that place."

Silas smirked. "Glad to see your priorities are in the right place, as usual."

"Time to bug out." Cleo gestured to the transport waiting at the front gates. Jamal would drive them to just outside the five-mile perimeter. They'd hike the rest of the way. From there, the mission was a question mark, a huge unknown.

Amelia was grateful she didn't have to part with Silas or Micah. She wasn't strong enough to do this alone. She needed them both beside her.

She watched Micah and Gabriel embrace like the brothers they were. The sight warmed her heart. That embrace—that closeness— had been hard-earned by both of them.

She glanced at the mountains above them, pretending not to listen as Gabriel whispered, "Just us," his voice hoarse, and Micah answered, "Always."

They were words meant for each other and no one else.

Micah pulled back, removed his glasses to give his eyes a quick, fierce swipe, and glanced at Amelia. His face was going lean, making him look older than his nineteen years. But there was still a boyish charm to him, his wavy dark hair spilling haphazardly across his forehead. His eyes behind his glasses were a warm and gentle chocolate brown.

"We'll wait for you," he said with a tilt of his chin at Gabriel. Then he jogged after Silas to the transport.

She turned to Gabriel, her cheeks already reddening. She felt his gaze on her as she walked the two dozen steps to reach him. He leaned against a small maple tree in front of a low concrete building, the windows boarded and covered with black, light-blocking paint.

"You know I would go with you if I could," he said in a low voice.

She dared to meet his gaze. She could drown in those dark eyes, full of longing, guilt, regret, and desire. Despite herself, she felt the responding tug in her own heart. "You risked yourself to save my mother. It was dangerous. You probably shouldn't have done it, but you did."

"And I'll continue to do it. I'll keep her safe, I promise you that."

She swallowed around the lump in her throat. "Thank you."

He attempted a smile, but it didn't reach his eyes. "I would do anything you asked. You know that, right? I—I owe it to you. But more than that, I want to."

The air thickened between them. There was so much—the past, the present, the possibilities of the future—it was all there, unspoken but still present. Her veins buzzed. Her breath quickened. "Gabriel—"

"I know this isn't the time." His features contorted in a pained expression, like he was forcing himself to hold back the things he really wanted to say. "What you're about to do is brave and dangerous and possibly incredibly stupid. But if you succeed, you can change the world for the better. You have to do it. And Micah will watch out for you. I know you're in good hands."

He swallowed, his hands fisted at his sides. "But if something happened to him or to you—" He looked away, blinking rapidly.

Part of her wanted desperately to go to him, to offer him comfort, to remember what it felt like to be wrapped in those strong, safe arms. But another, stronger part of her held back.

Because she couldn't forget what came after, either. The look in his eyes when he'd betrayed her. When he'd stood by as Kane dragged her by her hair from the *Grand Voyager* bridge, intent on violence.

"Gabriel—"

He turned to her with a groan in the back of his throat. His eyes filled with anguish. "I can't protect you in there. And that thought is killing me."

"We have to trust each other, then." He was so close she could have put her hands on his chest. To push him away or draw him closer, she didn't know.

Before she could react, he took her chin gently in one hand and tilted her chin up. His other hand cupped the back of her head. He bent down and kissed her mouth. His lips were hard and searching, hungry.

Her stomach flipped. The buzzing filled her whole body. She wanted him and she hated herself for wanting him and she was weak —but also warm and wild and falling from a dizzying height...

Amelia gasped. She pulled away. But for a moment, she hadn't. For the barest moment, the brush of his lips electrifying her entire body—she'd let it happen.

They were so close she felt his heartbeat thrumming through his chest, sensed the hard strength of his body, his arms and shoulders and stomach, could feel the coiled power in him.

His hands dropped to his sides. His body was tense, taut as a live wire, the muscle in his cheek jumping as he clenched his jaw. "Don't run," he said quickly. "Please."

She nodded, breathing hard. Not sure she could trust herself, trust her voice or what she would—or should—say.

"I'm sorry—no, that's not right." He smiled wryly. "I'm not sorry for kissing you, Amelia Black. I will never be sorry for every good moment we ever shared. It was selfish to kiss you now, I know that. I know I don't deserve you, not after—after what I did to you. I accept that. I hate it, but I accept it. I don't know what tomorrow will bring. I don't know if I'll ever get to see you again. I hope you can forgive me that one last kiss."

She cleared her throat, her cheeks burning. Guilt stabbed through her. It wasn't fair to give him what she wasn't sure she should. "I can. I do."

He moved toward her, then stopped himself. He nodded curtly, as if coming to terms with something deep inside him. When he spoke again, his voice was hoarse. "Until next time."

Gabriel turned and strode between the buildings toward the barracks, his head down, his shoulders hunched, his hands balled into fists at his sides. Exhausted but determined, bone-weary but resolute, doggedly walking into an oncoming storm.

In a way, they both were.

7

WILLOW

F inn nudged Willow's foot beneath the picnic table. "Look over there."

"What?" Willow asked, turning away from the game she and Finn were playing, a holo version of chess featuring red and blue shimmering medieval knights on horseback, robed bishops, and foot soldiers wielding swords, axes, and bows. Willow was losing, badly.

"Cleo's staring at Celeste."

Willow narrowed her eyes. Celeste was leaning against the picnic table, her injured leg stretched out on the bench, her eyes closed against the cold sun.

Ten yards away, Cleo slunk in the shadows of the infirmary building, her arms crossed, a cigar in one hand. Finn was right. She was watching Celeste—like a cat watches a mouse.

Willow poked gently at the scabbing burn on her neck. "I bet she's a cannibal. She's probably imagining Celeste's leg as a rack of lamb cooking over a spit."

"First, that's a revolting image. Thank you so much for searing that into my brain."

"You're welcome."

"Second, I'm pretty sure that's not the reason she's interested in Celeste."

Willow glanced between them again. This time, she noticed Cleo's furtive glances, the way she was gnawing on her bottom lip like she was biting into a juicy steak.

Willow shoved her hair behind her ears and groaned. "Is something in the water? Has some new brain-altering pathogen been released into the air? Wasn't the apocalypse enough? Amelia has her very weird, very unhealthy love triangle with Micah and Gabriel, even though none of them will admit it. Now Cleo the sociopathic cannibal has a thing for Celeste?"

"You hate her with the fire of a thousand suns?" Finn said, trying to distract her from the fact that his red knight had just knocked out her second bishop. The mounted knight's horse reared in triumph. Her bishop crumpled to the checkered board, grabbing his throat and gagging dramatically before disappearing in a puff of glittering blue mist.

Finn had already taken out ten pieces to her three. He was unfairly good. Or maybe she was just that bad. She rubbed her neck. The burn had started to itch like crazy. "I wouldn't use that particular phrase, but hell yes, I do. That psychopath branded me!"

"To be fair, she was undercover."

"Yeah, but *to be fair*, she enjoyed the heck out of it." She prodded at the burn, wincing. It was going to leave an ugly scar. She didn't care about the scar as much as she loathed the person who'd inflicted it. Cleo was manipulative and petty, cunning and cruel. She was hardly better than the Pyros, undercover or not. "I don't know what her problem is, but I bet it's hard to pronounce."

Finn grinned. "Yeah, she's mad as a bag of cats, alright."

She glanced back in time to see Cleo saunter across the yard toward Celeste. Celeste looked at her, a tiny smile on her perfectly symmetrical face. Celeste was all softness and elegance and beauty, while Cleo was solid muscle, battle-scarred, and tough as nails.

Finn was right, as always. In a bizarre sort of way, they made a good pair—as long as Celeste kept Cleo away from the cigars.

Finn swiped his massive hand through the tiny holos hovering over the game board. "There's something to be said for physical things you can hold in your hand. My dad used to have a board with real ivory pieces." He sighed dramatically. "We can't always choose our allies, Willow."

"How can you say that?" She checked the field, where Benjie and another little girl his age were sitting in front of the ragged soccer goal, their heads bent over a pack of playing cards. Benjie was overjoyed to have a devoted fan, eagerly teaching her every magic trick he knew.

Past the field, a handful of soldiers clustered in a circle near the barracks, laughing raucously. She couldn't believe Amelia and Micah were trusting these people. New Patriots. Terrorists. Thugs and criminals. Willow didn't care what they called themselves. "You know who these people are. What they are."

"They didn't create the Hydra virus."

Amelia had finally told the rest of the group the truth about her father, Declan Black, the chairman of the Unity Coalition. He'd turned out to be as power-hungry, malicious, and wicked as Willow always suspected. The elites had all the power, influence, and wealth they could ever need, and still they craved more. Their greed had destroyed the world.

But none of that changed the fact that the New Patriots were still violent radicals, plenty capable of taking innocent lives if it served their own agenda.

She shook her head. "They're the same people who attacked the *Grand Voyager*. I don't care if they say they weren't a part of it.

They're the *same*. And I don't care whether they planned to kill little kids or not. It happened. Your dad is dead because of them. My mom and sister—"

Her voice broke off. Her throat thickened. She blinked rapidly. The New Patriots had killed Zia. It didn't matter that it wasn't actually these people. For that, she would hate them with every fiber of her being for as long as she lived.

She didn't trust them. She didn't like them. She wanted to get as far away from here as she could.

She swiped her finger over the board to pull her rook out of Finn's reach. The lights in the castle tower flickered. Finn moved swiftly, barely fluttering his fingers as he captured her extravagantly-gowned queen with his bishop. She hadn't even seen it coming. The tiny queen shook her fist up at Willow, muttering incoherent curses. Willow gave her the middle finger. The queen burst into blue mist.

"And now they're allying themselves with the Headhunters," she continued. "The murderous psychos who killed Nadira. I mean, what are we even doing here? I know what Amelia is doing, what Gabriel is doing. But what are *we* doing?"

Finn looked at her, his expression turning serious. "What do you want to do?"

Willow shifted restlessly, unable to contain her frustration. She wanted to get away from the New Patriots and never have to see Cleo's savagely cunning face again. She wanted to protect the people she loved. To find a way inside the Sanctuary and make a safe place for Benjie to grow up. She wanted so many things, all of them outside her grasp. "I don't know! But I can't help feeling like this is all some kind of elaborate ruse. The most dangerous predators are the ones that draw you in."

"Like the Venus Fly Trap."

"Do you have to ruin every analogy? Plants aren't remotely scary."

Finn shrugged with his left shoulder. He still winced. The meds the New Patriots doctor gave him weren't enough to dull all the pain. "To flies, they are. I thought it was quite apt."

She destroyed one of his foot soldiers with a flick of her finger, her blue knight galloping across the squares and spearing the red soldier in the chest. "You thought wrong. Didn't we learn our lesson at Sweet Creek Farm? Nobody does something for nothing."

"It's not for nothing," Finn argued gently. "They want the cure from Amelia. She, Micah, and Silas are risking their lives to smuggle it out."

"And what if they don't get it? What if she doesn't have the cure in her blood after all? What will the New Patriots do to us then? The Headhunters? The Sanctuary? Hell, the Pyros are still out there somewhere. Let's throw them in the pot, too."

Finn narrowed his eyes at her. "You've got an idea rattling around inside that head of yours, don't you? Out with it. Before it drives you crazy."

The idea was half-formed, half-baked. She felt silly even saying it aloud. But the more she thought about it, the more she couldn't ignore the insistent, unsettling buzz in her gut.

Finn took out one of her soldiers. She took one of his. "I'm not sure. But maybe while Amelia's off saving the world at the Sanctuary, we need to do something, too."

He studied her face. "You want to find Raven."

She looked at him sharply, startled. She kept forgetting how perceptive he was, how well he knew her, like he could read her mind. Lately, she *had* been thinking about Raven and her enormous, half-tamed wolf, Shadow.

Raven had appeared out of nowhere in the middle of a thunderstorm, sending Shadow to save Willow from the infected stray outside the warehouse. Raven and Shadow had helped them again at Sweet

Creek Farm, herding the rabid dogs in a surprise attack against the Headhunters.

Maybe Raven could save them again.

Willow pulled out the wooden bird carving which Raven had given to Benjie. She had carried it for him in a cargo pocket of her pants. She ran her fingers over the smooth wood. "I doubt we could find Raven if we tried. But we could make it so she finds us."

Finn nodded. "And then what? You don't want to bring her here."

The Sanctuary was dangerous. The New Patriots were dangerous. But maybe they didn't have to choose between them. Maybe there was a third option. "She talked about a place called the Settlement, remember? She said they were good people. When Cerberus was negotiating with Cleo, he mentioned the Settlement, too. He said they had airjets and other weapons the New Patriots would want. I think it's the same place. I think maybe they could help us."

She half-expected Finn to laugh at her. But he didn't.

He grinned mischievously, his eyes glinting. "Maybe a quest is in order?"

"I'm serious."

"So am I." He pushed away the holo game board—it didn't matter, she was losing horribly anyway—and cleared his throat, his expression abruptly grave. "Wherever you go, I'll be right there with you."

She tilted her head, masking her suddenly hot face with a curtain of her hair. "It will be dangerous."

Finn's gaze slanted beyond Cleo and Celeste toward two Headhunters stalking the perimeter of the rec yard. One was a hulking beast in a German Shepherd pelt, the other tall, skinny, and draped in the sleek black fur of a panther. They paused, hands on their gun holsters, watching Benjie and the little girl playing.

Willow started to rise, outrage burning through her. What did those idiot thugs think they were doing, watching her brother like that? Were they thinking of stealing him, too? Selling him? She'd kill them both before they even took a step—

Finn gripped her arm. "Not now."

Slowly, she sank back down onto the bench. She didn't relax or take her gaze off the two Headhunters until they moved on, headed for the training center.

"It may be dangerous out there," Finn said, "but that doesn't mean it's not just as dangerous in here."

Willow nodded with a huff, blowing her bangs out of her eyes. "The New Patriots aren't just going to give us guns and supplies and let us waltz off into the sunset. You know that, right?"

"Gee," Finn said, "if only we could find someone clever and quick-witted and sneaky. Preferably short. Yeah, short is definitely on the list of requirements."

She kicked his shin beneath the table. "So you're not totally against it."

"I'm saying we should do this." He leaned forward and grasped her hand in his good one. Tingles sparked in her fingertips and shot up her arm. She tried to jerk her hand away, embarrassed, but he was too strong.

Finn was too intent to notice her sudden discomfort. "We were made for this. A crippled giant, a dwarf, and a kid with an ace up his sleeve: a trio of misfits wandering around in a strange and wild forest in the middle of winter." He flashed her his goofy, lopsided grin, revealing the adorable gap in his front teeth. "What could possibly go wrong?"

8

AMELIA

"I don't have a good feeling about this," Silas muttered.

"Do you ever?" Amelia shot back.

Silas managed a tight grin. "Touché, big sister."

They stood atop a large hill along the two-lane road leading to the Sanctuary. Jamal had brought them to the five-mile perimeter with a military-grade, off-road vehicle via an overgrown national park access road.

For the last four-plus miles, they'd trekked on foot. There was no way to determine the exact distance, since she'd turned off her Smart-Flex to avoid identification.

They had passed a dozen old-fashioned "no trespassing" signs and holos auto-repeating, "Nuclear waste facility. Hazardous material. Intruders will be shot on sight." Within minutes of entering the Sanctuary's safe zone, two sleek black drones had materialized on either side of the road, halting them in their tracks.

"Nighthawks," Micah said. "Military-grade, armored, weaponized."

The drones hadn't shot them, though several gun turrets swiveled in their direction. They simply hovered within ten yards, watching them, likely capturing them with invisible, embedded lenses and sending a live vidfeed back to Sanctuary command. The drones followed them silently, only the soft whirring of their lifting blades betraying their presence.

Finally, Amelia, Micah, and Silas had reached the Sanctuary. A valley spread before them, mountains bristling with old forest rising steeply to either side. In the distance, a shining band of river wound like a twisting snake. Nestled between the mountains, a pristine city gleamed beneath the winter sun.

The first thing Amelia noticed was the buildings. They were several stories and made of some sort of engineered white quartz, some domed, some spired, others circular and multi-terraced.

She sucked in her breath as her gaze lowered to the wicked purplish-blue plasma wall surrounding the city, thirty feet tall and crackling like lightning. At regular intervals, the walls were mounted by guard towers bristling with enormous cannons large enough to take out any aircraft stupid enough to invade the city's airspace. The barest hint of movement flickered; soldiers patrolled along the ramparts.

"I wasn't sure what to expect," Micah said, awe and dread in his voice, "but it wasn't this." He adjusted his glasses as if that might somehow change the forbidding view before them.

"More drones." Amelia pointed toward the plasma wall. Dozens—maybe hundreds—of armored nighthawks patrolled the wall, some as large as small cars.

"The New Patriots were right after all," Silas said. "No way in but through the front door."

Before Jamal left them several miles back, he had shown them the maps the Patriots had managed to cobble together of the exterior defenses and terrain of the Sanctuary. There was no section undefended. To breach the five-mile radius anywhere but the main entrance road meant death. According to Jamal, over the last several months, more than a dozen Patriots had been killed by drones, mines, or captured by Sanctuary soldiers to be interrogated and tortured, never to be seen again.

A secondary access road was two miles northwest. It was used by Sanctuary contractors, suppliers, and soldiers, but those soldiers' orders were "shoot first, don't bother with questions." Silas was right. There was no other way in. Not without a tank or an army. And even then, the Sanctuary appeared well prepared to defend itself.

Dread filled Amelia like lead in her bones. She'd heard the Patriots' warnings. She had clung to the faint hope that they could sneak in undetected, that she could find the scientists without the Coalition ever knowing her true identity. But that was a pipe dream, wishful thinking, a foolishness she couldn't afford.

She straightened her shoulders. "Let's go. Stay on the road." As if any of them needed the reminder.

They headed down the hill, passing several craters in the ground so large a truck could fit inside. Someone had tried to attack the Sanctuary. It hadn't gone well for them.

"How are you feeling?" Micah asked softly as they walked.

"As well as can be expected." That part was true, at least. She hadn't had a migraine—or even a headache—since her last seizure during their escape from the fire at the mall in Atlanta. Was that two weeks ago? Three? It was easy to lose track of time when every day felt like an eternity, when everything could change in an instant.

Another seizure could take her at any time. She was never safe.

Micah didn't touch her. He never touched her without asking first. But he was close, close enough that she felt the brush of his shoulder against hers, felt the warmth radiating from his body. He was here. He wasn't going anywhere.

She smiled at him.

"What's that for?"

"For coming with me when I know you're worried sick about Gabriel."

"Of course." She could tell he was biting the inside of his cheek. "We just have to trust him, right?"

"We don't have a choice." A shiver ran through her as she remembered their last meeting, the kiss. "He's changed. I believe he has."

"So do I," Micah said.

"Then we trust him."

Silas snorted behind them. "Good luck with that."

"Not helpful, Silas," Amelia said.

Ignoring Silas's jab, Micah turned to Amelia. "What do you think the Sanctuary will be like?"

"I don't know." She couldn't explain the knot of fear, hope, dread and determination tangled inside her. What if the guards refused to let them in, no matter who she said she was? What if her father was inside those plasma walls? What if the Coalition imprisoned or tortured her?

Worst of all, what if she really wasn't the cure? The Hydra virus would shatter what remained of the world, piece by desperate piece. Those with immunity would just keep killing each other, fighting over the scraps of a dying civilization. The thought broke her heart.

"What if all this is all for nothing?" she whispered.

"It's not," Micah said with conviction. "I have faith, Amelia. This is all happening for a reason, for a purpose. What we're doing here—what you're doing—is important. It's everything."

Without hope, without a future, there was only survival. And survival wasn't enough. Micah had taught her that. Amelia touched her charm bracelet beneath her jacket. "Tell me something beautiful."

He considered for a moment. "There is something good in this world, and it's worth fighting for."

"Who said that?" She always knew when he was quoting something.

"Tolkien. *The Lord of the Rings.*"

Of course. His favorite book. She glanced at him. "Is that what we're doing? Fighting?"

"I don't know. I hope not. But I'm willing to if we have to, if that's what it takes."

She kicked a stray rock. The winter air felt suddenly colder. She was grateful for Micah's steady strength beside her. She took a deep, shuddering breath. "Are we strong enough? Am I strong enough?"

"We are," he said. "You are."

Silas rolled his eyes. "You two make me physically ill. Have I ever told you that?"

There was no bite to her brother's words, no cruelty in his smirk. He was as tense and nervous as they were. Amelia smiled grimly. "Once or twice."

Silas had been slightly more subdued since the Pyros, since Jericho's death and their night in the Pyro prison, when he'd finally opened up to Amelia for the first time in years. He was still Silas, but maybe he wasn't quite as acerbic, maybe his armor wasn't quite as thick.

They crested another small hill. The plasma wall loomed over them.

"Stop right there!" someone shouted. "Hands in the air!"

Adrenaline shot through her. She, Micah, and Silas halted and lifted their hands. A dozen soldiers marched out to them, as many drones zooming over their heads.

The soldiers leveled plasma guns, their eyes hard above the clear masks fixed over their noses and mouths. They wore helmets and sharp, charcoal-gray uniforms with a patch over the right shoulder—a white triangle with a rippling American flag behind a sword.

She blinked hard. Looked again. The emblem was the same. These were Coalition security agents.

This was exactly what her mother feared. But it didn't matter now. The only option was to obey orders. She felt the cold metal of the charm bracelet against her skin beneath her clothes. It gave her no comfort.

A figure in a hazmat suit stepped forward to meet them. Amelia glimpsed nut-brown hair and a round, feminine face through the hazmat visor. "Nice and slow, please reveal your right wrist," the woman said to Amelia. She held a wand-like object in one hand and a holopad in the other. "We need to verify your identity."

Amelia carefully pulled back the sleeve of her jacket and tugged down her glove. Her wrist was slim and pale, mapped with thin blue veins. "I don't have a Vitalichip. Neither do my friends."

The soldiers were standing outside the ten-foot infection radius, but they still tensed. Their fingers tightened on the triggers of their pulse guns. Amelia felt the same tension coiling inside her own body.

The woman scrutinized her suspiciously. "We cannot immediately determine your infection status without a chip. Without a specified infection status, you are automatically registered as potentially hostile under safety regulation code 221.5. I am required to inform you that 99.6% of persons seeking asylum are unqualified and refused entry. I am authorized to direct you to the nearest regional FEMA medical center for help."

Silas snorted. "We need FEMA like we need a shot in the head."

Micah gave him a warning look.

"We aren't interested in FEMA," Amelia said evenly. "We need to speak to someone in authority inside the Sanctuary."

"Identify yourself and state your intentions." The woman swiped something into her holopad and held it out for Amelia to scan her thumbprint. Amelia knew the drill. A retinal scan would follow. The two biosignatures combined would confirm her identity.

Her heart slammed against her rib cage. This was it. Whatever waited for them—salvation or destruction—it started now.

She peeled off her glove and pressed her thumb to the glowing digital handprint on the scanner. Her name would either save them or doom them. There was only one way to find out.

"I have information of utmost importance to national security," she said in a loud, clear voice. "My name is Amelia Black."

9

GABRIEL

"Stop moping around, Rivera," Cleo said to Gabriel. She finished loading supplies in the back of the transport and slammed the door shut. "Let's move."

It was just past dawn, the orange glow of the sun barely creeping above the tree line. The sky above them was still the deep purplish-gray of a bruise. Gabriel wrapped his scarf tighter around his neck. His cheeks and ears stung in the chilly air.

Amelia, Micah, and Silas had left yesterday. Jamal Carter had returned last night, reporting that he'd dropped them off just outside the perimeter without incident.

Now, the New Patriots were departing on their mission to secure the Phantom. They took two armored, all-terrain Jeeps. General Reaver, Colonel Reid, and several other Patriots took the first transport. Cleo, Gabriel, Jamal, Cerberus, and two other Headhunters rode in the second vehicle. Gabriel rode shotgun.

Cleo punched in the GPS coordinates to the town nearest the location Cerberus had given them and sat back, letting the auto-drive sensors take over. "Pay attention," she said to Gabriel. "The auto functions get a bit jittery from all these hills."

The dirt and gravel roads were mostly clear. Up here in the mountains, they weren't obstructed by thousands of abandoned vehicles.

Thoughts of Micah and Amelia filled his mind. Anxiety roiled through him. What were they doing now? Had they made it inside? Were they safe? He tried to focus on something else. "Does your mother come on every mission?"

"Only the most critical ones," Cleo said. "The Phantom is a game-changer. She wants to see it for herself—and ensure we don't mess anything up," she added with an edge of resentment.

She glared at Cerberus in the rear-view mirror. He was a hulking giant hunched in the back seat, his meaty arms crossed over his chest, the white wolf pelt bristling across his shoulders. He looked for all the world like some futuristic Viking lost in time.

"You better not be lying to us," she spat, "or I'll gut you myself."

"You're welcome to try." Cerberus sneered. "It would be my pleasure to school you in the proper attributes of womanhood."

Cleo gave a mirthless laugh. "You Headhunters are probably thrilled the world's gone to hell. You can bring us all back to the stone ages with you."

Cerberus shot her a stony-faced glare and refused to answer.

Gabriel clung to the side door as the Jeep roared over the pitted, overgrown access road. They swerved around a fallen tree blocking the road, the vehicle angling dangerously near the edge of a steep ridge. Two hundred feet below them, a glittering river twisted at the bottom of the gorge.

With his other hand, Gabriel grasped the butt of his holstered gun. He had his handgun, his rifle, and his hunting knife. Plenty of weapons to defend himself—and to kill. He felt Cerberus's presence behind him, a dangerous, barely restrained predator. He loathed every second of it. The Headhunter was unarmed at present, compliments of General Reaver's command, but Gabriel didn't doubt the man was deadly with his bare hands.

Gabriel was dangerous, too. Nadira's scrap of blue cloth burned like a brand in his pocket. Silently, he vowed to kill Cerberus at the earliest opportunity, Cleo and her mother's orders be damned. Then, maybe some of the guilt he wore like clanking chains around his neck would fall away, finally freeing him. Maybe.

The hours passed in silence. He kept his gaze on the forest whipping by outside the windows, his jaw clenched. He tried not to think too much about Amelia and Micah heading for the Sanctuary. But he couldn't dispel the tightness in his chest, the terrible helplessness washing over him. He was separated from the people he loved at exactly the time they most needed his protection.

But neither Micah nor Amelia was helpless. Micah had grown stronger, both physically and mentally. He could fight when he had to. He would kill to defend their people. Gabriel didn't doubt his brother's will or his loyalty.

He didn't doubt Amelia's determination, either. She wasn't the same girl from the *Grand Voyager*. She hadn't been weak then, but she'd lived in shame and fear for so long she didn't recognize her own power. Now she did. She was a force to be reckoned with—strong-willed, confident, beautiful.

The memory of their kiss flushed through him. Maybe he shouldn't have done it. He'd told her he wasn't sorry. And he wasn't. He would never force her to do anything she didn't want to do. But some part of him had whispered that he might never see her again, that he'd regret this chance not taken for the rest of his life.

Whatever happened next, he wanted Amelia to know he loved her. Even though she couldn't love him back...he would always love her.

The transport shuddered to a halt. Cleo shoved the door open and jumped out. "We're here."

"We're in the middle of nowhere," Gabriel said.

Cleo unloaded a large, industrial-sized hovercart and looked at Cerberus. "How far?"

Cerberus just shrugged with a lazy, predatory smile. "Soon."

A three-mile hike over rough, rugged terrain later, they crested a small hill to find a mid-sized town sprawling in the distance. A hundred yards to the north stood a huge concrete block of a building topped with a blue metal roof. Gabriel recognized the big-box store brand emblazoned in bright, candy-apple red on the front of the building.

"It was a restock warehouse for commerce drone delivery," Cerberus explained.

With their guns in the low and ready position, they cleared the area. They found several dead bodies and a few infected wildlife—which they promptly dispatched—before entering the warehouse through a side entrance. The lock had already been bashed, the door pried open and squeaking on its hinges.

Gabriel flicked on the light attached to the scope of his rifle. The towering shelves were ransacked. Plastic wrap and torn cardboard littered the cement floor. He kicked aside several empty, discarded boxes.

The stench of rotting flesh filled his nostrils. He adjusted his mask over his mouth and nose. The others did the same. It did nothing to staunch the foul, rancid odor, but he hoped it would protect him from any bodies infected with the Hydra virus.

A rat squealed and scurried out from beneath an empty beer crate. Gabriel shot it with a shudder, memories of the rat-infested sewer flooding through him. "Be careful of those things. They're cunning little beasts."

"Back here," Cerberus said. He led them through the labyrinthine rows of shelves to a metal door in the back wall. Brown streaks smeared the door. Dried blood. Four bodies dressed in army fatigues and combat gear slumped in front of it. They were bloated, decomposing. No blood leaked from their eye sockets. Their veins weren't a dark topography spidering across their rotting, corpse-white skin.

They weren't infected.

"They were all knifed or shot," Cerberus said. "Two of them in the back. We dragged them against the door to discourage looters. Figured most folks would decide it wasn't worth the risk to scavenge an office when there was plenty to plunder out here."

Jamal covered his masked mouth with the sleeve of his jacket. Coughing, he used a crowbar to push and prod the bodies out of the way. He pried open the locked door. Gabriel and two others cleared the office quickly.

The rest of the New Patriots crowded into the office.

It was unremarkable. Two integrated computer desks, a holo-screen, a couple of moldy-smelling sofas, a dusty coffee bar, an employee-only bathroom in the back.

"Here we go!" Jamal gave a low whistle as he crouched behind one of the sofas.

The Phantom was hidden between the sofa and the wall. It was huge, about six feet long, and sinister. It reminded Gabriel vaguely of a gun-shaped torpedo.

"Someone was lugging it around," Cerberus said. "Ex-airmen who took it from their abandoned base. They stopped here for supplies, got ambushed. Whoever took 'em out didn't know the value of this thing, figured it was too big and heavy, and just left it."

General Reaver stood with her arms crossed over her chest while two of her soldiers examined it. Cleo stood next to her, watching nervously, her expression tense.

"It's legit," one of them reported.

"What exactly does it do?" Gabriel asked.

"You know what an EMP is," Jamal said.

"An electromagnetic pulse," Gabriel said. "North Korea used a nuke like that to decimate part of Japan, set them back a hundred years. That's why we nuked them in return."

"An EMP burst fries electronics within a certain radius," Jamal said. "But it takes out everything. The Phantom is a HERF, an EMP gun that fires an intense, controlled electromagnetic pulse that takes out a narrow target."

"Won't everything in the Sanctuary be hardened?"

"Not necessarily," General Reaver said in her deep, throaty smoker's voice. She squatted next to the weapon, stroking its sleek black side with her free hand. In her late forties, she was a tall, stern-faced black woman with hard, shrewd eyes. Gabriel didn't doubt she shared her daughter's single-minded dedication to the cause, no matter the cost. "The Phantom is future tech. It's stronger than anything we've seen. It can burn right through Faraday cages and lead shields three inches thick."

"We can't penetrate the plasma wall without neutralizing their cannons first," Cleo said. "That's what this baby will do."

"Can't they just repair it?" Gabriel asked.

"Of course." Cleo flashed a wicked grin. "But it will take time. And a little time is all we need."

Something scuttled in the shadows behind the desk. Gabriel whirled, aiming his gun at the sound.

A furred, hump-backed shape scurried beneath the desk and popped out only a yard from where General Reaver squatted. Her hands and face were unprotected but for a thin pair of gloves and a paper mask.

"Get back!" Gabriel shouted. His first shot struck the desk leg a foot above the rat's head.

The rat darted toward General Reaver. The general jerked back, instinctively raising her arms to protect her face and neck. The rat leapt, launching its muscled, bristling body straight at her.

It was too close. There was no clear shot. Gabriel watched in horror as the creature struck the General's right hand and latched onto her thumb, scrabbling with its tiny claws for purchase. It sank its gleaming razor teeth deep into the flesh of her thumb.

She tried to fling the vicious creature off, but it was too strong.

"No!" Cleo lunged forward and slammed the butt of her gun against the rat—and her mother's hand—with a loud crack.

The rat tumbled to the floor with an outraged screech. It scrambled to its feet but faltered, its hind legs limp and useless, likely shattered. Cleo struck it a second time, bashing its head and spine.

It let out a terrible, high-pitched sound as it writhed in agony. It twitched, then lay still.

General Reaver inhaled a sharp breath, but she did not cry out. She clutched her damaged hand to the chest of her navy wool peacoat. "I think you just broke half my fingers."

"I was saving your life," Cleo said.

General Reaver climbed heavily to her feet. "Let's hope so."

"Did it bite through the skin?" Colonel Reid asked. He was a heavy-set man in his fifties, his middle bulging against his coat, his jaw blurring into his neck. Gabriel had only met him a few times, but he had a weak, conniving look about him.

Colonel Reid's olive-toned skin was ashen, his thick black brows lowered in alarm. He took a step back from General Reaver.

The general looked down at her hand. "Possibly." She spoke in a calm, controlled voice. "The virus is passed through saliva and other bodily fluids."

"Was the beast even infected?" Cerberus asked. "It doesn't look like it."

Gabriel nudged the limp body with the toe of his boot. He didn't see the tell-tale bloody saliva around the jaws. But that didn't mean it wasn't infected. Normal rats weren't aggressive. Normal rats didn't attack human beings. "I'm not sure."

Cleo stared down at the thing in revulsion. A tremor ran through her. She shook it off. Her whole body vibrated with barely restrained rage. "It's not. It's just a stupid rat. It's fine."

"Bag the creature," the general said. "We can test it at the lab in the infirmary."

Jamal pulled a few plastic bags from his backpack and gingerly wrapped it in several layers. Everyone watched General Reaver warily, as if they half-expected her to spontaneously leak blood from her eyes then and there.

"Load up the Phantom," General Reaver ordered, her voice rough as gravel, her expression impassive. "We have a war to win."

10

AMELIA

"Whatever happens, we can't let ourselves get separated," Amelia muttered.

"I won't let that happen," Silas said beside her.

On her other side, Micah nodded. "We're with you, always."

She wished she could find more comfort in their words, but the dread coiling in her stomach was a living thing, voracious and insatiable. It gnawed at her hope like a cancerous rot.

They were inside a large, multi-domed tent assembled beside the gate in the plasma wall, separated from the outside world by a ring of wicked-looking barbed wire fencing. The containment center, the woman in the hazmat suit called it.

"The medical safety department oversees and evaluates all outsiders," the woman had said briskly. "Wait here."

The containment center was larger inside than it appeared, filled with rows and rows of small square cells with transparent, tent-like walls. Each cell served as a separate quarantine zone. The cement floors in each cell contained a drain—for reasons Amelia didn't wish to contemplate—a single cot, a slot for food delivery, and a partitioned, non-transparent area for a latrine.

The cells Amelia could see were all empty.

The acerbic scent of antiseptic and bleach stung her nostrils. The smell was so strong that for a moment she felt lightheaded. They waited anxiously in the center of a ring of soldiers, all in hazmat suits, guns still pointed at them, while the woman conferred with two other officers with Coalition insignias emblazoned on their gray uniforms. She repeatedly gestured at the data on her holopad—the data that had appeared after she'd confirmed Amelia's identity.

One of the officers glanced over at Amelia, his expression grim. He tapped his earpiece and spoke softly to whoever was on the other end, his gaze never leaving her face.

Amelia tensed. The sharp scent of antiseptic pricked her nostrils. Her breath stuck in her throat. But there was nothing she could do, nothing any of them could do. They were surrounded, outmanned and outgunned. The Sanctuary soldiers could do anything they wanted. There was nothing Amelia could do to stop them.

A second figure in a hazmat suit approached them. "Put these three in containment," he said, gesturing at Amelia, Micah, and Silas.

"I'm not going in there," Silas growled. "You can't lock us up."

"It's not a prison," the man said with a sigh. An Indian man in his mid-sixties, his grizzled face and thick gray eyebrows were visible through his helmet visor. "I'm Dr. Veejay Ichpujani. These isolation units are for the safety of everyone involved."

"We're not sick," Amelia said.

"We don't know that," Dr. Ichpujani said. "You aren't chipped. We cannot determine your health status without a seventy-two-hour quarantine for observation and testing."

"Please don't separate us." Amelia despised the pleading in her voice but couldn't help herself. Panic closed iron-fingers around her throat. She didn't want to attempt this mission without them. She needed Micah and Silas. She couldn't do this alone.

"You should count yourselves lucky," Dr. Ichpujani said. "The Coalition has mandated automatic rejections for anyone without chips and all non-essential personnel." His gaze lingered on Amelia, his expression intrigued. "The only reason we aren't tossing you out on your backsides is because of her. The daughter of the Coalition chairman. A *Grand Voyager* survivor. Who would have thought, after all this time? Good on you for making it, when so many billions of others didn't."

"What am I, chopped liver?" Silas muttered.

But the doctor ignored him. He seemed only interested in Amelia.

Amelia's lungs constricted. Did he know about her father? Did he suspect something? But he was already turning away, losing interest. She couldn't let paranoia get the best of her. He didn't know anything. "When will we get out of here? I need to speak to whoever is in charge. It's of critical importance."

He glanced back at her and waggled his eyebrows. "Relax, girl. You got in. That's what you want, isn't it? You're safe. Seventy-two hours, we'll let you in. No problem."

Three days was too long. She couldn't wait here, trapped in these tiny cells, the walls closing in while outside people were sick and dying. Now that she was finally here, anticipation thrummed through her, the tension about to explode inside her chest. She had to know the truth. Whatever it was—she needed to know.

Two suited, helmeted soldiers grabbed Micah's arms and jerked him roughly toward one of the containment cells. Two more reached for Silas. He reared back, scowling and furious. "Get your hands off me, you filthy cockroaches—"

"Silas!" Micah hissed.

"Wait!" Amelia said. "I'm immune."

"Many of the remaining survivors are. Unfortunately, their blood has proved useless in the search for a cure." Dr. Ichpujani merely flicked his wrist, dismissing her.

"Mine isn't."

But the doctor kept striding away, his focus back on his holopad. A soldier took hold of her arm. She shook him off. She wasn't going to be ignored. Not now. She raised her chin and spoke loudly, projecting her voice. "I've had the Hydra virus."

The soldiers stiffened.

"That's unfortunate," Dr. Ichpujani said over his shoulder. "I'm sorry you came all this way, only to perish like all the rest." He didn't sound sorry so much as resigned, like he'd said those exact words a thousand times. He'd seen his share of suffering and death, especially out here—so close to the Sanctuary but not safe inside its walls.

"You didn't hear me." She spoke over her hammering heart, the blood rushing in her ears. He had to listen. She had to *make* him listen. "I said I *had* the Hydra virus. I recovered more than a month ago."

The doctor whirled and strode back to her, his expression incensed behind his visor. "Your lies are not appreciated here. Don't think you can shirk the rules, just because you're an elite used to getting whatever your little heart desires. The world has changed. No one escapes the Hydra virus except the immunes. Everyone who gets sick, dies. Everyone." His lip twisted in barely restrained derision. "Not even your money can save you now."

"Do you know who we are?" Silas snarled. "You won't get away with treating us like this!"

"It's true," Micah said. "I was there. So was Silas. She had every symptom—even bleeding from her eyes. Then she got better."

Dr. Ichpujani only shook his head, disbelieving. "I will not waste another moment on you lot. I don't care who you are. As far as I'm concerned, the Outlands can have you. All of you."

"I am not lying." Amelia spoke calmly, keeping the trepidation from her voice, the tremble from her fingers. She met his irritated gaze without flinching. She thrust out her right arm and peeled back her sweater. "Test me right now."

"I told you, without the microchip, it takes seventy-two hours—"

"You have microscopes, don't you? Disease-identifying vectors? Take a sample of my blood. It won't take much time or effort. A chance at hope—however small—is worth it, isn't it, doctor?"

Dr. Ichpujani hesitated, indecision flashing across his features. Finally, he sighed heavily. He swiped something into his holopad. "Fine."

An oblong-shaped med-bot with a half-dozen tentacled arms zoomed to the doctor's side. It carried a tray with a needle and stretchy tube. "Pull up your sleeve and hold your arm steady."

The bot swiped an alcohol pad over the inside of her forearm with one tentacle, held her arm steady with another, scanned her skin with a soft beeping and flutter of red lasers with a third, wand-like appendage, and pricked her vein with a fourth.

It was over in a moment. The needle was so tiny, she barely felt the sting.

Deep red blood gushed into the glass tube. It looked no different than the blood she'd always bled from every scrape and cut her entire life. Was it really special? Could it really contain the antibodies that would lead to a cure? She hid the doubt from her face as the bot slapped a strip of med-glue over the needle prick and zoomed away, dodging expertly between the clusters of soldiers.

"Wait in there," Dr. Ichpujani ordered. He pointed at the containment cells before stalking off in the same direction as the med-bot.

Amelia allowed the soldiers to put her in a cell. Micah and Silas were placed on either side of her, but the sides of the tent walls weren't transparent. She couldn't see them.

Through the transparent exterior wall, soldiers and doctors and med-bots passed by without a glance in her direction. The door was sealed and locked with a biometric scanner.

An air compressor near a ceiling too tall for her to reach distributed fresh oxygen and circulated out the stale air. The walls puffed in and out like sails. She pressed her hands against the walls. No one pressed back.

"Micah," she said. No answer. "Silas!"

They couldn't hear her. She couldn't hear them. The walls must be made with sound-dampening fibers. With a sickening wrench of her stomach, she realized the doctors didn't want to hear the screams of their patients.

She punched the wall a few times. The fabric was strong and coarse, and scraped her knuckles even through her gloves. Still, there was no responding touch or push on the opposite side. There must be a hollow space between each containment cell.

It didn't matter that Micah and Silas stood only feet away. It might as well have been a thousand miles. Her palms were damp inside her gloves. A heavy sense of foreboding settled over her.

When they'd been quarantined at the naval base in Florida, at least they had been together. This was different. This was isolation. She was surrounded by people and yet completely, totally alone.

It had only been ten minutes, and she already hated it. She took a breath, steeled herself. She would be strong. She would be brave.

This was only the beginning.

11

WILLOW

"What do we do about the guards?" Willow asked under her breath.

She and Finn stood near the rear gate of the perimeter fence, feigning interest in the small, dormant garden Benjie and a few other children were digging in about ten yards away.

Benjie glanced up at her, mud on his hands and streaking his pant legs, a question in his dark eyes. He knew to be ready to run as soon as she said the word.

She gave a small shake of her head. *Not Yet.*

They had told him they were going on a surprise adventure, a secret quest. The wilderness was dangerous, but it was more dangerous here. There was no way Willow was leaving Benjie behind.

She was *Ate*, the eldest sister, the responsible one. Her Filipina mother had put her in charge of her siblings. But now she was responsible for all of them—her friends, her family. She couldn't fail them.

She'd been worried about supplies, but luckily, the New Patriots collected the extraneous belongings of new recruits and rescued families and kept them in a single room, reallocating items as necessary.

She'd spent last night breaking into the storage room and scavenging up the supplies they'd need for the trip.

The wooden door had been padlocked with a small biometric scanner. Instead of messing with the lock, Finn used his multi-tool to unscrew the hinges and held the door aloft while she scurried inside. Luckier still, the Patriots were anti-surveillance. There were no drones zooming about, no holo ads scanning Smartflexes, and the old prison security cameras were all dark.

Willow had quickly found and stuffed two hiking backpacks with a small camping stove, gloves and masks, enough self-heating meals to last them two weeks, water bottles, extra ammo for her rifle and hand-gun, a fire starter, tarp, rope, filtration straws, and a tiny three-man tent, but it was all they had.

They had briefly considered grabbing an all-terrain vehicle or hovercraft, but stealing something of value increased their chances of being hunted and caught. It was better to take only themselves and what they absolutely needed. Hopefully, the Patriots would decide they weren't worth the trouble.

Now, their packs were hidden behind a garden shed only a few yards from the back gate. Even Benjie had a school-sized backpack stuffed with a change of clothes for each of them. The extra sweaters, mittens, and scarves, they wore in layers or stuffed in their pockets.

They were ready to go—except for the two guards that manned the rear gate 24/7.

The guards were mostly for external threats—they usually faced the hills, sweeping for movement. But the guards were equally effective deterrents to keep new recruits or kids from sneaking off.

Willow and the others had been allowed outside the fence for Jericho's funeral, but not since then. Burdened with two enormous packs of supplies, there was no way the guards would believe they just wanted to go for a little stroll.

"I don't know how we're going to get past them," Finn said. "Don't they ever leave? Get bored and decide to take a nap?"

"Not from what I've seen. I checked several times last night, and they were always awake."

"'We could drug them."

Willow cocked her brows. "With what? Somehow, I think the pharmaceuticals are more heavily guarded than discarded sleeping bags."

"You could knock them out with your ninja moves."

"Maybe. But there are too many people around now. If we tried that, it would have to be at night. But even then, it's risky." She knew her own limits. She couldn't take out two armed guards by herself before either of them sounded the alarm.

If she had Silas helping her...but he was already gone with Amelia and Micah. Gabriel was here, but he'd become fast friends with Cleo. Willow had never trusted him completely. Now that he was back in the fold of the New Patriots, she trusted him about as far as she could throw him. And Finn, bless his damn heart, was a pacifist, so he wasn't any help at all.

Jericho could have pulled it off with ease. But Jericho wasn't here anymore. The thought brought a fresh pang of sorrow and regret. She had always felt safe with him. Now there was no one but herself.

Carrying a glass of water, Celeste sauntered between two buildings. Balancing in the stiletto-heeled boots she'd found somewhere, she bent down to whisper something to Benjie. He glanced up at her, an eager grin on his face, and laughed.

Celeste had been different since Atlanta, since the two nights she'd spent wounded and alone after Tyler Horne stabbed her in the leg and left her for dead. She was still Celeste, a spoiled and vain elite to the core, but she was somehow less irritating. She'd stopped complaining so much and actually pitched in to help with cooking, cleaning up, and other tasks.

But now here she was, waltzing up in those ridiculous boots, dressed in skin-tight leather leggings and an oversized fuzzy salmon-pink sweater that would've looked absurd on Willow but somehow looked adorably chic on Celeste's lean, nearly six-foot frame. Her springy, cranberry-red coils haloed her face.

Willow gaped at her. "Wait—is that lipstick you're wearing?"

Celeste grinned. "It sure is." She fluttered her long, slender fingers in Willow's face, her fingernails painted a sparkly scarlet.

"*And* nail polish? Really?"

Celeste sniffed airily. "There's no reason not to look your best."

"In case you haven't noticed, the world just ended."

Celeste pursed her perfectly bowed lips. She swept out her arms in either direction. "But it hasn't. We're still here, aren't we? That's something. That's an accomplishment we should celebrate, if you ask me."

"No one asked you," Willow muttered. She kicked a rock and sent it tumbling into a snowbank melting against the garden shed.

Finn grinned at Celeste. "I think you look very nice."

Celeste swept into an elegant little bow. "Well, thank you."

Jealousy flared in Willow's chest. Why was Finn looking at Celeste? Did he like her? Of course he did. Who wouldn't? She was tall and thin and beautiful, and Willow was short and dumpy and... ugh, she hated this feeling, like some dark and ugly monster sucking at her insides. She hated that she felt it, hated how small and petty it made her.

She'd survived an apocalypse, damn it. This wasn't who she was, who she wanted to be.

Celeste shot Willow a sharp look. "At least someone remembers their manners."

Willow sighed. "What do you want?"

Celeste fisted her hands on her hips. "Y'know, a little kindness wouldn't kill you. I came out here to help you."

Willow leaned back against the fence, one eye still on the guards at the gate. "Thanks, but no thanks. Don't you have somewhere to be? Like in front of a mirror?"

"Willow," Finn said reproachfully.

"Before you scoff," Celeste said with a self-satisfied smirk, "I know what you're doing."

Willow stiffened. All the casual sarcasm drained out of her. If Celeste decided to tell someone, it was all over. The Patriots would double the guards or lock them back up in the quarantined barracks with the Headhunters.

Then they'd be stuck here, surrounded by enemies, helpless and utterly useless. "We're not doing anything—"

Celeste gave her a knowing look. "You're planning to escape."

12

AMELIA

A melia stood in the center of her containment cell, fighting down panic. She touched her charm bracelet beneath her clothes, searching for the tiny violin charm. She pressed her finger against the pointy edge through her sweater. *Breathe. Just breathe.*

It didn't matter. There was no reason to panic. Micah and Silas were right next to her, even though she couldn't see them or feel them.

They wouldn't be in here long. It was only a matter of time. She believed that. She had to believe it.

She sank down on the narrow cot. The mattress was sealed with some sort of soft, impenetrable plastic shell. She imagined all the people who'd sat here before her. Scared, alone, worried for children, parents, and friends, possibly sick, possibly dying.

Time passed. Maybe an hour, maybe two. It felt like much longer.

A woman appeared in front of her cell. The woman wasn't wearing a hazmat suit. She was dressed in a cranberry-red wool skirt and fitted suit jacket. Latina and roughly in her late twenties, she seemed pleasant and well-groomed, her black hair pulled back in a neat bun at the base of her neck.

The woman smiled. "Amelia Black. How wonderful to meet you! Let's get you out of here, shall we?"

Amelia stood up slowly, her hands clasped in front of her.

The woman stepped up to the biometric scanner, placing her palm on the bottom half of the scanner. She stilled, unblinking, as it also scanned her retinas. The door hissed open.

The woman held out her arm. Amelia took it politely as she stepped out of the containment cell. "Thank you."

"My name is Vera Longoria-Castillo. Call me Vera. I work directly for President Sloane and the Coalition."

"It's a pleasure to meet you," Amelia said automatically.

"President Sloane is very eager to meet you."

Amelia nodded mutely, not trusting her own voice. She'd suspected President Sloane was here. Now she knew for sure.

Vera tugged her away from the row of cells. "I'm sure you're tired and would like to rest. As we speak, a room is being prepared for you right in the capitol, and—"

Amelia halted. "What about my brother and my friend?"

"They'll join you soon enough, but now—"

"I'm not leaving without them."

Micah and Silas both stood behind the transparent doors of their cells. Micah's hands hung limply at his sides, his glasses slipping down his nose. He smiled at her, offering steady encouragement like he always did.

Silas looked like he was barely containing his rage. His jaw was rigid, his gray eyes sparking, his hands balled into fists at his sides.

"Oh, honey," Vera purred, "they're not immune like you. They'll be released after the quarantine period. Coalition rules, for the safety of everyone."

Her throat closed. She swallowed. "I don't want to leave them behind."

Vera only smiled wider. A smudge of red lipstick marred her symmetrical white teeth. "I'm sure you understand. President Sloane knows they're here. She'll make sure they're given special priority."

"But—"

"They aren't immune, and they aren't chipped." Vera's voice cooled considerably. "If we let them in before ensuring they aren't infected, we would endanger thousands of innocent men, women, and children."

Amelia forced herself to nod, when what she really wanted to do was lunge past Vera and the soldiers and rip open Silas and Micah's cells. But that wouldn't help anything.

She focused on their mission, their purpose: to get the cure. To save everyone. She knew it would require sacrifices and risks. Still, she hated the thought of abandoning them in this place with every fiber of her being. "May I at least say goodbye?"

"You'll get to see them in only a few days, so don't worry your pretty little head!" Vera patted her back, her smile bright and friendly again.

Amelia repressed a flinch. She still disliked being touched, especially by strangers.

Amelia gave Micah and Silas a small wave, the only thing she could do. Silas snarled something, his face contorting, but she couldn't hear him. Micah tapped his chest, that warm, comforting smile still on his face, telling her it was going to be okay.

Her hand flitted to the bracelet around her neck. It was attached to the leather thong Micah had made for her. She still had a piece of him. It would only be a few days, like Vera said.

She steeled herself, fighting down the flicker of apprehension, of panic. She could do this. She had to do this. If she had to do it alone, then so be it. "I understand."

"Good girl!" Vera steered her past a cluster of soldiers and several sealed compartments. A blast of cold air struck her as they exited the containment center. She shivered, drawing her jacket more tightly around herself.

"Impressive, isn't it!" Vera gushed as she led Amelia through the towering, fifteen-inch-thick steel city gates that controlled access to the Sanctuary. Dozens of armed soldiers, military drones, and several tanks flanked the entrance. The plasma wall rose on either side, impossibly tall and imposing. The electrified plasma crackled and hissed.

The gates closed behind them without a sound.

"We could have taken a transport, but I thought you'd want to see our glorious city," Vera said eagerly. "This is a government-operated safe zone, like Raven Rock, Cheyenne Mountain, Mount Weather. But people can't live for long underground. It's just not natural.

"I'll tell you a secret. When I first heard we were coming here, I thought it was going to be just another awful underground bunker of concrete and stale air, but I was so wrong! The government built this place to last not for months, not for years, but for decades. And who would want to leave? We have everything we could possibly need!"

Vera guided Amelia onto a moveable sidewalk. They passed people walking, chatting, studying their Smartflexes. Just like before— though even in here, many still wore masks.

The Sanctuary was laid out in a series of expanding concentric rings, like the cross-section of a tree, only shaped more like an oval, Vera explained. Each ring was tiered and separated further into districts. The outer rings were for food, energy, and manufacturing production, the middle rings for worker and soldier housing, the inner rings for "critical infrastructure elements and our most important citizens, of course."

As they walked, Amelia couldn't stop staring. The luxury apartments on her left were column-shaped, with large, circular terraces jutting out on each level. Transparent spheres curved over the terraces, enclosing a riot of colorful gardens and lush, verdant plants.

Only a few hundred yards from the gates, an enormous square with an impossibly green lawn spread before them, flanked on either side by business and luxury apartment buildings. At the far end rose three impressive structures, taller and more beautiful than all the rest. "What are they?" Amelia asked.

"BioGen headquarters, City Hall, and the Capitol," Vera said. "The heart of the Sanctuary. Pretty much everything is controlled within those three buildings." She gestured at a manicured rose bush, delicate petals of primrose-pink, deepest ruby, and flaming orange in full bloom. "We use the latest genetic modifications to keep the foliage flourishing even in winter. Amazing, isn't it?"

Drones zoomed through the air above their heads—delivery, security, surveillance. Auto-transports hummed to and fro. Emblazoned on the sides and fronts of nearly every building were giant holoscreens playing ads for VR games, popular vlogs, designer brands, holofilms, and networking apps.

Amelia gaped. After months of no or very little power, the gleaming lights and vibrant pixels and shimmering holos danced in front of her eyes like vivid, almost grotesque apparitions. Did those commodities even exist anymore? Were the ads simply a comfort thing, a promise that the world was still the same, even though everyone knew it wasn't?

"No dinosaurs or outdated tech here," Vera went on briskly. "Everything has been built to the latest safety and tech standards. Residences and offices are designed to be ultralight, modular, and made from eco-friendly organic material, mostly quartz and bamboo. They run all the new applications and appliances. Plug-and-play, hot-swapping peripherals, all of it with a twenty-four-hour wireless uplink to the Net. Energy lines, plumbing, security, fire, structural integrity, indoor air quality, lifestyle data —it's all built-in, all auto-maintained. If you misplace your designer shades, your house will tell you where to find them. Wicked cool, huh?"

Amelia didn't know the correct word for it, for what she was feeling. She was used to the silence of a broken world, not the hustle and bustle of so much busyness, so many people all at once and so close together. She was used to the roads and highways cluttered with the carcasses of dead cars and trucks, the decomposing bodies of their owners still locked inside. She was used to hulking buildings empty of all life but rats and vermin, used to houses and apartments and businesses with busted windows and shattered doors, every surface filmed in dust and dirt and rubble. She was used to scavenging and hunger and a constant, wary fear.

She didn't know if she could ever get used to this again. After so many months of destruction and ruin, all this order and beauty was almost too much to bear.

Vera patted her shoulder. "Listen to me patter about nothing when you must be exhausted! Luckily, we're here!"

A brick circular driveway arced in front of a palatial mansion reminiscent of the architecture of a century past—four stories of majestic white stone, towering fluted columns, a multitude of ornate terraces crowned by a steep, turreted roofline.

Amelia followed Vera up the stone steps to the cedar doors inlaid with panes of stained glass. Eight secret service guards flanked the doors. One of them scanned Vera's wrist, then moved aside as the doors opened.

Amelia stepped inside. An ornate crystal chandelier gilded everything in a golden glow. She took in the grand hall, arched ceilings, the black granite floor so highly polished she could see her own ragged, unkempt reflection.

A smartwall to her left greeted her while an unobtrusive door slid open in the wall to her right, a service bot appearing to take her coat and gloves and store them in the hidden closet.

Vera turned to Amelia, that wide smile still pasted on her face. "We'll get you cleaned up for dinner with President Sloane and the Coalition chairman!"

She reached out and fingered Amelia's short, jagged hair.

Amelia couldn't help it. She jerked back.

Vera didn't even notice. "It must have been so horrible out there in the Outerlands! But don't worry. We can fix your hair. Get you bathed and dressed and looking back to your best in no time!"

"Thank you."

"Anyway, I bet you're just ecstatic!"

"To meet President Sloane?" She was still half-numb, in a mild state of shock. Everything coming at her at once. "I've met her before. When she was vice-president, of course."

Vera squeezed Amelia's arm, bouncing on her heels in excitement. "Oh, didn't I tell you? So sorry! What an 'oops' on my part!" She leaned in close, like she was imparting a vital secret. "Someone else will be at dinner. And he cannot wait to see you! You'll just be tickled pink, I just know it. Your father—Declan Black—he's here at the Sanctuary."

13

GABRIEL

Halfway back to the compound, the second transport's tire blew, punctured by a rock hidden beneath the snow. Jamal and another Patriot worked on changing the tire while the rest of the group grabbed a water break and stretched their legs.

The first transport continued on, hurrying General Reaver and the dead rat back to the infirmary to be tested and examined.

"Is your mother okay?" Gabriel asked Cleo in a low voice.

She scowled at him, her scar twisting the left side of her face. "She's fine. If you think a filthy rodent can take down someone as formidable as my mother, then you're more stupid than you look."

"If the rat that bit her was infected—"

"It's just a scratch!" Cleo whirled away from him. "I'm gonna take a piss. Try to keep a lid on things until I get back."

Gabriel leaned against the vehicle, scanning the hills above them. He breathed in the sharp winter air. Rafts of white clouds drifted over the sun. Behind him, a couple of Patriots joked about something he couldn't hear, laughing among themselves.

Twenty yards ahead of the transport, a streak of movement snagged his gaze. Cerberus. His white pelt glinted as he slipped into the shadows between a clump of pine trees.

Gabriel glanced around, scanning the road in both directions. No one else was watching.

Silently, he followed Cerberus into the woods. He kept a safe distance, winding between maple and birch trees, stepping over roots and jagged rocks. A twig snapped beneath his boot.

Cerberus spun around. A slow sneer spread across his face. "Can't a man piss in peace anymore?"

Anger flared through him like an electrical current. His hand strayed to the rifle slung over his shoulder. "How can you live with yourself?"

"You're going to have to be more specific."

He clenched his jaw so hard his teeth rattled. "You're the problem with the world. You buy and sell human beings. You trade in suffering and slavery."

"You think they don't?" Cerberus gestured behind them, in the general direction of the Sanctuary. "Their city—our entire civilization —was built on the backs of others' suffering. You know it as well as I, better than I. Your choices are to die a victim or see the world for what it is and adapt to fit that world, to dominate that world, to take what's yours by force and violence."

"There's another way." Gabriel struggled to restrain his anger. "That way leads only to destruction and suffering and death. Violence is sometimes necessary, but it is not the answer. Domination and force are not the answer."

"Those are empty words you don't really believe," Cerberus sneered. "We're the same."

Gabriel bristled. "I am not."

Cerberus leaned against the slim trunk of a birch tree. "You want to kill me right now."

"That's no secret."

"You would kill an unarmed man who's not an immediate threat. That's murder."

"I am not a murderer."

Cerberus's lip curled. "I heard what you did on that ship. You're a killer. That's who you are. No one changes."

Gabriel's fingers tightened on the stock of his rifle. He could do it right here, right now. No one was close enough to stop him. He could drench the ground with this psychopath's blood. He could finally avenge Nadira. The desire was so strong he was nearly blinded with it.

He took a deep, shuddering breath. He was no murderer. "I've changed."

"Have you?" Cerberus smiled, revealing his sharp teeth. "We shall see."

"Rivera!" Cleo called sharply. She stepped between the trees into the clearing, her glare lethal. "A word."

They stood on a rocky outcropping, overlooking a shallow valley about fifty yards below them. The Blue Ridge Mountains loomed in the distance, huge and shadowy blue, like great sleeping giants.

"I know what you're doing." Cleo lit a cigar and stuffed the lighter back in her cargo pocket.

Gabriel watched her warily. "Is that so?"

"You're planning to kill the Headhunter," she said flatly. "And I can't let you do that."

"You don't know what he did."

"I know exactly what his kind does, and who they do it to."

"He murdered my friend." The words were like barbed wire in his mouth. The memories seared through him—cradling Nadira in his arms, her body impossibly light and fragile, the blood spreading across her chest, her head nestled against his chest like she was only sleeping.

Sometimes, we get what we don't deserve, she had whispered, blood bubbling from her lips. *Sometimes, we don't get what we deserve.*

She had thrown herself in front of the bullet intended for Gabriel. A bullet shot by Cerberus. That moment had broken Gabriel's heart wide open. That moment he would give almost anything to do over, to switch places, to take the punishment he'd deserved.

That choice had been taken from him. But Cerberus was still here. Still living and breathing in a world where Nadira wasn't. Out of all the injustices plaguing the world, this was something he could—he would—do something about.

Cleo blew out an icy circle of smoke. "You think I don't understand. I do. But you need to put your revenge aside. For now."

"We've found the Phantom. Cerberus served his purpose. He's dead weight now."

"He's not. He has hundreds of armed, trained fighters. He's a skilled, organized leader. His lot would fall apart if we tried to take him out and lead them ourselves. It doesn't matter how much you hate him—we need him to fight the true enemy." She pointed into the valley with her cigar. "Look."

Gabriel followed her gaze. A cluster of buildings huddled in the center of the valley—three large farmhouses, several barns and storage sheds, with fenced areas for farm animals. Except for a large metal garage, the buildings were blackened husks. Something—or someone—had burned this place to the ground.

"Use your scope," she said, her voice husky.

He swung his rifle by its strap, set the butt against his shoulder, adjusted the scope, and peered through the glass. Scattered here and there across the muddy ground were blackened skeletons. Two large ones together, with two small ones in-between. A family. Children.

There were other bodies—some charred skeletons, others badly burned but still recognizable as human. A flutter of auburn hair. An apple-green dress rippling in the breeze. A tiny arm flung out, an ash-covered stuffed bear lying next to outstretched fingers.

He staggered back, revulsion roiling in his gut. Acid burned the back of his throat. He was sickened, horrified. "What the hell happened here?"

"These people weren't infected. This was a safe zone. The Sanctuary killed them anyway. Our government committed this atrocity and a thousand others like it. They act in fear—destroying anything and everything they view as a potential threat to their power and control."

Gabriel's outrage burned white-hot. His whole body went rigid. His hands balled into fists. He wanted to fight, to destroy something, to rip this depraved and rotting world apart with his bare hands.

"You think I don't have compassion or empathy or whatever," Cleo said. "I see it in your eyes whenever you look at me. But you're wrong. I have compassion for them." She jabbed her finger at the valley, at the charred and blackened skeletons. "I knew them. We gave them food a few times, lent them one of our extra generators. I tried to get the daughter to convince her parents to join us. But they wouldn't. They wanted peace, freedom. They didn't get it."

She paused for a moment, her jaw working, the cigar clamped between her teeth. "President Sloane and the rest of the Coalition did this. They saved their own and left the rest of us to die. They are the true enemy. The only enemy. Do you understand?"

His insides were full of cut glass. He felt shredded. "This has to end."

"Then help me end it." She turned to him, her eyes smoldering coals. "You don't like me. Maybe you even hate me. I don't care. You hate the New Patriots. I don't care. You hate the Headhunters. I don't care.

"What I need is your help, not your adoration. You're skilled. You're smart. You did what needed to be done on the *Grand Voyager*. You have what it takes to lead, to fight."

He spat out the words. "And Cerberus?"

"We use him as long as he's useful. After we've taken the Sanctuary, you can have your revenge. On the Headhunters. Kill them all if you want. I'll even help you."

"You promised him peace."

She shrugged. "I lied. It's called strategy, Rivera."

"You lied to me, too." He kept his gaze on the terrible scene below him. He refused to allow himself to look away. "About your plans to attack the Sanctuary."

"I owe you nothing," she scoffed. "Not a damn thing."

He wasn't so naive as to believe she wasn't using him just as she was using the Headhunters, just as she used the Pyros. When she was done with him, would she discard him and his friends just as easily?

Was there someone worth redeeming within all of that anger? Someone fierce and loyal and brave as hell? He wanted to believe there was. "If we're allies, if we're going to work together, then we have to trust each other."

She tapped ash from her cigar and scowled. Her gaze drifted back to the scene below them, to the apple-green dress fluttering in the breeze. "Fine. You have my trust. Do I have yours?"

He hesitated. Cleo and the New Patriots were offering him everything he'd been denied before—vengeance, justice, the promise of creating a new and better world—but the cost was still as high as ever.

She tossed her cigar on a rock and ground it out with her boot. "You have a choice to make, Rivera. The question is, which side are you on?"

14

WILLOW

"What are you going to do?" Willow asked Celeste, hardly daring to breathe.

Celeste rolled her eyes. "You're as bad as Silas sometimes, you know that?"

Willow frowned. "Thank you?"

"You're off to do something brave and heroic, right?"

"Or incredibly stupid," Willow said.

"It's too soon to tell," Finn said brightly.

"I don't need details." Celeste sidled up next to Finn and lowered her voice. "It's probably better if you don't tell me. I'm gonna go out on a limb and guess you need to bypass those bozos over there."

"You have any ideas?" Finn asked.

"Yeah, actually." Celeste turned and pointed to a spot about twenty yards past the fence where a rocky outcropping and a thick copse of pine trees would provide good cover. "You just need a minute of distraction to get through the gate and make it over the open ground to those trees."

"And how are we going to do that?" Willow asked, still feeling sour and prickly.

Celeste crossed her long, lean legs. She flipped her mass of tightly coiled curls over her shoulder and winked seductively at Willow. "Why, with the art of flirting, of course."

Willow flushed. She crossed her arms over her chest. "I don't flirt."

Celeste's bright laugh rang out in the cold winter air. Both guards glanced over at them. "I didn't mean you. I mean me. *I'll* do it. I'll distract them with my scintillating charm, and you three will scurry into the woods and disappear."

"You can distract them for that long?" Willow asked, still dubious.

Celeste tsked. She cocked one hip coquettishly. "Oh darling, you've never seen me at my best."

"What about opening the gate? It's locked."

Celeste's simpering expression dropped from her face like a mask. She spun in a slow circle, pretending to look at everything but focusing on the fence, the guards, the gate, and checking for any other Patriots nearby. Willow watched her, stunned.

Celeste turned to Willow, suddenly serious and determined. "I'll get it done. You just be ready to go."

Shame skewered Willow. How petty she'd just been. Acting snotty, jealous of Celeste's beauty, wallowing in her own self-pity—it was pathetic. A ridiculous thing to be worried about at the end of the world, with life and death and everything she cared about hanging in the balance.

It was a flaw she just couldn't seem to get rid of—no matter how much she despised herself for it. And here was Celeste, doing her best to change, to be a better person. To help them.

"Thank you, Celeste. I mean that."

Celeste's smile was dazzling. "You're welcome."

Willow huffed her bangs out of her eyes. If Celeste could be a better person, so could she. The words weren't easy to say, but she forced them out. "Do—do you want to come with us?"

Celeste shook her head with a laugh and fluttered her fingers again, her scarlet nails flashing blood-red in the sun. "I *cannot* handle one more day in the wild. Been there, done that. It royally sucked. No, I'll stay here and keep an eye on things. Keep Gabriel on the up and up, take care of Amelia's mom, and help the Patriots with whatever they need."

Gratefulness overwhelmed her. She resisted the sudden urge to hug Celeste. That would be entirely too awkward. "Be careful."

"You, too. I want to see you guys again. We belong together—our group, I mean." She paused, daintily biting her lower lip, careful not to smear her lipstick. She glanced at Willow again. "It feels like a family."

"We are a family," Willow said, and meant it. "We'll be back. I promise."

"I'm going to hold you to it." Celeste looked between Finn and Willow. "Are you ready?"

Willow looked over at the garden, where the kids were still happily digging in the red Georgia clay. She caught Benjie's eye, lowered her hand to her thigh, and flashed the secret hand signal they'd devised last night. He wiped orangey-red clay smears on his already stained pant legs and gave her an enthusiastic thumbs-up.

"As ready as we'll ever be," she said.

"Well then, stand back and prepare to be amazed." Celeste spun elegantly and flounced across the grounds, swaying her hips. Not enough to look weird or unnatural. Just enough to be alluring, tantalizing. She knew what she was doing.

The first guard turned from his post by the fence. Celeste waved as she approached them. Willow couldn't hear what they were saying, but Celeste was speaking animatedly, pointing outside the fence at something. The other guard laughed. The guards were both young, in their early twenties; one red-haired and bearded, the other a good-looking Asian guy with a low ponytail. Celeste tilted her head, leaned in, and said something softly.

Willow tensed. She kept her head turned toward Benjie, but watched Celeste out of the corner of her eye. The kids were distracted, and there were no other adults nearby. She wiped her damp palms on her pant legs and held her breath.

Celeste asked a question. The bearded guard shook his head. She leaned in, her fingers barely grazing his arm as she flashed him an enchanting smile. He noticed. She pointed again at something beyond the fence. This time, the ponytailed guard nodded. He actually moved to the gate, swiped a passcode into the padlock, and opened it.

"I want her magical powers," Willow said under her breath to Finn, who was pretending to be engrossed in some sort of ridiculous stretching exercise. "I think she just cast a spell on them."

The guards looked like they were going to stay at the fence line. Just as the bearded guy was about to relock the gate, Celeste grazed his elbow again, gently chiding him with a giggle and a toss of her hair. This time, they both followed her, lock forgotten, entranced.

Celeste led them toward a grouping of boulders about fifty yards to the northwest, where Willow could just make out a small thicket of bright purple violets poking through a bare patch of earth.

Celeste had done it. The gate was open. The guards' backs were turned. And they were plenty distracted, attracted to Celeste like moths to a flame.

"Now," Willow said.

They sprang into action—but without running, so they wouldn't attract undue attention. It was one of the most excruciating minutes of Willow's life. Despite the chilly air, sweat dripped down her spine.

She walked stiffly to Benjie and thrust out her hand. "Can I borrow you for a minute, buddy?"

Finn strode behind the shed, hauled two packs over his good shoulder and gripped the straps of the third pack, lifting it easily. He met Willow and Benjie at the fence. They slipped through the opened gate. Willow paused to click the lock back into place. The guards would forget they had left it open.

She glanced back at the kids playing in the dirt. None of them were watching. The voices of the guards drifted through the air. Celeste's clear voice rang out in a peal of girlish laughter.

"Go!" Willow hissed.

They sprinted up the steep hill behind the compound. There were twenty yards of open ground before they reached the tree line. The hairs on the back of Willow's neck prickled. She felt vulnerable, exposed. She half-expected to hear a shout or even a gunshot behind her.

Finn reached the tall rock outcropping first, ducking low behind it. Benjie's foot struck a small stone. It tumbled down the hill. Willow seized the back of his jacket and lunged for the outcropping, diving behind it with Benjie in tow. She landed on top of her brother with a grunt.

"Ouch!" he gasped, but in a whisper.

Good boy.

She scrambled to her hands and knees on the cold, uneven ground, rocks and twigs digging painfully into her kneecaps, her heart surging in her chest. She held one finger to her lips. Benjie nodded, eyes wide.

In the pine tree beside them, a bird chirped. The breeze rustled the pine needles. Celeste's voice carried, high and bright. She sounded happy. Willow risked a peek over the side of the rock.

Below them, Celeste was leading the guards back to the fence. She clutched a handful of the delicate purple flowers, holding them to her nose and gushing over their beauty. Both guards were nodding, enthralled by her every word.

"She's talented, no doubt about that," Finn whispered.

"Are we starting our epic quest now, Mister Finn?" Benjie asked.

"You bet, Sir Benjie." Finn rubbed his numb right arm. "Let us not tarry a moment longer."

"We're not out of the woods yet," Willow said, rolling her eyes at the irony of the phrase. "Stay on your hands and knees and crawl right behind me, okay? The trees are thick here and should cover us, but just in case. We're going to get a safe distance, then skirt around the compound in a big circle before heading southeast."

So began their quest.

Whether it ended in glory or disaster remained to be seen.

15

GABRIEL

C leo and Gabriel stood in the compound's garage, a huge warehouse with ten garage bays and room for more than a hundred vehicles. They were still waiting for General Reaver's test results. Cleo hadn't stopped scowling in two days, her entire body vibrating with the tension.

"We have three hoverchoppers and two tanks, but no airjets." Cleo gestured with her cigar toward several rows of Humvees, Jeeps, a few trucks, and ATVs. "The Settlement has plenty, but we have no way to get them."

"Who exactly are these people?" Gabriel asked.

"They call themselves the Settlement. They're not the most creative. We call them Undergrounders. Moles. They live in an underground bunker. Which makes them idiots, but well-fortified idiots. Rumor is they have their own aircraft armada. The bunker is an ancient abandoned air force base. The government knows about them, but they're pacificists, harmless crazy hippies spouting love and peace and some such crap."

"Pacifists?" Gabriel asked, thinking of Finn. "With an armada?"

"They want to be left alone, but they'll defend themselves." She grunted and blew out a puff of smoke. "We learned that the hard way."

"Did you try talking to them?"

Cleo gave him a scathing look. "Until we were blue in the face. Then we tried stealing an airjet. We lost seventeen good soldiers. Trust me. They won't help us."

"What if they knew about the cure?"

She rolled her eyes. "Forget about them. They're a non-starter."

"Captain Reaver." A Patriot stood in the opened garage doorway. "There's news."

Cleo stiffened. "What are you waiting for, Nguyen? Out with it."

Bao Nguyen stepped inside, shuffling his feet nervously, refusing to meet Cleo's gaze. He was Vietnamese, with a wide, round face and the stubble of a beard ghosting his weak chin. He was a New Patriots' foot soldier in his early thirties, but his hesitant, uncertain manner made him seem much younger.

Nguyen cleared his throat nervously. In a slow, halting voice, he told them the news. It wasn't good. The Patriots' blood test needed seventy-two hours to detect sufficient virus levels in human blood, but rodents were quicker.

The results were in. The rat was sick.

Even then, if the rat's claws had scratched the general rather than its teeth, Cleo's mother might still have escaped, since the virus was passed through bodily fluids.

But the test results didn't matter now. General Reaver had begun to cough.

She was infected with the Hydra virus.

Cleo's face turned ashen. Her fingers clenched the hilt of her knife. She yanked it from the sheath at her hip, whirled, and hurled it at the wall. The knife spun through the air at an incredible speed, flying end over end before nailing the wall a hairs-breadth above Nguyen's head.

Nguyen ducked with a curse.

The blade lodged three inches deep into the drywall, vibrating from the power of her throw.

"Get out!" she screamed at him.

Nguyen fled, running his hands over his hair as he ran, checking to make sure it was still there.

"What a pussy," she snapped. "It wasn't even close."

"I think our definitions of 'close' differ," Gabriel said.

"Colonel Reid and Colonel Willis are probably thrilled," she said, ignoring him. She paced in a tight circle. Her face was carved in stone, expressionless. Only her eyes burned with a desperate, helpless fury, emotions Gabriel knew all too well. "They've been vying for command for years. With them grappling for power and fighting among each other, it will be chaos."

"I'm sorry," he said.

She jerked her knife out of the wall and slammed it back into its sheath. She remained there for a moment, both hands flattened against the wall, her back stiff, her shoulders quaking. A sound escaped her, so soft he almost didn't hear it. A low moan, the terrified cry of a trapped animal.

He wasn't sure what to say. Micah was always better at this stuff. He wanted to help her, even though he knew his words were useless. "I'm sorry about your mother."

"What do you know?" She turned and faced him. She attempted a smirk, but her lips quivered, the mask she always wore slipping. Cleo was hard, tough, a soldier willing to do whatever it took to get the job done. She was a skilled liar, fighter, and killer. She was dangerous.

She was also a daughter with a dying mother.

"I lost both of my parents, too."

She looked at him with hollowed eyes. "Did you know she's not really my mother? Not biologically, I mean."

He had noticed that Cleo was Indian while her mother was African-American, but he had no idea who her father was. These days, families came in so many shades it hadn't really even registered. "I didn't know."

"My brother and I were foster kids, just products of a broken system. My dad was a mean drunk, and my mom was just mean." Her lips curled back from her teeth. She gestured at her face. "Bet you wondered where I got this."

"It's none of my business."

"Damn right, it isn't. But it's your lucky day. Most people here think it's a war wound from one of the homemade bombs we used to blow up government buildings. I let them think that. They don't want to know that truth. Nobody wants to know that my dad believed in corporal punishment, that he thought pouring boiling water on his seven-year-old daughter's face was a reasonable discipline for sass. They don't want to know it was my mom who held me down and let him do it." She glared at him, the burned side of her face shiny in the florescent lighting, challenging him. "The truth is a lot less glamorous, a lot more ugly. Like me."

Gabriel's chest tightened. No wonder she was so hard. She'd had to be. It sickened him, all the cruel ways parents could destroy their own children.

But she didn't want pity. So he didn't give it to her. "What happened?"

"The state took me and my brother away. But group homes aren't exactly an improvement. The government didn't give enough stipend to cover adequate food, let alone clothes and toys and whatever else kids are supposed to have. Hell if I know. We fought over food. Only the meanest had full bellies at night. I always made sure me and my brother had something to eat, no matter what.

"The workers were as broken as we were. You don't want to know what happened there. I ran away five times."

"Did they catch you?"

"My brother, he—my mother pushed him down the stairs when he was four. Broke both his legs. They never healed properly. So he couldn't run away with me. I never got caught. Each time, I came crawling back on my own. Couldn't bear to leave my brother."

Gabriel nodded. That, he understood. Cleo might act like a sociopath, but she was capable of love. She clearly loved her brother, had sacrificed and suffered for him. Gabriel felt the same ferocious, protective love for his brother. He'd do anything for Micah.

"I was twelve when this woman comes in," Cleo continued. "Short, middle-aged, but she's got this presence, you know? You notice her. One of the older boys said she'd adopted two kids a few years ago. She took her time, talking to the workers and visiting with every kid, all of them acting sweet as sugar even though they were really monsters.

"I didn't like her. I didn't trust her. When it was my turn, I didn't act any way but myself. No nice old lady was ever going to pick a scarred, ugly girl with bruises and scratches all over her arms and face from fighting.

"But then she came up to me and looked real hard at me without saying anything for a moment. She asked me how often I won. I said, 'As often as I need to.' She laughed. Then she said, 'I'm looking for troublemakers who will grow up to make trouble, to change how things are, to make them better. Are you a troublemaker?' And I said, 'You can see that for yourself.'

"So she chose me. She picked me, out of all of them. I said I'd go with her, but not without my brother. She said that was an acceptable arrangement, and went to fill out the paperwork.

"That was over a decade ago." She gave a rueful smile, her expression sharp-edged as a knife. "My mother is tough. But so am I. I haven't lost her. Not yet."

She pushed off the wall and ran her hands through her purple braids, shoving them over one shoulder with a heavy sigh. The sleeve of her jacket slipped up her arm, revealing a line of scars, each about an inch long, laddered from her wrist to her forearm. Some were bunchy and white, others an angry purple, a few red—fresh cuts, not yet scars.

She caught him looking. Her face hardened, the mask slipping back into place. "To track my kills."

"What for?"

"To remember," she said with a snort, "that no one gets in my way. No one." She strode forward until she was inches from Gabriel. He could feel the body heat pouring off her—an unquenchable fire of hatred, fury, and conviction. "We can't wait. We have to take the cure by force. We have to attack the Sanctuary now."

16

AMELIA

Hot water streamed over Amelia's head, neck, and shoulders. She turned the temperature so high it was nearly scalding. Steam billowed all around her.

The walk-in shower was tiled in intricate patterns of teal, aqua, and shades of blue, from palest egg-shell to the deepest cerulean hues of the ocean. Twelve sprayers massaged her body from the sides, while overhead, a rain shower head spilled a hot waterfall over her head and shoulders. The personalized scent of honeysuckle and jasmine—her mother's favorite flowers—infused the steaming room.

After months of cold and caked dirt and sweat, with only a few lightning-fast showers in freezing water, she finally felt clean for the first time since the *Grand Voyager*. How desperately she'd missed this —warmth, cleanliness, comfort, and beautiful, sumptuous surroundings.

Weariness filled her bones like cement. She was so tired. Tired of always looking over her shoulder, perpetually tense and anxious, unable to sleep, fear her constant companion.

She raised her head and closed her eyes as rivulets of warm, soapy water ran down her face. For all those years, she'd misjudged her mother, believing she'd stayed with Declan for money, prestige, power. Amelia hadn't valued safety because she already had it. She'd never had to feel its lack. But safety was a powerful thing, a precious thing.

She understood this now as she stood beneath the warm, soothing rain, tears pricking the backs of her eyelids, in a way she'd never understood before.

How much would she give to stay here? To never have to go back to the cold, the discomfort, the dirt and the hunger, the constant danger and fear and death?

How much was safety worth?

But you're not safe here.

She leaned against the tile wall, her eyes still closed. The powerful massage sprayers pummeled her stomach and thighs, so strong it almost hurt.

With all the worrying she'd done over the last months, she should have been prepared. But she wasn't. She felt the shock of it in every cell of her body, in her bones.

Her father was alive. Somehow, someway, he'd escaped from the international terrorist syndicate that had abducted him from the *Grand Voyager*.

Her father was here.

And she would be forced to face him.

Her father, whose cold and calculating manipulations brooked no weakness. Her father, who used shame as a tool to humiliate and control. Her father, who exploited her beauty and charm as a tool to beguile his political allies.

She had spent years checking mirrors compulsively, ensuring she was perfect enough, good enough, for her father. But whatever she did, it was never enough.

It wasn't until his final rejection on the *Grand Voyager's* bridge that Amelia finally understood that her father might be incapable of loving her.

Despite everything he'd done to her, he was also her savior. He was the one who had introduced her to the violin, who'd glowed with pride at her concerts and competitions. And he was the one who had saved her from brain damage and certain death with the illegal medication he'd developed for her deadly form of epilepsy.

A cold, dull dread stole over her. She wasn't ready. She had thought she was, but she wasn't.

Her knees buckled. She collapsed hard, slipping to the wet, slick tile. She dragged in harsh, rasping breaths. Her belly cramped, her knees knocking against each other, her shoulders shaking, her whole body trembling.

She drew her legs to her stomach and wrapped her arms around her shins. She rocked back and forth, numb and terrified and alone. Water pounded her head and back, pooling around her feet.

Fear and despair clawed at her. Beneath it all, beneath the slow-burning shame and betrayal and anger, there was a terrible kind of devotion. She both feared and hated her father—and loved him. How could she possibly reconcile such competing, disparate emotions inside her without being torn apart?

How was she possibly going to do this?

When the first tears came, she barely noticed them. They blended with the water pouring down her face. They came harder and faster, until she was sobbing, heaving, unable to stop them. Unable to stop anything.

It might have been an hour before the grief wrenched every tear from her body. The warm water never ran out.

Numbly, she unfolded her limbs and forced herself to stand.

She waved her hand over the dryer sensor. The sprayers retracted, replaced by the auto-dryers. Billowing clouds of heat enveloped her, wicking the liquid from her body. In moments, she was dry from head to toe, even her hair.

The temperature was warm as she stepped into the bedroom. She nearly fell into the opulent, king-sized sleep pod. The curved lid of the sleek, egg-shaped pod was open, beckoning to her to lay down, to succumb to her exhaustion. With the pod's simulations, she could choose to sleep on decadent silks and furs, luxurious feather-soft velvet, or drift in a calm, moonlight-drenched ocean. The advanced haptics and pressurized air nodules could replicate the weightlessness of floating in outer space. In the sensory deprivation of a sleep pod, she could sleep for three days straight.

Her gaze was drawn to the velvet box wrapped in a bow laying in the cushioned center of the sleep pod. She unwrapped it to find a simple pair of powder-blue underwear and a bra. *Hope this is your size! Dinner is at six! Love, Vera!* read the attached digital card.

She couldn't let herself rest yet.

Amelia stepped behind the discrete privacy shield in front of the closet. She waved her SmartFlex over the body scanner. Nothing happened.

If it were working, the scanner would have scanned her height, weight, and measurements and projected the latest runway fashions over a rotating holographic image of her body. Through a chute in the wall, her selection would be delivered in a lavender-scented box.

But that was the old world. Or, that was the old world of the elites. She knew better now.

The closet was barely visible but for the rectangular cracks in the sleek white wall. "Open closet," she said.

The door slid open, revealing a pre-selected dress draped on the single hanger. Of course. That was why the scanner hadn't worked. Her father had chosen for her.

Carefully, slowly, she slipped into the supple, indigo-blue asymmetrical gown. It rippled above her knees, silky as gossamer, but hung loosely at her chest and hips. She'd lost weight from the Hydra virus, from the weeks and months scavenging to survive. She wasn't willowy like Celeste or sturdy and muscular like Willow. She looked sickly.

She wrapped a luxurious sable shrug around her bony shoulders and glanced down. A delicate, midnight-blue clutch lay on the vanity next to a familiar-looking benitoite necklace gilded with diamonds. The rich indigo facets of the rare jewel glinted bright and fiery in the light.

Amelia sucked in her breath. She'd worn this necklace—or one eerily similar—on the *Grand Voyager*. Like everything else, her father had picked it for her.

Her hand hovered above the necklace, trembling. He wanted her to wear it. He would be upset if she didn't.

She took one last glance in the mirror. Her hair was a ragged mess, cut in jagged chunks around her ears.

She didn't miss her long hair. Cutting it short had been symbolic of so many things. It had freed her from the gilded prison of perfection her father had forced on her. She no longer needed to be beautiful and graceful and articulate and utterly dazzling.

Until now.

Now, she was right back inside that gilded cage. Her hair hadn't made a mote of difference. The cool air against her bare neck made her feel exposed. Her heart was cold as a block of ice. Her mouth was dry, her palms damp.

No. She didn't have to be afraid anymore. *Don't forget who you are.*

Even though Declan Black was still alive, she wasn't his daughter anymore, not the one he knew. She wasn't the scared, weak little girl he expected. She was someone else now. Better, stronger, braver.

She grasped the diamond charm bracelet still bound to the leather thong around her neck. She pressed her index finger against the point of the violin charm. It didn't fit her elegant dress. She would wear it anyway.

Someone knocked on the door. "Vera Castillo-Longoria is here to see you," the room AI purred in a rich, sophisticated voice.

Amelia left the blue benitoite necklace on the vanity and went to meet her father.

17

GABRIEL

Fear stuck in Gabriel's throat like a hook. He stared at Cleo in horrified disbelief. "You can't do that! You can't attack the Sanctuary now! Amelia is going to smuggle the cure out, just like she promised. You have to give her time! You have to—"

"I don't have time!" Cleo's dark eyes glittered. "Did you not just hear me? My mother is *infected*! She's dying!"

It was too dangerous. She was insane. They couldn't put Amelia, Micah, and Silas at risk like this. "And Amelia and my brother?" he roared.

"We'll be careful. We won't hurt the labs, the scientists, or Amelia. We'll take over, and the scientists will get us the cure."

"What about anti-virals?" Gabriel asked, scrambling for ideas. "Don't they hold off the symptoms and delay the onset indefinitely?"

"Only for a month or two at most," Cleo said. "The Sanctuary lied. Big surprise. Besides, we don't have any. I already asked Cerberus —and checked their supplies for veracity. They're out. They'd planned to stock up when they reached the Sanctuary. We prevented that."

"So we find a way to get more. We have what—almost two weeks before the final stage of the disease?"

Cleo shook her head. "The anti-virals only work if taken before the coughing starts, within the first forty-eight hours."

Gabriel thought of Harmony. She'd betrayed them to the Head-hunters for a case of anti-virals for her infected, dying nephew. Her nephew, who had already suffered through the advanced stages—the incredibly high fever, the bleeding from the nose, mouth, and ears.

A sharp, bitter pain flared in his chest. Harmony had betrayed them for absolutely nothing. The anti-virals wouldn't have worked. Her nephew died anyway. Nadira was killed for nothing.

Something shriveled inside him. It was all so crushingly pointless. He blinked back the stinging in his eyes.

"I will not let my mother die," Cleo said. She patted her breast pocket for a fresh cigar and growled in frustration when she found it empty. "We move up our plans. We attack the Sanctuary and get the cure now."

He felt sickened, dread coiling in his gut. "What about the rest of the Patriots' leadership? They won't agree with such a rash action. You're putting too much at risk!"

Her eyes flashed. "I'll make them agree."

Something crashed behind them. Gabriel and Cleo spun, yanking their guns from their holsters and aiming into the shadows of the garage. Something—or someone—was hiding around the corner five yards to their rear, in the hallway that led to a pair of offices, bath-rooms, and a back door.

Gabriel's heart hammered against his ribs as he inched forward silently, Cleo right beside him. He and Cleo crept to the wall, then swiftly rounded the corner. The hallway was empty but for a metal shelving unit containing packs of paper towels, microfiber clothes, and cleaning supplies. A bottle of industrial cleaner had fallen to the floor. Gabriel prodded it with his foot.

Cleo nudged his shoulder, tilting her chin at something at the other end of the hallway. The steel-reinforced back door was wide open, daylight forming a long rectangle on the concrete floor.

"Damn it," Cleo whispered. They rushed through the hallway to the doorway. Outside, the sun peeked through a raft of gray clouds. A strong breeze whipped the bare trees and kicked up a swirl of dead leaves in the patches of ground where the snow had melted.

The sounds of children laughing and screaming as they played soccer drifted from the rec yard. A kitchen worker escorted a hovercart filled with potatoes freshly harvested from the greenhouse thirty yards to their left. To their right, two military Jeeps were parked in the empty, weed-infested lot beside the garage.

They checked the Jeeps, but found exactly what they were expecting—nothing at all. Whoever had been spying on them had gotten away. Who was it? And what were they going to do about what they'd just heard?

A boy dressed in army fatigues with a rifle slung over his shoulder rounded the corner of the garage along the inside fence line.

He shook his head when Cleo questioned him. He'd ducked around the corner to take a piss. He hadn't seen a thing.

"I'm sorry, sir," he said to Cleo nervously, his eyes darting from her to Gabriel. A spray of pimples peppered his forehead and chin. A feather-light dusting of blonde hairs brushed his upper lip. He was just a kid. Maybe fifteen.

"What's your name?" Gabriel asked.

The boy snapped to attention. "James Hunt, sir. Ready for orders, sir."

Cleo gave him a tight smile. "You ready to fight for your freedom?"

There was fear in the kid's eyes, but also determination and boyish enthusiasm. "Yes, sir."

"We'll need your services soon, soldier. You're dismissed."

The boy turned smartly and marched back to his patrol along the eastern perimeter fence line. Gabriel clenched his jaw. "What's he doing here?"

"What do you mean?"

"He's a kid. He's too young. He's—"

"We need every able-bodied soldier," Cleo snapped. "This is his future, too. We've trained him. He has every right to be here. Though he just screwed up royally. The intruder escaped. Whoever they are." Her gaze trained on Gabriel. "It better not be one of your people spying on us."

He saw the defiance in her eyes, the hard resolve, the intensity that burned everything it touched with a consuming fire.

It would burn him, too, if he wasn't careful.

18

AMELIA

"You look lovely, Amelia." President Sloane greeted her with a prim hug and an airy kiss on each cheek. "You must have an incredible story to tell."

"Something like that," Amelia murmured.

A humanoid service bot pulled out a carved, plush chair. She smoothed her dress and sat at the ornate mahogany table. Crystal lights dripped from the domed ceiling. Opulent paintings of former presidents adorned the far wall. On the three remaining walls, pastel colors swirled to the beat of jazz music playing softly from invisible speakers.

President Sloane took her seat at the head of the table. She was dressed in a tailored chartreuse pantsuit. Tall and svelte, she was in her mid-fifties, though she looked younger, lines just beginning to crease her mouth and the corners of her eyes. Her auburn hair was clipped short and slicked behind her ears. She had a brisk, efficient manner. Everything about her oozed competence and authority. "Welcome, my dear. Please, make yourself comfortable."

"Thank you for having me, Madam President. This is truly an honor."

President Sloane gestured at the four other people at the table, who were all watching Amelia with interest. "These are a few of my closest advisers and cabinet, all members of the Coalition." The President introduced them as Senator Steelman, General Daugherty, and her Chief of Staff, Selma Perez. Vera Castillo-Longoria sat further down the table, her head bent as she typed something into her holopad.

"It is a pleasure to meet you all," Amelia said politely.

"Likewise," Senator Steelman said. She was in her late forties, whippet-thin and blonde, her perfectly styled and polished hair cut in a crisp bob to her chin, her makeup precisely applied, her posture ramrod-straight. Her eyes were frank and assessing as she studied Amelia without smiling.

Several members of the president's security team ranged the room semi-discreetly. A hulking man stood behind her. President Sloane followed Amelia's gaze and gestured vaguely. "This is Angelo Bale, my head of security. Impressive, no?"

The man's muscular arms strained the seams of his tuxedo. His oiled black hair was streaked with silver. The shadows playing across the sharp angles of his face gave him a brutal, sinister look. Slowly, he lowered his gaze to meet Amelia's.

Despite herself, she flinched. Angelo Bale's beady eyes reminded her of Kane—the psychopathic New Patriot terrorist who'd enjoyed killing, who took pleasure in others' pain. Who'd taken pleasure in her own.

The memories she'd worked so hard to defeat flashed behind her eyes: Kane and his rough, scrabbling hands, his predatory eyes, his vicious leer as he hovered over her in the captain's quarters on the *Grand Voyager*.

Kane had tried to break her. He almost succeeded. But she'd fought back. She'd beaten him, stabbing him right through the eye with the needle of her auto-injector.

Amelia looked away from Bale, drawing a breath she hoped the president didn't hear. *When among wolves...*she remembered Cleo's words clearly. She didn't doubt for a second there were wolves here, stalking the shadows with beatific smiles set upon their deceptively benevolent faces.

But who were they? Were any of them here right now, watching her with malice in their hearts?

She picked up a linen napkin and spread it over her lap, willing her fingers not to tremble. The table was set with fine china and wine glasses. A cluster of orchids in a glass vase glistened in the dim glow of the crystal lights. A service bot placed a steaming cup in front of her.

"Green tea, correct? Declan said that was your favorite. He suggested we begin, though he will be here shortly. He's very eager to get started on your bloodwork—"

Selma Perez, the president's chief of staff, leaned over and whispered something in her ear. She was a thin, stuffy-looking woman with a horsey face, a pinched mouth and watery eyes.

President Sloane sat back, a wide smile creasing her face. She looked friendlier—and kinder—when she smiled. "Forgive my manners. I have to say, you've brought a fair bit of excitement and hope into a place in sore need of it. Eat, my dear, eat. You must be famished."

Amelia was suddenly starving. The service bot whisked the cover from her plate, revealing steaming beef risotto tarts, succulent lemon chicken, and crisp zucchini fritters. The delicious scent of real, freshly cooked food filled her nostrils.

Her empty stomach cramped. Her mouth watered. Grateful tears filled her eyes. "I—thank you."

She took a bite of chicken, sinking her teeth into the juicy, spiced meat. It was the best thing she could remember eating. Ever. After several hurried bites, she forced herself to remember her etiquette training and set down her fork. "You said my father is here."

President Sloane nodded. "Yes. And with any luck, he'll be able to formulate a cure from the antibodies in your blood. How extraordinary that you, of all people, are the only survivor of the Hydra virus, considering who your father is." President Sloane's eyes were bright and intelligent, her gaze gentle but with a sharpness around the edges as she studied Amelia. "Simply extraordinary."

"But—how did he get here? He was kidnapped on the *Grand Voyager* by the Southeast Asian terrorists." Amelia cringed, remembering Cheng and the thick, purple scar slicing across his face, the way he'd offered her to Kane like a prize, a spoil of war. *Be my guest,* he'd said, the last words she'd heard before Kane dragged her from the bridge by her hair. Before he'd—

Her gaze flickered to Bale again, those beady, viper eyes. She swallowed. She had killed Kane. She wasn't back there, trapped on the *Grand Voyager*, terrified for her life. She had saved herself, then. This time, she would do everything in her power to save everyone else.

She forced herself to focus on President Sloane, on the here and now. To consider the facts dispassionately, clinically. Her father had been their target, but Cheng and his soldiers had planted explosives on the *Grand Voyager*, attempting to destroy everyone on board: elite men, women, and children, ship staff, New Patriots, even his own men.

Gabriel had said Cheng was the one in direct contact with the mastermind behind the Hydra virus. The person or persons who had crossed Declan Black, taking care of loose ends while simultaneously using the New Patriots' attack on the *Grand Voyager* as a ruse, blaming the bioweapon's release on the New Patriots.

They were still out there, whoever they were. Nameless, faceless shadows. A shiver of dread ran through Amelia. Maybe she was staring at one of them right now. Sloane had become president because of the Hydra virus, after it infected and killed President Morgan.

It could be her. It could be anyone.

Senator Steelman was watching her intently. General Daugherty bent and whispered something to Selma Perez, their gazes flickering toward Amelia before darting away. The back of Amelia's neck prickled.

President Sloane wiped her mouth primly with her linen napkin. "This country could not allow terrorists to torture and murder such a valuable leader as the chairman of the Unity Coalition."

"Once we realized the gravity of the situation, we sent our elite Delta Force unit to rescue Declan," General Daugherty said, his voice like gravel. He was a solid, thickly built man in his early sixties, his face craggy, his close-cropped beard streaked with gray. He was a four-star general, his uniform decorated with medals, pins, and badges.

"It was a delicate mission, especially with tensions so high, populations all over the world succumbing to the virus, governments destabilizing; chaos, confusion, and blame running rampant—but our brave troops got it done.

"We rescued your father and brought him here," President Sloane finished. "He's been working with our scientists on finding a cure for the virus ever since."

Amelia nodded around the lump in her throat. There were too many competing emotions swirling inside her. She couldn't even begin to untangle them all.

Senator Steelman leaned forward in her seat. Her dinner was nearly untouched. "I assume you came here because you realized the immunological properties of your blood may be our best chance at synthesizing a cure."

Amelia nodded. "Once we realized no one but myself had survived, yes."

"You are correct," Senator Steelman said. "Others have claimed to be survivors of the virus in an attempt to gain admittance to the Sanctuary, but upon examination, their blood proved to be as useless as everyone else's. Please forgive Dr. Ichpujani for his skepticism."

"Of course." Amelia took a bite of zucchini fritter, forcing herself to chew slowly when she longed to inhale the whole thing.

President Sloane turned to her Chief of Staff. "How soon before Declan will be ready for her?"

Perez glanced up from her holopad. "First thing in the morning, you'll report to the lab. Our virologists can tell you more regarding the specifics tomorrow."

"Oh," President Sloane said, as if disappointed. "Tomorrow I'll be overseeing a food drop for some of the Outerland survivors in the northern suburbs of Atlanta. In the afternoon, I promise to drop by to check in on you."

Amelia frowned at the mention of Atlanta. She pushed back the memories of the rats, the fires, Tobias Moruga and the Pyros. Jericho's death. If she could help it, she'd never set foot in Atlanta again. "What about the rest of the country? What are things like?"

Sloane took a sip of wine. Her expression turned grave. "General Daugherty, you want to take this one?"

General Daugherty coughed and cleared his throat. "There are pockets of survivors all over America. Cheyenne Mountain Complex in Colorado is still functional, along with a few other government and military outposts. There are other countries with functioning governments. Australia and New Zealand were the first to cut off domestic and international travel, so they survived, though they've taken losses in the hundreds of millions. Russia survived, of course. Some parts of Canada are still functioning, albeit barely. Pockets of Africa. They know how to survive. Europe has fallen. Mexico and South America. And Asia. The populations were simply too dense. There was nowhere to run."

Amelia wasn't surprised. Not after what they'd learned from the survivors at Sweet Creek Farm. Still, the words sent a cold, slithering dread through her. The zucchini turned to mush in her mouth.

"I'm with a group of survivors," she said. "Two of them are in the containment center outside the Sanctuary, including my brother. The others are...somewhere else. It's beautiful and safe here. May they come here as well?"

President Sloane smiled. There was something oily about it, like it might slide off her face. She rubbed her eyes. It was then that Amelia noticed the bags under the President's eyes, the unhealthy pallor of her skin. She looked weary—exhausted.

And why wouldn't she be? She was busy protecting the Sanctuary, doing everything she could to keep the surviving government afloat.

Or maybe there were other, more sinister reasons.

"Of course, we'll bring your brother here as soon as we can," the president said.

"What about the others?" Amelia asked. "There are still survivors out there—women and children. Why aren't you looking for them? Why aren't you bringing them here? You seem to have plenty of space —and food."

The other Coalition members seemed to be staring at her so hard she felt their gazes like heat on her skin. Their expressions were pinched, grim, hard to read.

President Sloane leaned forward, pushed her plate aside, and folded her hands on the table. Her eyes softened. "I would love to do that, Amelia. I can't tell you how difficult it has been to close our gates to survivors. But ninety-nine percent of the people outside these walls are contaminated—essentially, they're reservoir hosts."

It was suddenly difficult to breathe. "What do you mean?"

"Reservoir hosts may not be symptomatic—they may not get sick themselves—but the virus has already infiltrated their cells. And if they contact other humans, they'll spread the virus. If we let them inside, we would kill thousands of innocent people and destroy everything we've worked so hard to protect.

"We very carefully screen for any potential candidates we can allow inside our gates, but my most important job is to keep my people —the people already inside—safe, first and foremost. That's one of the reasons every citizen volunteers to receive the monthly antiviral shots our scientists have developed. We're hopeful that over time, the antivirals will strengthen our citizens' immune system in case of accidental exposure—which we do our utmost to prevent, of course."

"We're a fairly well-oiled machine by this point," Senator Steelman said with a prim smile.

Amelia felt light-headed. She couldn't make sense of it all. "But how can—"

"Of course, we do everything we possibly can for those poor souls suffering outside our walls." President Sloane made a flicking motion with her wrist. "Activate wall-screen. Show last week's outreach efforts."

A holoscreen flickered to life on the west-facing wall, in a space between a gilt painting of President Morgan and one of the last-century presidents, President Reagan.

The holo showed a vidclip of President Sloane, Senator Steelman, and General Daugherty on a hoverchopper with several soldiers and figures in hazmat suits. They lowered a huge crate of bottled water and boxed, canned, and powdered food into a clearing. Thirty to forty survivors, mostly families with children, converged on it. The vidclip zoomed in on a young girl of six or seven clutching a bottled water and waving giddily at the camera.

"Screen off." President Sloane turned to Amelia, her expression strained, her eyes full of compassion. "I assure you, as soon as we're able, I'll be the first one on that chopper distributing a vaccine or a cure. But for now, this is all we can do. I have twelve thousand civilians and eleven hundred soldiers I'm responsible for. Do you understand?"

Everything President Sloane said made sense. Were the New Patriots wrong? Had they made a mistake? Or maybe they had their own motives. A benevolent Sanctuary didn't fit into the agenda Cleo and General Reaver wanted to push.

Maybe everything the New Patriots had told them were lies. It wouldn't be the first time. Anyone could be lying for their own sinister reasons. She would have to be at her best to untangle the truth from deception.

"I want to do everything I can to help," Amelia said. "I want to help everyone inside *and* outside the Sanctuary."

"I would expect nothing less of my daughter," came a deep, rumbling voice from behind her.

19

WILLOW

The air was sharp and brittle. Every sound was crisp. The crunch of their boots over snow. The crack of a twig. The soft thud of powdered snow falling from a tree branch.

It was so cold even Willow's blood felt frozen. She stamped her feet on the snowy ground, her boots crunching a layer of frosted pine needles.

The first several miles, they'd jumped at every sound, but now they were used to the rhythm of the woods, the creak of the bare branches against each other, the soft patter of creatures moving in the snow, the dense trees and the shadows that seemed to dog their every step.

"We've been wandering around in the woods for two days now," Finn said. He'd been complaining all afternoon—good-naturedly, but still. He winced, pressing his good hand to his side. "I prefer a more leisurely pace."

"And I'd prefer to sip mai-tais on a Caribbean beach," Willow snapped, "but alas, here we are."

"You get what you get, and you don't throw a fit," Benjie chimed in behind them.

"Listen to the kid," she said with more patience than she felt. They were just now far enough south of the Patriots' compound that her shoulders were relaxed a bit, the tension in her gut beginning to unwind.

She checked the Smartflex she'd borrowed from the Patriots' storage room before they'd left; both the GPS and the compass still worked. It was top of the line, plated in smoky platinum and crusted with rubies. In her old life, she could've paid for four years of college with this. Or maybe a house with more than one bathroom.

But the old world was long gone. Now she'd be thrilled to have an outhouse.

They'd traveled about twenty miles in two days, which was a lot for an eight-year-old kid and Finn, who was still recovering from his gunshot wound.

They were all exhausted. Willow's thighs ached. Her eyes were red and gritty.

Last night, she'd barely slept. Between watch shifts, with the eerily disconcerting forest noises and Finn's giant body nearly squeezing her out of the too-small tent, sleeping was pretty much a lost cause.

She had stayed awake, staring into the living darkness of the woods, wishing the yellow eyes of Raven's wolf would appear, and thinking of Silas, of their last conversation before they'd parted ways.

They had been sparring outside near the compound's training center. Willow had managed to land a particularly nasty punch. Silas stumbled back, clutching his nose. Blood gushed between his fingers. "Damn, princess."

"Are you okay? Let me see." She went to him, gripped by guilt, and tried to pry his fingers away. He flinched from her touch like she'd burned him.

Irritated, she spoke without thinking. "You can have friends, you know. It's not a weakness."

He spat blood on the ground. "To my father, everything was a weakness."

She hid her surprise at his response. It was real—with feeling behind it. He'd never brought up his father before. "He's not here anymore. You are. Believe it or not, there are people who actually care about you."

He wiped the blood from his nose with the back of his shirtsleeve and half-turned toward the tree line, staring off into nothing, his whole body tensed like he was ready to run, to flee.

The conversation had suddenly gotten too serious. She had no idea how to handle it, so she just shrugged in mock indifference. "Not me, of course. Other people. Someone. Somewhere."

He was silent for so long she wondered if she'd said something wrong, if her sarcasm had been a mistake. She was terrible at this sort of thing. Where was Amelia or Micah when you needed them? They were both the sensitive sort.

"I didn't mean that," she muttered. "It was a joke. You know, a lame attempt at...something."

He smirked. But it seemed like an automatic reaction, not something he really meant. He scrubbed more blood from his face. Only a trickle dripped from his nose. He stared down at his bloody hands as he flexed his fingers, popping his knuckles one by one. "I'm aware of the definition of a joke."

"I just—" She scrambled for words that would mean something to him. "You're a good teacher."

The corner of his lip twitched. "I know."

"Humble, too."

"Not to mention extremely good-looking."

Willow laughed.

The tension leaked from Silas's shoulders. He gave her a lazy half-smile.

"You aren't alone," she said. "You don't have to keep pretending that you are."

She expected him to go all sullen and sarcastic, spit out some nasty barb, but he didn't. He clenched and unclenched his fists at his sides. But there was something thawing inside him, a softness in his eyes she didn't remember seeing before. "I'll try to remember that."

"In the Sanctuary...don't get yourself killed, okay?"

"You either." He touched his nose gingerly. "I know a particularly fine sucker punch I'm looking forward to flattening you with. You'll be in a world of hurt."

"It's a date."

They had grinned at each other. Real smiles. Like real friends.

She missed his smirks and snark already. She missed deflecting knife thrusts and eye gouging, breaking choke-holds, and practicing the fine art of throat-punching. She didn't have Silas to spar with, and she didn't want to accidentally hurt Finn's arm, but she still needed to train. She couldn't let herself go soft, not even for a moment.

Out here in the wilderness, she was responsible for both Benjie and Finn. She was *Ate*. She couldn't let anything happen to either of them.

That night, after they made camp and enjoyed a self-heating dinner of spaghetti and faux-meatballs that tasted vaguely of sawdust, she found a small clearing between a grouping of trees and practiced.

She slid into her fighting stance. Legs slightly bent at the knees, left fist up and back to protect her face, right fist up and leading, elbows tucked in. Springy on her feet, muscles tensed. Strike. Block. Punch. Feint. Spin, drop into a lunge. Kick. Repeat.

She punched and kicked and lunged, again and again, knife out, stabbing invisible enemies until her heart was pounding, her muscles warm and loose, and her breath coming in ragged, steaming puffs.

"Nice ninja moves," Finn said when she returned to the campfire. She felt his eyes tracking her.

She tossed more sticks on the fire, then leaned against a nearby tree, half-facing the darkness that swirled and thickened just outside their ring of flickering light.

He still wanted to say something to her. She felt it in the way he studied her, his jaw working, hesitant and unsure in a way he normally never was. He had started a conversation back at the compound on Christmas Eve, when he'd stolen the box of brownie mix and made her an unbaked cake. But she hadn't been ready for it.

Deep down, she was terrified of things changing between them. He was Finn, her best friend. Her family, her person. She couldn't bear the thought of losing him.

In some ways, she was still a coward.

20

AMELIA

Amelia leapt out of her seat, shoving back her chair and nearly spilling her goblet of wine. General Daugherty watched her impassively. Senator Steelman gave a tiny frown of disapproval. Selma Perez didn't bother to look up from her holopad.

Amelia straightened, smoothed her gown, and pasted a brittle smile on her face. She forced herself to turn around. "Father."

Her father's presence was just as regal and commanding as she remembered, if not more so. He drew all the energy in the room. He was tall and broad-shouldered, finely dressed in a dark wool peacoat, a black designer suit, and diamond cuff-links. His brown hair and spade-shaped beard were threaded with silver. But it was his eyes, iron-gray and hard as stone, eyes both cunning and cruel, that undid her.

A tsunami of emotions flooded her, too much for one soul to bear. Declan Black was her father in everything but genetics, the man she had been raised to both fear and adore.

He had forced her to live in shame and fear. He'd hurt and humiliated her mother and brother. He'd intentionally designed the Hydra virus as a bioweapon, intending to murder over one hundred thousand people to further his own agenda and clinch his bid for power.

And yet—some childish part of her she could not deny still loved him. He was her savior. She both loathed his cruelty and craved his approval, felt both terror and elation, joy and grief, hatred and hope, all knotted in a mess she had no chance of untangling.

Her lungs constricted. "Father," she whispered again.

Declan Black grasped her shoulders and crushed her to his chest. He released her, standing back, a broad smile on his handsome, dignified face. "You're my daughter. A survivor. I knew you were still alive."

"So is Mother. And Silas," she said before she could stop herself. Maybe that was a mistake. She didn't know. She didn't know anything, standing there staring at her father, his eyes glowing with pride and admiration, looking at her the way she had longed for her entire childhood—like he finally approved of her, like she'd finally done something worthy of earning his love.

"Silas is here," she said. "He's in quarantine—"

"We'll get them and bring them here where they belong. But first, you and I have work to do." His smile broadened. "I knew it would be you."

She started to ask him how he could possibly know such a thing, but the words died in her throat.

His gaze flicked to her hair. His smile faltered. "We can do something about this?" he asked President Sloane, though it sounded more like a demand than a question.

"Of course," President Sloane said pleasantly, gesturing to the service bot to clear the table. "I'll send my personal stylist to her quarters."

Amelia licked her dry lips. She felt the eyes of everyone in the room on her. "I don't think this is the time to worry about my hair—"

"Nonsense," Declan boomed. "I demand only the best for my daughter."

Some part of her cowered before her father's overpowering presence. A stronger part of her hated herself for such weakness. She straightened her shoulders. "I like my hair."

Declan's gaze flicked to President Sloane, then to General Daugherty and Senator Steelman, before returning to Amelia. His gaze lowered to her throat, to the leather thong she wore instead of the benitoite necklace. His eyes sharpened, though the broad smile never left his face. For a moment, she thought he would criticize her, point out her disobedience, her every flaw and shortcoming.

But he didn't. He waved a hand dismissively. "Months in the wild must have muddled your sensibilities, daughter. But no mind, we'll get you up to par in no time."

Vera Longoria-Castillo cleared her throat. She stepped forward, looking up from her Smartflex. She smoothed her cranberry-red wool skirt. Every hair was tamed and yanked back into a tight bun at the base of her neck again. "President Sloane, a call for you. It's urgent."

"Of course. Please excuse me." President Sloane rose and shook Amelia's hand. "It is a great pleasure to meet you, Amelia. You are a tremendous asset to the Sanctuary. The people are going to love you."

"Thank you," Amelia said demurely, dipping her chin.

The other Coalition members also rose. They shook Declan's and Amelia's hands as they filed out of the room.

"You have a lovely daughter," President Sloane's chief-of-staff said to Declan before hurrying out of the room after the president. President Sloane's head of security, Angelo Bale, followed them silently, his movements surprisingly fluid for such a huge man. After a moment, they were alone in the room but for the remaining security agents.

Declan grasped Amelia's arm.

Unease jolted through her. Was he still upset about her hair? The necklace? He'd always saved his most lethal criticisms for when he had her alone. What was she thinking? She should have just worn it. She should apologize—

No. Those were the thoughts of the anxious, fearful girl she used to be. Not who she was now.

She nearly jerked her arm back, but she restrained herself. "What is it, Father?"

"I knew you would need this." He thrust something hard and round into her hand. A plain white pill bottle. "I formulated some of your medication here in the lab."

She looked down at it, stunned. Her pills. Her father had brought her pills. Her mind couldn't even process it. The hope that had niggled at the back of her mind since she'd learned he was still alive— it was real.

"I ran out. I had a seizure. A bad one. I was—" She stopped herself. "Thank you."

Her father smiled gently, his eyes softening. "You're welcome."

She could have wept in relief. After all this time, the weeks and months spent coming to terms with the fact that her epilepsy was going to kill her, going to tear her brain apart, piece by broken piece— and suddenly, out of nowhere, her father had placed hope into her open palms.

Once again, her father had saved her.

"Get your rest, daughter," her father said. "Tomorrow, we save the world."

21

WILLOW

Willow, Finn, and Benjie spent their third day hiking along a creek bed, fording it in a shallow area, leaping from slippery rock to slippery rock. They climbed one steep ridge after another, Finn keeping a firm grip on Benjie with his good hand. Willow slipped more than once, sending tiny avalanches of loose pebbles and scree down the incline. Once, Finn stumbled, ramming his right shoulder against the trunk of an elm tree.

Willow did her best to help him back up, but he was simply too heavy. "How's your arm?"

He clambered to his feet with a heavy sigh. "Fine. I didn't really feel it."

She looked at him in alarm. "It's still numb? You can't feel anything yet?"

He shrugged. "It's still useless. I think this is it. I don't think it's coming back."

"Are you okay with that?"

He managed a half-grin, but she could see the strain in it, how hard he was working to make it seem okay. "It is what it is, right? At least I'm alive." He swatted the crumbling stump of an oak as they skirted its fallen trunk. "How exactly are we going to find Raven?" He asked to change the subject.

"We aren't." A tangle of thorns tugged at her pant legs. She kicked herself free and shoved aside a thick pine branch, the scent of sap thick in her nostrils. "We couldn't."

Finn whacked the trunk of a maple tree with the walking stick he'd whittled yesterday with the knife on his multi-tool. He was extremely proud of it. "Then what?"

"She needs to find us."

Finn just stared at her, aghast. "That's your genius plan?"

"In fact, it is." Willow smiled. Her lips were chapped and split from the cold, so the smile hurt. She pointed at the carved wooden bird Raven had given Benjie, which Benjie was now zooming around like a toy airplane as he clambered over tree roots buried in the snow. "We need to leave signs so she knows it's us. We have no hope of tracking her and Shadow. We wouldn't even know where to start. But Raven's a tracker, a hunter. We need to make it so she can find us."

"Like Hansel and Gretel left crumbs in the woods to find their way home?" Benjie chimed in.

"Kind of like that, only without birds eating our crumbs. I was thinking we should carve little birds in the tree trunks every so often while we make our way in the general direction of this settlement. We know it's somewhere around Jasper and Elijay. That's not too far from I-575, where she told us she'd wait for us. Though I doubt she's waiting anymore."

Benjie's eyes lit up. "And you think she'll know it's us because she gave me this bird and her name's Raven?"

"Exactly."

Benjie scrunched up his nose, just like Zia used to do, and parroted a high-pitched voice. "That's a ridiculous idea!"

"You're ridiculous," she snapped back, a pang in her chest flaring brightly for a moment. Her grief over Zia wasn't as constant as it used to be, but it was always there, a hidden blade ready to cut at any moment.

"Now who's being mature?" Finn gave her his lopsided grin, the one she could never get mad at.

She huffed her bangs out of her eyes and wrapped her scarf more tightly around her neck. The scabbing welt from Cleo's cigar burned. She winced. "Sorry, Benjie."

"I think it's a great idea!" Benjie said. "Can I carve the first bird?"

"Okay, but no running with a knife," Willow warned as Finn handed Benjie the multi-tool and flipped up the small blade. She was lucky Benjie was so good-natured and obedient. Like Zia was, she thought with another pang.

He seldom whined. He was always willing to help with chores. And he knew how important it was to obey her and Finn at all times in this dangerous world. Her mother would be so proud of how Benjie was turning out.

That thought brought more pain, a bruising ache beneath her ribs.

"Um, Mister Finn, what kind of footprint is that?" Benjie asked, pulling Willow out of her morose thoughts. He pointed down at a print in the snow beside a broken-topped pine tree.

Finn squatted down next to him. "Well, Sir Benjie, that's some big animal, isn't it?"

"Do you think it's Shadow?" Benjie asked.

Willow peered over Benjie's shoulder, hopeful until she saw the massive size of the thing. Large pad bigger than her head. Five distinct toes. Claw prints. It had left a deep impression, whatever it was.

"Shadow is big, but not that big. This was something else." She suppressed a shudder, not wanting Benjie to see the trepidation flushing through her. Hopefully, it was a harmless mod.

Modded animals had been engineered by scientists, first created to replace endangered species in zoos as their wild counterparts went extinct. Scientists modified the animals, even the apex predators, to be as docile as sheep. Demand rose on the black market, of course, for the elites enjoyed parading their pet cheetahs and leopards around their marble mansions.

After the collapse, many mods were released from zoos, wildlife sanctuaries, and personal homes. They weren't dangerous. But a few of the remaining real wild animals had been released as well—tigers, leopards, wolves, bears.

"Let's go," she said brightly, tugging Finn back to his feet.

They trudged on.

"Do you think it was a bear?" Willow asked in a low voice so Benjie couldn't hear.

Finn whacked another tree. "I don't know."

Willow scanned the dense trees on either side of them. The forest seemed suddenly darker, though it was only mid-afternoon. A large shape moved deep in the shadows. Or was it only a tree branch? She squinted, but could see nothing more.

Finn nudged Willow's shoulder and pointed. Ten yards through the trees to her right, a large elm looked different than all the rest. The trunk had been clawed. Great scrapes raked the bark from at least ten feet up all the way to the roots. Clumps of brown hair clung to the bark in several places.

Willow swallowed. She never wanted to meet whatever had done that.

The freezing wind whipped across her bare cheeks. She inhaled an icy breath and shivered. "How many grizzly bears do you think are in this woods?"

"None," Finn said.

Willow sighed, more relieved than she wanted to admit.

"I've seen two tigers, though."

"Damn it, Finn!" She whirled on him. "Why didn't you tell me?"

But Finn was doubled over, his face contorted with silent laughter. Benjie giggled right along with him, even though he had no idea what was going on.

She fisted her hands on her hips and glared at him. "You just made that up."

"I confess," Finn wheezed, wiping tears from his eyes with his good arm. "But the look on your face was priceless. It was totally worth it."

Willow rolled her eyes, fighting to keep a matching grin off her face. "We'll see about that."

22

AMELIA

"Please remove your clothing and put on your custom temp-adjusted medical gown, Amelia," the room AI instructed in a brisk male voice. "I am increasing the room temperature now for your comfort. I do not detect a Vitalichip. I will request a technician to remedy this issue immediately. In the meantime, when you've reached your ideal comfort level, please let me know with a verbal command."

"Thank you," Amelia said politely, her years of decorum training kicking in automatically. "I'm fine."

After a light breakfast of muffins and yogurt, two soldiers had escorted her a few blocks from the capitol to the sixth floor of the BioGen research facility. From what she could see, the place was a series of long white corridors branching off into equally white research labs filled with rows of stainless-steel counters and scurrying figures in lab coats or hazmat suits. Machines beeped and hummed in every room, multi-armed bots of all sizes working with sterile efficiency.

Her own small room was white and empty but for her bed, two swivel office chairs, a couple of beeping machines, and a counter against the far wall. The wall was a sleek white polymer, with various charts and scans and anatomical diagrams projected over the width of it.

"Please make yourself comfortable," the AI said.

She breathed in the sharp smell of antiseptic and bleach and lay gingerly on the hospital bed, an elongated pod-shape without a lid. It was filled with a spongy cushion that conformed to the contours of her body, but it was still chilly. The smooth coldness leeched the warmth from the bare skin of her arms, legs, and the back of her neck.

She felt vulnerable, exposed.

Especially with the two soldiers standing guard just inside the doorway. They stood like sentries, pulse guns holstered at their sides, wicked-looking rifles cradled in their arms. They wore charcoal-gray uniforms with the Coalition's emblem stitched on the right shoulder.

The female guard on the left looked to be in her mid-twenties, with mouse-brown hair yanked back in a tight ponytail. She was medium height, medium build, medium everything. Easily missed, easily forgotten. She didn't seem like much of a soldier, but maybe that was her advantage. Maybe she would surprise you, just like Willow.

In contrast, the second guard looked every inch a soldier. Broad, straight shoulders, a clean-shaven, angular face, with faint lines creasing his startlingly green eyes. His skin was a deep olive tone, his hair so dark brown it was nearly black, and shorn close to his skull. His jaw was set, his gaze alert and stoic, aimed somewhere over Amelia's head.

"Hello," she said politely.

"Hello," the woman on the left said. The guard on the right barely nodded, still not meeting her gaze. A soldier through and through.

"Oh, you're here!" gushed a familiar voice. Vera stepped into the room, clapping her hands together and grinning from ear to ear. She wore three-inch suede heels and a lavender, knee-length dress embroidered with tiny gold buttons. Pearl earrings glinted at her earlobes.

"Look at you! Not a drop of makeup, and you look like you belong in a holo-ad! Except for that hair, of course."

She ignored Vera's subtle jab and smiled graciously. "Thank you," she said, because it was expected of her. "Where is my father?"

Vera looked at something on her Smartflex, swiped it away with the flick of her finger, and glanced at Amelia with another blinding-white smile. "Any moment now. Don't you worry about a thing! We're going to get you your Vitalichip—you'll love it! I adore mine. It does just about everything but brush your teeth—and then we'll get started. Are you excited? I just can't even describe how I'm feeling right now..." her voice trailed off as another ping sounded and her gaze darted back to her Smartflex.

"Why do I have guards?" Amelia asked.

"They're not *guarding* you, hon. They're *protecting* you. You're a precious asset, you know. Very important."

"I see." Though she wasn't sure she did. She changed the subject. "When can I see my friend and my brother? It's been two days."

"I have instructions to bring them to you as soon as they're released. Don't you worry about a thing!" Vera clapped her hands again. "Ah, here's the technician."

The technician swept into the room with an air of impatience, a med-bot zooming behind him. Not even remotely humanoid, the med-bot gleamed with chrome and steel, its multi-jointed arms like an insect's—bristling with scalpels, clamps, syringes, and other medical instruments.

The technician, a slight, balding man in his forties, plunked down on a swivel chair beside Amelia. "Right arm, please," he instructed in a bland, disinterested voice.

Amelia sat up and held out her arm as he picked up several objects from the stainless-steel medical tray that slid out of a slot in the med-bot's belly. He swiped a disinfectant swab over the inside of her forearm. He unsealed a small rectangular object and fitted it inside a metallic instrument that looked like some kind of spring-loaded gadget. He pressed it against her skin.

Something sharp pierced her. A thin wafer sharp as a razor blade slid deep into her flesh.

The technician swabbed the wound with an antiseptic wipe. He gestured to the med-bot, who slid the scanner over her arm. It beeped softly. She could almost make out something tiny, reddish, and rice-shaped glowing faintly beneath her skin.

"It reads your vitals, monitors activity, sleep, breathing, heart rate, blood cell count, and most importantly—viral load. It can detect the virus within four hours of exposure." His words were brisk and clipped, as if he were in a rush to get to more important projects.

"Four hours," Amelia murmured, staring down at her arm and remembering the endless days they'd spent isolated at the naval base in Florida.

The technician slapped a smartbrochure into her hand. "Report to Suite 113 in City Hall in the morning and they'll walk you through setting up financial accounts, ID records, smart programming for your home, work, and transport."

"Thank you," she said, even though she had none of those things. Not anymore.

"It's a good thing, the Vitalichip." He paused at the door, not bothering to turn around. "You know how many people out there would kill for this? You should be grateful."

She opened her mouth, at a loss as to how to respond, but he was already gone, the med-bot chirping behind him. In his wake, four other people crowded into the room, all wearing lab coats and clutching holopads. One of them was her father.

Declan gestured behind him at the three doctors. "This is Dr. Hobbs, Biomedical Research and Development, U.S. Army Medical

Research Institute of Infectious Diseases. Dr. Weinstein, infectious disease specialist. And Dr. Ponniah, a leader in research for live attenuated vaccines from John Hopkins."

"Formerly," Dr. Weinstein said with a pained expression. He was in his mid-sixties and balding, with a trim mustache and spectacles sliding halfway down his nose. He wore pressed chinos and Italian loafers beneath his pristine lab coat.

"Nice to meet you. What, ah—" she cleared her throat and wiped her damp palms on her hospital gown. "What exactly is going to happen to me?"

"We do our best to keep invasive harvesting procedures to a minimum," Dr. Ponniah said crisply. She was a short, plump Indian woman somewhere in her forties.

Amelia paled. Invasive? Harvesting? But what had she expected? She knew it wouldn't be easy or simple. Or painless. She kept her back straight and her chin up. She wouldn't show them her fear.

"We'll do our best to take care of you." Dr. Hobbs gave her a reassuring smile as he moved next to her hospital bed. He was a friendly-looking black man in his late fifties.

Declan glanced down at his holopad, flicking through reports and charts, frowning slightly. Beneath his lab coat, he wore an impeccably tailored suit, with a crimson handkerchief tucked neatly in the breast pocket of his suit jacket. "We've been analyzing the clinical data for months. Every avenue is a dead end. Until now."

"Holoscreen on," Dr. Hobbs said.

The wallscreen over the right wall lit up with a display of graphs, blips, numbers, and words she didn't recognize. "Cardiac monitor is steady. Blood oxygen levels good." Dr. Hobbs smiled at her like she'd succeeded at some marvelous achievement.

"This is the initial bloodwork from her intake exam." Dr. Weinstein tapped his holopad and flicked the data to the wallscreen. Her father examined the DNA sequences rotating slowly in front of him. He swiped his hand and brought up a datapack of research studies and patient files. He enlarged a segment of DNA, highlighting a series of amino acids. He spoke softly to the other doctors. Amelia caught only a few words: gene sequencing, white blood cell counts, pH levels.

"How long will it take?" Amelia asked Dr. Hobbs, who stood the closest to her.

"Unfortunately, we are unable to field test potential vaccines on rats or primates in any rigorous fashion," he said. "There simply isn't time. But since every single infected patient dies, there is no adverse risk we need to take into consideration. It shouldn't take too long to develop an antigen from your blood, in combination with the ideal adjuvant, stabilizers, and preservatives we have been exhaustively testing over the last several months."

"We hope to begin the first patient tests within twenty-four hours," Dr. Ponniah interjected.

Amelia raised her brows. "That quickly?"

Her father beamed at her. "We have virologists analyzing the data from your blood samples as we speak. The protective antibody levels are simply astounding."

A med-bot zoomed into the room with a mechanical chirp. Declan gestured at it. "We need to keep her vitals in tiptop shape."

The med-bot was about three feet tall and bullet-shaped. A compartment in the med-bot's side slid open and dispensed several pills in tiny paper cups on a small silver tray. Another hatch opened, and a mechanical arm with a needle appeared. It dispensed pain-relievers, non-inflammatories, immune-boosters, vitamin supplements, and who knew what else. Amelia swallowed the pills and gritted her teeth against the injections. This was only the beginning.

"If you don't mind, time is of the essence," Dr. Ponniah said. "We'd prefer to begin immediately."

Amelia nodded as the med-bot jetted away.

Dr. Ponniah prepped a large twenty-gauge biopsy needle. Dr. Weinstein started an IV attached to her arm via a clear tube.

"Dr. Weinstein will start with the blood samples," Dr. Ponniah said. I'll take liver and lung tissue samples, as well as extract a biopsy of your lymph nodes."

"We've prepared local anesthetics and a mild sedative to keep you as comfortable as possible," Dr. Hobbs said, squeezing her hand and giving her a warm smile. He had a gentle bedside manner, like someone's favorite grandfather.

"Thank you."

"I took the liberty of piping in some of your favorite music," Declan said as Dr. Weinstein inserted a sedative into her IV drip. Classical music filled the room.

Amelia's heartbeat slowed. Her hands unclenched. She rested her head against the backrest and closed her eyes.

She'd injected herself dozens of times with her emergency auto-injector. Somehow, this was different.

Maybe there were some things it was better not to see.

23

MICAH

"Congratulations," the guard said, gazing at his holopad with a scowl. "You don't have the Hydra virus. Though you do appear to have some important friends in high places. Guess we have to let you inside after all."

Micah elbowed Silas in the ribs before he could make some smart retort. They had spent the last three days stuck in those cramped isolation cells devoid of sound, touch, or interaction. Three times a day, a metalhead slid a plate of slop through a narrow slot that immediately sealed shut again—beef stew or lentil soup or chicken something, but it all tasted like overcooked cardboard.

Micah had spent the time sitting on the uncomfortable cot, watching the figures in hazmat suits hurry by, not even pausing to glance at him. He'd gone over the plots of his favorite books in his head, trying to recall subplots and minor character names. That and praying constantly for Amelia and Gabriel. It had been harder than he'd imagined to go seventy-two hours without speaking to a living soul.

But if it had been rough on Micah, Silas looked absolutely

wrecked. Judging by his sweat-stained shirt and the stench of him, he'd spent the time training.

"I thought you'd like it in there, seeing as you hate people," Micah murmured as they were led out of the containment center, a guard flanking either side of them.

Silas just gave him a sullen stare. "No one likes prison, not even a misanthrope."

"Can't you smile? At least look a little more pleasant?"

"If I did," Silas retorted, "you wouldn't recognize me."

They passed through the massive gates into the Sanctuary. Everything was pristine, new and functional, beautiful. Gleaming white cylindrical buildings, newly planted trees somehow still green, clean streets. A sani-bot on the corner suctioned up dead leaves and a stray bit of trash.

Moving sidewalks hurried pedestrians to their destinations. A mother gripped a toddler's hand, a stroller hovering beside her. Three teenagers crowded a bench, giggling at something on one of their SmartFlexes.

In the distance, tall buildings spiraled with circular terraces, many of them bursting with greenery and colorful gardens. Even the sky seemed bluer here.

"Get your head out of the clouds." Silas pinched Micah's arm, pulling him from his awestruck gawping, and pointed with his chin.

The armored military drones—nighthawks—patrolled the inside of the Sanctuary as well. Smaller surveillance drones flitted here and there. Soldiers in dark gray uniforms were everywhere, marching with purpose in twos and threes, guns slung over their shoulders. Two Humvees blocked the street ahead of them, turret-mounted machine guns pointed toward the gates.

Micah nodded silently. This place wasn't safe. Not for them. Not for anyone here. He couldn't forget that, not even for a moment.

He turned to the guard closest to him, a bald, burly black man in his forties. "Where are you taking us? We need to see Amelia Black. They would have taken her to—"

"You don't give the orders here," the burly guard said. "First you get the Vitalichip, then we'll see about the rest."

"We'd prefer to abstain," Silas said.

The second guard sneered. He was a young white guy, short and stout, the buttons of his uniform straining against his gut. "You Outerlanders are all the same. No one gets in without the chip. Coalition law."

"Coalition law?" Micah asked.

"They run things now," the burly guard said. "If you ask me, if they'd taken over years ago, none of this would have happened. Our country would still be ruling the world."

He kept talking, but Micah was no longer listening.

Across the street, a heavy-set boy leaned against a lamppost, arms crossed over his chest. He wore a cap low on his forehead, baggy cargo pants, and a fitted leather jacket. An apple-red scarf fringed with gold was wound around his neck. He was staring straight at them. When he caught Micah's gaze, he nodded slightly.

Their New Patriot contact. It must be the brother, Theo. Just as Cleo had said.

He and Silas exchanged looks. Silas had seen him, too. Time to get out of here. They couldn't get the chip-implants. They couldn't be tracked. They needed to move freely inside the Sanctuary.

Slowly, Silas lowered his hand to his thigh, counting with his fingers. *One, two, three.*

Micah nodded, adrenaline and apprehension spiking through him. Gabriel would be a hundred times better at this.

But Gabriel wasn't here. This was up to Micah. Too many people were counting on him to fail now.

On three, Micah raised his arm and jackhammered his elbow into the burly guard's throat with all his strength. Simultaneously, Silas turned and aimed a savage kick at the other guard's kneecap. There was a sickening crunch as the man collapsed. He let out an agonized scream. The burly guard staggered, clutching his throat, gasping for oxygen that wouldn't come.

It would take too long to steal their weapons, precious seconds Micah and Silas didn't have. They had to trust that Cleo's inside guys would help them.

They ran.

Micah searched across the street for their contact in the red scarf—but he'd disappeared. Maybe they were on their own, after all.

The mother with the toddler and stroller yelped as they pushed past her. "Sorry!" Micah called over his shoulder.

"Officer down!" came the shout from behind them. The guard with the shattered kneecap. "Two male hostiles on foot, armed and extremely dangerous, approximate GPS location is—"

"There!" Micah cried, pointing at a cluster of circular residential buildings. Maybe they could lose their pursuers in the side streets. They were in a strange city, with no idea where they were, where to go, or how to get there. They were vastly outnumbered, about to be hunted by dozens, maybe hundreds, of armed soldiers and drones. Would the soldiers shoot to kill? Micah didn't intend to find out.

They turned sharply between two round buildings and raced down a side street, searching frantically for an escape. There were rows of tall—and very green—bushes between each apartment. In the back alley of one, he glimpsed a large blue container, some kind of communal recycling bin. Maybe they should try to hide—

"Over here!" Abruptly, someone reached out and seized Micah's arm, nearly wrenching it from its socket. Micah was jerked into the shadows between two apartment buildings.

A second figure grabbed Silas. Micah glimpsed a girl with a mass of russet hair. She shoved Silas against the exterior wall and placed her hand on either side of Silas's shocked face.

Micah gaped, too stunned to react when a second figure plucked the glasses off his face and yanked a huge, pumpkin-orange trench coat over his shoulders. The white-furred fringe tickled his cheeks.

"What in the world?" was all he could manage.

"Go with it," the guy said, shoving Micah's folded glasses into the pocket of his lime-green peacoat. He pulled Micah against the wall and thrust an unfurled Smartflex into his hands. A holofilm was already playing, a tiny holo fighter jet shooting at a larger ship in outer space. The guy leaned over him, ostensibly to get a better look at the movie, but it also partially shielded Micah's face.

A dozen guards rounded the corner, stun rods and pulse guns in their hands, a squadron of nighthawks gliding silent and deadly over their heads.

"Don't enjoy this too much," the girl said to Silas with a wink. Then she leaned in and kissed him.

24

AMELIA

Amelia was desperate for a break.

The last few days had passed in a haze of swirling voices and gently rolling music, mixed with stinging pricks and the repeated sensations of intense pressure and discomfort. The sedative helped. The pain would be much worse without it.

"May I use the restroom?" she asked.

"Of course." Dr. Hobbs leaned back in his wheeled office chair. He rolled across the room to a counter with an integrated computer. He was the only one left in the room besides the med-bot and the guards at the door. She hadn't noticed her father leaving. Or the other two doctors, for that matter. "When you return, we'll get started on the next round of bone marrow samples and organ biopsies."

She stood, steadying herself against the bed for a moment as a wave of dizziness washed through her. Her brain felt thick and fuzzy. It must be a side effect of the strain all this was taking on her body.

The female guard stepped forward and held out her arm. "I'll escort you."

Amelia managed to wave her hand. "No, thank you. I can manage the bathroom by myself."

The guard smiled tightly. "I'm sorry, but I must insist. Orders from President Sloane."

Amelia sighed. "Why am I not surprised?"

She allowed the guard to take her arm as she tried not to wince. Her inner forearm burned and stung. Yellowish-green bruises marred her skin. The bone marrow and organ biopsies would be far from pleasant. But this pain was nothing compared to what she'd already endured.

She was willing to go through far worse if it meant a cure.

The female guard escorted her through a series of blank white corridors. All the doors they passed were closed. As they rounded a corner, two doctors in hazmat suits brushed past them, their suits crinkling. The doctors hurried into a door emblazoned with a red biohazard sign and the words "Authorized personnel only."

A Biosafety Level 4 lab. This was where the virologists would examine her blood and tissue samples. This was where they would expose her samples to the Hydra virus, where the cure would be discovered—or not.

The pressurized door closed behind the doctors. As it sealed, air was sucked out of the chamber, leveling the pressure. Along the edges of the door, a long, thin rubber bladder inflated to seal the seams. Through the narrow glass partition, she could make out the decontamination chamber with banks of nozzles, and beyond that, a lab teeming with figures in hazmat suits peering through microscopes and bent over thermocyclers, DNA sequencers, centrifuges. The bright light fixtures overhead were encased in airtight boxes and sealed with epoxy to prevent pathogens from escaping.

The guard tugged her arm and led her away. "Here." She pushed the bathroom door open and followed Amelia inside.

The counter was white quartz, the floor and walls long rectangles of gray tiles. Amelia chose one of the three stalls and did her business while the guard leaned against the bathroom counter, waiting.

Amelia came out and washed her hands. When she pulled her hands from beneath the faucet, the guard leaned in close, shaking her head. "Keep it on," she said in a low voice.

Amelia obeyed.

This close, the guard's skin was a field of pink, her blunt nose spanned by a network of faint freckles. A spray of pimples dotted her forehead. "My name is Harper Atkins." Her voice was as soft and inconsequential as her appearance. "I'm here to help you."

"To wash my hands?"

Harper frowned, her forehead wrinkling. "They told me you were smart."

The realization struck her. "You're with the Patriots."

Harper smiled. She was pretty when she smiled. "They'll keep a close eye on you. But I can get messages in and out. As soon as you have information, or even better, the cure, let me know and I'll smuggle it to them."

The hissing water drowned out their voices, but Harper still spoke in a whisper. So did Amelia. "Who's them?"

"The resistance here in the Sanctuary. I answer to Theo Reaver. I think you know of him?"

"Cleo Reaver's brother."

"Right. Whatever you do, don't trust the other guard. His name is Quentin Forester. He's one of President Sloane's personal security guards. She assigned him to you to keep an eye on things, if you know what I mean."

She nodded, relieved to not feel so alone. But could she trust this girl? She didn't know her at all. She could be anyone, say anything.

"Are you going to help the people I came with? They're still stuck in quarantine—"

"Micah Rivera and Silas Black. We know. We are helping them as we speak, I promise. I'll give you an update as soon as I can."

"Thank you," Amelia said.

Harper leaned over and switched off the water. When she spoke again, her voice was curt, her demeanor detached and professional. "Ready to go, ma'am?"

"Yes," Amelia said.

As she followed Harper back to the lab, she felt lighter than she had in days.

Maybe this whole thing would really work.

25

MICAH

Micah's pulse hammered in his throat. Even in the winter chill, sweat beaded his forehead. If one of the soldiers noticed...

The first guards rushed past, banging on doors and searching between and behind the buildings. Several of them wore tactical goggles with infrared sensors. Micah repressed a shudder, imagining the outcome if they had attempted to hide behind the bushes or beneath the recycling bin.

The guy beside him guffawed loudly and punched his shoulder. "Look at that move! Wicked awesome, am I right?"

Micah said nothing. He didn't trust his voice not to crack under the tension thrumming through every cell of his body.

A nighthawk glided past, pausing briefly to scan them with a red, gridded laser. Micah stiffened, unable to breathe. The drone moved on, floating away with a faint whir of its rotors.

The girl pressed her body against Silas, kissing him with passionate abandon. At least Silas had the presence of mind not to shove her away in disgust. Or maybe he was enjoying it. Who knew with Silas?

"Hey, you seen two hostiles run through here?" asked one of the soldiers.

"Nah, man," the guy next to Micah said in a bored, disinterested voice. He barely lifted his gaze from the holofilm.

"No loitering," a second soldier demanded. "Get yourselves inside. Don't forget about curfew."

The girl stopped kissing Silas and half-turned, still ensuring her head blocked most of the soldiers' view of Silas's face. "Yes, sir," she said with a demure smile.

"We'll have HQ check the videofeeds." The first soldier gestured to the rest of his squad. "Move out. They may have sought cover in the manufacturing sector."

No one moved until the soldiers and their drones had disappeared from sight.

"Get off me," Silas snapped at the girl.

The girl stepped back. "You should be thanking me."

Silas wiped his mouth with the back of his hand and spat. He glared at her, breathing hard. "I have one word for you. Boundaries."

"I'm sorry, I couldn't quite hear that," the girl said, returning Silas's scowl with a beaming smile. "Oh, you're so grateful that my quick thinking saved your life?"

"Thank you," Micah said with feeling.

"You're so very welcome." She turned her mega-watt smile on him. She was tall, only a few inches shorter than Micah, thick-waisted and curvy. A span of freckles sprayed across her snub nose and cherub cheeks. Her heart-shaped face was framed by a bushel of wild red hair. Her expression was open and friendly. It was hard to determine her age; she could have been fifteen or twenty-five. "I'm Fiona Walsh."

Micah sagged against the wall, closing his eyes in relief. "Would they really have shot us?"

"They're supposed to use non-lethal force first." The guy next to him reached into his pocket and handed Micah his glasses. "But everyone's a bit trigger-happy these days. My name's Kadek. Kadek Tedjasukmana."

He was Indonesian, and looked around Micah's age. He was tall and gangly, his long black hair dusting his slightly stooped shoulders. His sharp chin gave him a distrustful, ferret-faced look. In addition to his brightly colored wool coat, he wore fingerless leather gloves and a fedora hat.

"Who was the boy in the red scarf?" Micah asked. "Was that Theo?"

"That was me." Fiona flashed an impish grin. She pulled the red scarf out of her coat pocket and fluttered it at Silas. He swatted it away with a scowl. "Kadek and I are masters of disguise."

"That was smart," Micah said. "Hiding in plain sight."

Fiona stuffed the scarf back in her pocket. "No one is looking for four recalcitrant teens standing around doing nothing."

Silas stuffed his hands in his pockets and glowered sullenly at everyone. "So, where's this Theo then?"

The door of the apartment directly in front of them swung open. "Right here."

An Indian guy rolled out onto the sidewalk, his arms flexing as he worked his wheelchair. He was dressed in a wrinkled white T-shirt and jeans. His upper body was broad and well-muscled, tapering to a trim waist and slender legs. His thick black hair was disheveled, the beginnings of a scruffy beard along his jawline.

"I'm Theo." His dark eyes shone with intelligence as he examined them, a wry grin tugging one corner of his mouth. "Cleo's twin brother. Not quite what you expected?"

"No, I mean, um..." Micah stammered.

"No worries. Let me guess. Cleo told you nothing about me."

Micah had expected Cleo's brother to be a male version of her—tough, ferocious, and scary as hell. This guy seemed...nice. "Not really."

Theo winked at Micah. "Sounds about right."

"She said you were a hacker," Silas said.

"That I am. And a damn good one." Theo ran his hand through his rumpled hair. "I take it you got away before they chipped you."

"We did," Silas said.

Micah turned to Fiona and Kadek. "Thanks to your friends."

Fiona beamed. "I like them, Theo. Especially this one." She reached out to pinch Silas's cheek. Silas darted out of reach, an expression of abject mortification on his face.

"You should know there are cameras, microphones, and surveillance drones everywhere," Theo said in a low voice. "President Sloane declared martial law the day they announced the Hydra virus was a bioweapon. It's supposedly part of the Safe and Secure Act they passed in emergency session right after that ship blew up. She hasn't lifted it, even in here."

Fiona gave a flippant shake of her hair. "She claims law and order is even more critical while we re-establish civilization, or whatever."

Micah scanned the area nervously. "Are we being watched now?"

Fiona pointed to a tiny, barely visible camera lens nestled in the eaves over the front porch. "Unfortunately, this particular camera lost an argument with a rock. Maintenance hasn't made their rounds to repair it yet."

"We have a place off the grid to stash you, but we need to wait until after curfew," Theo said. "Until then, you're guests in my house. This is the first and only time we can stay here. We're very careful to move locations frequently when we meet."

Micah and Silas followed the Patriots into Theo's home. It was small and spare—four white walls, functional furniture, nothing extraneous or decorative. It wasn't at all what Micah had expected.

"Only the elites live in true decadence," Kadek said wryly.

"Sleep mode, please," Theo instructed the house AI.

"Certainly, sir. Powering off now," the AI said.

"I've hacked the home monitoring system to actually turn off," Theo explained. "Unlike the original version, which records every word spoken inside its walls 24/7." He pulled five cold sodas from a small, old-fashioned fridge and placed them on a stainless-steel table. "Take a seat."

Micah sat down across from Theo. Kadek took a seat to his right, Silas to his left. Fiona slid into the seat on the other side of Silas with a mischievous smile. She winked at him. Silas's scowl deepened.

Behind Micah, a bunch of synthetic grapes rested on the counter —impossibly huge and almost day-glo green. There was a bag of half-eaten chips and a bottle of salsa, the label advertising 5% real tomatoes.

"How do you eat here?" Silas asked.

Kadek shrugged his narrow shoulders. "We order on our Smart-flexes or apartment AIs; the drones deliver it. Sectors five and above get the real deal, soil-grown fruits and veggies, real cheese and even real meat. We get the printed crap that leaves that stale, gritty taste in the back of your throat."

Fiona tossed a bag of dehydrated vegetables on the table. "They add sugar to make them edible."

Micah took a handful of shriveled carrots gratefully. After months of hunger and homelessness, he would never turn away food again.

"Let's talk." Theo popped the lid of his soda and took a long swallow. "Let me start with us. I'm Cleo's twin brother, as you know. My mother, General Reaver, helped me infiltrate the government from the inside. We altered my identity before the mandatory Vitalichip ended all that. I've been working in tech security for BioGen for four years, since I was eighteen. By the time I finished acing their screening exams, they didn't care that I never took a single college class.

"I worked my way up to higher security clearances, eventually earning some government contracts. None of that matters to you except that my skills earned me a spot here. For now, I keep my head down and do my job. But I've been waiting for my chance to play my part. We all have."

"How many of you are there?" Micah asked.

Kadek sipped his soda. "Eleven."

"Only eleven?" Micah asked, deflated. He'd hoped for an army.

"We can get the job done," Fiona snapped, her beaming smile faltering. "We'll do our part."

"Most of our operatives are sleepers," Kadek said. "They do nothing until we activate them. We have an undercover guard— Harper Atkins—in President Sloane's security team. We made sure that she was assigned to Amelia's detail. She'll be passing us messages from Amelia while she's interred in BioGen's labs."

Micah held his breath. "So she's safe?"

"No harm will come to her," Fiona said. "They know how valuable she is."

Micah and Silas exchanged relieved glances. At least now they knew where she was. She was okay, and they could reach her if they needed to. And she had someone on the inside she could talk to. Right now, that was the best they could hope for.

"Harper's father is a Lieutenant Commander in President Sloane's Coalition forces," Kadek said. "All military—air force, marines, army, National Guard—have been combined."

"Kadek's father is a scientist for BioGen," Theo said. "And Fiona's mother is a hydrologist, a water specialist who ensures the Sanctuary maintains its aquifers and other supplies. Anyway, that's how they earned their spots in the Sanctuary."

Kadek watched something on his Smartflex. He flicked it closed and glanced at Fiona. "Fiona works in manufacturing and supplies. She's our resident thief. She siphons techy parts and pieces, and I'm the one who makes something wicked out of them."

Fiona ducked her head, her cheeks blooming red as she flashed a proud grin. She had a sweet, pixie-ish quality about her. Her gaze strayed to Silas for a moment before darting away. "Happy to be of service."

"I work in engineering," Kadek said. "I aid Theo with hacking, tech support, and whatever else he needs. But mostly, I'm the one that builds stuff."

Theo clasped his hands on the table. "Your turn. My sister told me you have information of critical importance pertaining to the origins of the Hydra virus." He glanced around the table. "We are extremely interested in what you have to say."

Micah took a swig of soda, relishing the burn as he swallowed the fizz. He told them who was really behind the Hydra virus. He told them everything, from the events on the *Grand Voyager* to the truth Amelia had revealed about her own father, Declan Black, and their suspicions about the Coalition.

The three Patriots listened, frowning silently.

When Micah finally finished, Theo drummed his fingers on the table. "Cleo is all blood and destruction. I love her, but we fundamentally disagree on many things."

"I can't imagine," Silas muttered. He slouched further in his seat.

"She thinks we need to take the Sanctuary by force, killing everyone inside. But I think there's room for all of us. I think there's a better way."

"What do you mean?" Micah asked.

"We can tell everyone inside the Sanctuary the truth." Theo's eyes brightened, his face filled with hope. "We can tell them their own government purposely unleashed the bioweapon, the very people they're following and trusting right now. If we can get the Sanctuary to revolt and turn on Black and Sloane and the rest of the Coalition, then this war of Cleo's never needs to happen."

"Most of these people aren't bad," Fiona said as she wound a red curl around her finger. "They just want to be safe. That's why they're keeping everyone else out."

"Sounds like rainbows and unicorn dreams to me," Silas said. "I know these people. I *am* these people. They won't care about anybody out there as long as they're safe in here, no matter who it is that keeps them safe—or what they've done."

"That is a horrible vision of humanity," Micah said.

Silas's eyes went flat. "That's the world. Always has been, always will be. The apocalypse isn't going to change that."

"If it avoids bloodshed, it's worth a shot, isn't it?" Theo asked. "I love my sister and my mother, but their first response to everything is to fight, to kill. I don't want to resort to that unless we absolutely have to."

Micah stared at Theo. He really was nothing like Cleo.

Theo took another swig of soda and slammed it down on the table. "We're all here because we believe in the ugly truth over pretty lies. I for one believe there are others who feel the same way."

"So how are you going to do this thing, then?" Silas asked dubiously. "How exactly are you going to show everyone the ugly truth?"

Theo grinned, seemingly oblivious to Silas's tone. "With a little work, I can access the Sanctuary network. That's every single screen, holo-ad, wallscreen, and Smartflex."

"But it won't mean anything coming from us," Kadek said. "There has to be proof."

"We can get it." Theo's voice rose in excitement. He took a small object out of his pocket—a thumb drive. He held it aloft on his opened palm. "That's where your sister comes in, Silas. She can get her father to confess the truth. If Amelia Black films it, I'll show it to every single person inside the Sanctuary."

26

AMELIA

"Would you like some water?" Harper asked Amelia from the doorway. "You look rather faint."

Amelia nodded weakly. She did feel exhausted, as weary as after a seizure had knocked her flat, rattling her internal organs and scrambling her brain.

"Don't be long," the other guard, Quentin, said with a slight frown.

"Of course," Harper said briskly. She helped Amelia to her feet.

Amelia pulled her hospital gown tighter around her bare thighs. She'd undergone another round of biopsies, scans, and blood draws all morning and afternoon. It was the sixth day of testing. She hadn't seen her father today, but technicians and med-bots had been in and out of her room throughout the day.

She was tired. So tired.

She nodded politely as they passed two virologists in lab coats, their heads bent over a holopad. They glanced up, watching her until she shuffled into the bathroom. A few moments later, the faucet water was flowing into the sink. Harper pulled something from the pocket of her uniform.

But Amelia was only interested in one thing. She met Harper's gaze in the mirror. "Where are Silas and Micah?" she whispered.

Last night, she had dined with President Sloane, a slew of advisers, and the five remaining Coalition members, including her father.

President Sloane had pulled her aside after the meal. "I just wanted to let you know that your brother and your friend managed to get themselves lost. They slipped away from their protective escort before they could undergo their chipping procedure. Unfortunate, since we could have used it to find them."

"Why did they need a protective escort?" Amelia had asked.

President Sloane brushed a stray hair back into place. "It was precautionary only. They're special VIPs, just like you. Declan is overcome with worry. I'm sure you can imagine." She patted Amelia's shoulder. "But don't fret. You focus on the cure; we'll focus on finding your brother."

Amelia forced her mouth into the shape of a smile even as doubts filled her mind. Just what kind of escort was it? Were Silas and Micah safe? Did President Sloane know they'd fled on purpose? Did she guess the ulterior motives at play? Or was she busy hiding her own?

"I'm incredibly grateful," she said as sincerely as she could. "Thank you so much."

"Of course, dear. Don't you worry about a thing. "You're Declan's daughter. That makes you practically family." President Sloane gave her a kind smile. She reached out and touched a strand of Amelia's newly lengthened hair. "I promised you my stylist would get everything back to normal, didn't I?"

Only nothing was normal anymore. It never would be again. Amelia touched the new extensions that fell in a sleek, waist-length white-blonde curtain. Though she had worn it this long for most of her life, her hair felt strange now, alien. She'd gotten used to the lightness of short hair, the feeling of fresh air on her neck, the freedom of not having to worry about its maintenance and upkeep.

Now it felt like a weight around her shoulders, a heaviness tugging at her skull. A reminder of her father's control over her life. She hadn't wanted it. But her father had gotten his way. She'd gritted her teeth and endured it because in the end, she had no choice. Her hair preferences meant little compared to the importance of her mission. *When among wolves...*

Now Amelia kept her gaze trained on Harper. She barely felt the hot water gushing over her hands. "Are Micah and Silas safe?"

"Keep your head down," Harper murmured, dropping her own gaze. "So the camera above us doesn't read our lips. And yes, they're safe. They're with our people."

Relief flooded through her. "Thank goodness. Where are they? What's happening?"

"I can only tell you what you need to know." Harper pressed herself closer to Amelia and thrust an object at her beneath the counter. "This is a thumb-drive with an embedded camera and microphone. It's a recording device. It can hover if you need it to, or you can hide it in a plant or something."

"What is it for?"

"We need you to get your father to confess to developing the Hydra virus."

Amelia inhaled sharply. "What?"

"There's no evidence unless he confesses. Get him to confess, and we'll show it to everyone inside the Sanctuary. Theo hopes the citizens will turn on the Coalition themselves."

Fear slid down her spine. Her mouth went dry. "He won't do it. He confessed on the *Grand Voyager*, but only with a gun to his head. He'll never tell me the truth."

"I know it's hard," Harper said gently. "And dangerous. But we have a chance to avoid bloodshed and still get what we want."

"But I'm going to steal the cure and smuggle it out—"

"Isn't that even more dangerous than what we're asking you to do now?"

Amelia went silent. Of course, Harper was right. But the thought of confronting her father sent tremors of terror rippling through her body.

Images of the *Grand Voyager*'s bridge flashed in front of her eyes—Simeon with the muzzle of his gun pressed against her temple, Simeon kicking her, punching her, explosions of agony racking her body. And her father, tied to the captain's chair, bruised and bloodied yet still defiant, refusing to give in to the terrorists—not even for his wife, not even for his daughter.

"You don't understand," she whispered. "I'm not the right person for this—"

"You're the only person we have." Harper thrust the thumb drive into her hands, then closed her own hand over Amelia's. "We're depending on you."

Amelia had no choice. She knew it. She knew this was the right thing to do. She took a breath and nodded.

Harper straightened and stepped back. She folded her hands in front of her stomach, a disinterested, bored look painted on her face.

Amelia said nothing as she allowed Harper to guide her back to her room. She faltered. Harper steadied her. "You all right, miss?"

"I'm fine."

But she wasn't. All her blood rushed to her toes. Her mind spun, dizzy and lightheaded. Could she really do this? Could she face her father, confront him? After all she'd endured, was she strong enough?

She wished Micah were here. She missed him with a physical ache. She missed his warm eyes and his smiles and his soft, full laugh.

She missed the way he was always fixing his crooked glasses, his determination to never give up hope, no matter what.

She missed Benjie's sweetness and Willow's sarcasm and her brother's sullen but steady presence. She missed Finn's goofy jokes, Celeste's attitude, and Gabriel's strength. She missed her mother's arms around her, promising her it would all be okay.

But that was a lie. Nothing was okay. It might never be okay.

No. That wasn't true. They could change things. They could make this world a better place for everyone. But nothing would change without risk, without sacrifice, without pain. She couldn't expect anyone else to shoulder that burden for her. She had to do her part to help. She had to be strong. She had to be brave, just like she'd told Benjie.

"I can do this," she said, meaning so much more than a walk down the hallway.

This was her brave thing.

27

MICAH

"What now?" Micah asked Kadek.

Kadek shrugged one narrow shoulder. "Now, we wait. Amelia gets the confession, Harper gets the recording to us, then we hack into network security and play it. Easy-peasy."

Night had fallen. The air was chilly but just above freezing. Micah dug his gloved hands deep into the pockets of his jacket. Theo had waited until almost eleven p.m., several hours after curfew to hack a transport to take them somewhere to hole up.

Kadek led Micah and Silas to a biodome in the agricultural sector. Rows and rows of biodomes stretched in front of them in the darkness. "All the hydroponic farming is done in biodomes to protect crops from the blights," Kadek explained. "All those from this street down are empty."

There were dozens—maybe hundreds—of them. How could they all be empty? "Why?"

"We've got plenty to feed the thirteen thousand or so people here. We could double our capacity, even triple it easily."

Micah's stomach twisted at the thought of all the people the Sanctuary could feed and shelter here—and were purposefully choosing not to.

Kadek gestured to a large glass dome directly in front of them. The door hung open on its hinges. One of the glass panes was broken. "This biodome malfunctioned a few months ago. Since they have so much excess inventory, they didn't bother to fix it. We've scanned it, and there are no active cameras or listening devices. So, this is your new home away from home."

Silas glanced around with an expression of derision. "Looks cozy."

"It'll have to do." Kadek thrust a duffle bag into Micah's arms. "Here are five days' worth of self-heating meals and water. We've already stashed sleeping bags inside for you along with a solar heater. It's risky to come out here, so we won't come back for you until we're ready to broadcast."

"So we're stuck here?" Silas grumbled.

Micah shot him a look. "We understand," he said to Kadek.

"Hopefully, it won't be long." Kadek turned and jogged into the darkness, quickly disappearing.

The biodome was empty and steeped in shadows, the cement floor still cluttered with dirt, old planter trays, and cartons, a hose coiled in one corner. It was divided into sections by glass walls, some transparent, some covered with a privacy film.

The sleeping bags were rolled against the wall closest to the entrance. Two old, threadbare chairs stooped in one corner, separated by an ancient and dusty desk. Micah squatted, shivering, and switched on the solar lamp and small heater. Instant warmth radiated against his skin.

He unrolled the sleeping bags and smoothed out the wrinkles. No pillows, but Micah had long since learned to appreciate whatever comfort he could find.

Silas tugged off his gloves and scarf and threw them atop Micah's sleeping bag. He dug around in the duffle bag and pulled out a self-heating meal pouch. He tore off the top and tossed it on the ground. He tilted his head back and poured some kind of brownish soup into his mouth.

Micah folded Silas's gloves and scarf and slipped them inside the duffle bag. He slanted his gaze at Silas's discarded trash. "You're not an ape. You don't have to throw your crap everywhere."

Silas just about choked on his soup. "Have you not taken a look at your surroundings, dude?"

"I'm just saying, if we're going to be living together for days—"

"Don't worry. I'll keep my crap on my side of the biodome. How's that?"

Micah pulled off his gloves, placed them neatly on his sleeping bag, and held his hands over the heater. It was the best he was going to get from Silas. "Deal."

"It's not going to work, you know," Silas said when he was finished with his soup. He tossed the empty pouch on the cement floor—but in the corner, away from Micah. "This whole recording thing."

Micah looked up, irritation surging in his veins. "Why do you always have to be like this? We're all worried. Of course, it might fail, but we're going to try. It's worth trying."

"You and your insane commitment to hope." Silas snorted. "It doesn't matter."

"Of course, it matters. Everything matters. It all matters. We're here for a purpose."

"What purpose? You think God is going to come down and save us?" Silas stretched out his arms, as if encompassing everything. "Even after all this? Humans destroying each other, killing each other? We're savages. Criminals and killers. We destroy everything good. Even if He existed, He'd turn His back on humanity and never look back."

Micah stared at him. "No, He wouldn't. God is love. He loves humans even though they're broken and ugly and lost. God believes humanity can be redeemed. So do I."

Silas rolled his eyes. "Your stubborn belief is going to get someone you care about killed."

"You mean Amelia."

Silas's shoulders stiffened. "She's not going to be able to do it. Not against my father."

"She's stronger than you give her credit for."

"I know her. I know what my father does, what he did to her, to all of us."

Compassion stirred in his heart. Despite their elite status, neither Silas nor Amelia had it easy. "She's told me some things—"

"You have no idea. She can't help herself. She turns into our mother. Sniveling, cowed. Weak."

"I have faith in her," Micah insisted stubbornly. He couldn't let doubt creep in. Doubt was toxic. The worst part of being afraid was the fear itself. He wouldn't give in to either of them.

Silas sneered. "Like you had faith in your brother?"

Micah winced, but didn't back down. "Yes."

"And how did that turn out for you?"

"Gabriel has changed. He's worked very hard to prove that."

"Except now he's with his old buddies, the New Patriots. How long do you think that change is going to last, huh? He's running around with Cleo, who wants to annihilate every elite she sees. You don't think that's going to rub off on him? You don't think he's gonna go right back to his old ways?" Silas's gray eyes sparked. "You know what they say. A dog always returns to his—"

"Not Gabriel." Micah shook his head, adamant. He'd had his worries, his private doubts. But he refused to be controlled by them. He chose to trust Gabriel. He chose a better way. "At some point, you have to believe in something. You have to trust someone. Otherwise, what is life?"

Silas slouched against the glass wall. He buried his fists in his pants' pockets. "I don't trust anyone."

"That's exactly my point."

A shadow passed across Silas' face. He turned and stalked deeper into the biodome, rounded one of the glass panes, and disappeared from view.

For a moment, Micah thought he was gone for good. The same old Silas, always running from his problems, the same way he'd disappeared when Amelia contracted the Hydra virus—too much of a coward to face harsh reality.

Something crashed. Several loud thuds followed the first noise. Then the sound of glass shattering. Silas must be punching inanimate objects.

Micah considered going to check on him, but decided against it. At some point, people were in charge of themselves. No one could make them change. No one could make them be better people, to leave their old, destructive ways behind.

That was a choice only Silas could make.

Several minutes later, Silas materialized out of the shadows. His hands were balled into fists at his sides, drops of blood leaking down his fingers. His shoulders were trembling. His mouth contorted, a flash of raw pain crossing his face.

Micah stood. "Silas? Are you okay?"

"I'm not there," he said in barely a whisper. "I'm not there to protect her."

Silas's veneer had cracked wide open. The snarky anger was gone, replaced by naked fear. Micah understood the desperate helplessness in Silas's eyes. He felt the same way. They both loved Amelia. They were both powerless to do a thing to help her.

"I know."

"No, you don't." Silas shook his head. "Don't you get it? I'm the one who should be suffering all this. I'm the asshole! Why is she the one our father tormented the worst? Why was she the one dragged off to be nearly raped and murdered by a psychopathic terrorist? Why is she the one cursed with migraines and seizures? Why is she the one who got sick?

"Now she's trapped, scared and all alone, surrounded by enemies, back with our monstrous father, and it's all on her *again*. How much can one person take? How long until she breaks?" He stared down at his trembling hands. "It should be me. I should be there. Not her."

"She's not going to break," Micah said quietly. "And neither are we."

Silas raised his head, his eyes glittering in the glow of the lamplight. "And how can you possibly know that?"

"Because she's loved." The moment he said the words, he knew they were true, all the way down to the marrow of his bones. "And she knows she's loved. By you. By me. By Gabriel and Benjie and Willow and everyone else. Even if we can't be by her side, she has us here." He tapped his chest. "And we have her. It's love that gives us strength, courage, and hope. It's love that's going to get us through this."

He expected Silas to keep arguing, to hurl insults or sneer in contempt. But he didn't. Silas slumped down on the sleeping bag opposite Micah. "You really believe that."

"I do."

"Okay," Silas said, breathing deeply. "Okay."

"Even the darkest night will end, and the sun will rise. Victor Hugo wrote that."

"*Les Miserables*," Silas said.

Micah looked at him, surprised.

"I do read on occasion," Silas said irritably. "When the apocalypse isn't around to distract me."

Micah climbed into his sleeping bag and switched off the solar lamp. He listened to Silas breathing in the darkness.

Weariness descended over him. His eyes fluttered closed in spite of himself. He was almost asleep when Silas spoke. "Maybe you're right."

Micah blinked. He could make out the dim shape of stars in the dingy glass over his head. "Silas—"

"If you say a word, I'll punch your teeth down your throat."

Micah smiled into the darkness.

28

AMELIA

"I'm pleasantly surprised that you suggested this, Amelia." Declan turned from the window to survey her with his sharp gaze.

"I—I thought we should spend more time together." Amelia forced confidence into her voice. "Outside of the lab."

"Your timing is impeccable." He gestured for her to sit at the glossy quartz table in his penthouse suite on the top floor of the BioGen building. Her father had ordered the guards to wait outside the penthouse. They were alone. "I have a gift for you."

She sat gracefully in the magnetic floating chair, adjusting the skirts of her silk peacock-blue gown. Her newly long hair was bound in a French twist, curled wisps fluttering about her face. Carefully applied makeup accentuated her ice-blue eyes and delicate cheekbones.

Despite the external perfection, inside she was a mess. Her father had promised no migraines with this medication, but a lesser headache throbbed dully at the back of her skull.

She forced herself to keep it together. She couldn't falter now.

She allowed her gaze to stray as her father poured expensive wine from a crystal decanter into two goblets. Where the capitol building was sumptuous and decadent, her father's quarters were sparse, minimal, but still pristine. The enormous suite was open, sectioned off into a spacious living area, dining room, and office space. The kitchen was hidden behind a floor-to-ceiling aquarium undulating with exotic, luminescent jellyfish.

The entire west side of the penthouse was a wall of glass, revealing the gleaming city below them and the mountains beyond. The white polymer walls pulsed with cerulean ocean waves.

Her stomach tightened at the idea of elites painstakingly preserving jellyfish but caring little for the suffering human beings outside their walls. She forced herself to look away before her anger got the best of her.

She was here for a purpose. She couldn't forget that.

"I remembered." Her father watched her closely. "The ocean was always your favorite."

She blinked back a sudden stinging behind her eyelids. "Thank you."

She glanced at the bouquet of lilies she'd brought, now placed on the table beside her plate.

His eyes dropped briefly to the bouquet. "Beautiful flowers."

"Vera gave them to me on the way here."

Earlier in the evening, Amelia had pinned the thumb-drive camera to the stem of a lily just inside the bouquet. She carefully adjusted it to just the right angle, so that her father was in clear view.

He grunted, his attention already drawn elsewhere, as she knew it would be. "I have a gift for you."

Her eyes widened. "A gift?"

Her father snapped his fingers. "Bring it now."

"Of course, sir," the penthouse AI said in a clipped British accent. "Fetching the gift now."

"Activate privacy mode," Declan commanded.

"Powering down," the AI said before falling silent.

A humanoid service bot appeared from behind the aquarium wall and handed her a gold-wrapped rectangular box tied with a silk bow. She opened it, her fingers shaking, her pulse beating in her throat.

"An 18th-century Guarneri, like your last one," Declan said grandly. "You have no idea how much time and expense went into procuring that."

She cradled the violin in her hands, running her fingers over the delicate stem, grazing the strings with her fingertips, permanently indented from her years of dedicated practice.

In her former life, she'd wanted to attend Juilliard to become a professional violinist for the Vienna Philharmonic. All that had died with the Hydra virus, but not her love for this instrument, for the beautiful music she created with it.

Her blood quickened, anticipation and excitement thrumming through her. She tenderly plucked a few strings, too overcome for words.

"Play something for me," her father commanded.

She could not disobey him. In this, she didn't want to. She shook her head to clear her mind. Both to play, and for what came after. She considered Korngold's and Mendelssohn's violin concerto before settling on Beethoven's "Moonlight Sonata."

She tucked the instrument beneath her chin. She went quiet and very still. Then she began to play. She drew the bow across the strings, and the first exquisite notes floated through the air, flowing over her, around her, through her. The song was sensuous, dark, and soulful.

The music filled her, swallowed her whole.

The tension in Amelia's jaw and around her eyes faded as she played. She closed her eyes, lost in the concentration of her art, her fingers moving with a beautiful fluidity and grace. This was what she knew, what she loved with all of her heart and soul.

She thought of Bach's "Gavotte," the first truly difficult piece she'd mastered at eleven. She thought of her music room, where the sunlight streamed through the floor-to-ceiling windows, the warmth of the sun seeping into the scarred hardwood floors, dust motes dancing as she played, and played, and played. It was her favorite room in the house, the rest of which was huge and cold and empty.

Her bowing intensified. The intricate melody underscored the emotions warring inside her, the splendor of the notes soaring through the air, the darker undertones weaving a tapestry of anguish around her heart.

She lost herself to the music, the way she always did. She pushed out the fear and dread, pushed out the knowledge of what she was about to do, how strong she needed to be.

Instead, for this brief respite, she soared to some invisible place free of pain and despair and heartache, a place only of beauty, of peace. Her heart squeezed as the music flowed through her fingers, building and swelling and filling the entire room until it calmed and centered her, bringing her back to herself.

As the last haunting note faded, there was a moment of complete stillness.

Her father clapped heartily. "That's my girl!" he declared, delight and pride thrumming through his voice.

Amelia opened her eyes, blinking as if coming out of a daze. She tucked the violin inside its case with the utmost care. She cleared her throat. Had to clear it again before she could speak. "Thank you. I love it. But what is this for?"

"This is a celebration!" Her father smiled broadly. From his pocket, he pulled out a long, rectangular aluminum case latched on both ends. He pressed his thumb to the biometric scanner. The latches released with a hiss.

He removed a vial full of clear liquid and held it up. "We did it, my girl!"

Her breath caught in her throat. "Is that what I think it is?"

"We tested this serum on a twelve-year-old boy on the ninth day of infection—after the fever set in but before the hemorrhaging. Yesterday, his viral count had dropped by half. By this afternoon, his fever had broken, he was speaking coherently, his white blood cell count had increased, and his viral load had fallen below day-two threshold levels.

"This morning, we administered the cure to twenty more infected patients. Their viral counts are already dropping." Her father turned to her, his face shining. "We've finally found it, Amelia. We have the cure."

29

GABRIEL

"They're ready for you." Jamal gestured for Cleo and Gabriel to follow him into the conference room. The room had a slightly musty smell to it. The Patriots' leadership sat around the scarred conference table, just like last time.

Only General Reaver was conspicuously absent.

"And how would we even get close enough to take out the missiles?" Colonel Reid swallowed the last dregs of coffee from his styrofoam cup. Empty cups littered the table. The strategy meeting had already been going for well over an hour. "Even with a Phantom, as soon as we strike one cannon, the others will blow us into the next universe."

Cleo stalked around the table, sat down hard in an empty seat, and shoved in her chair. She sat straight, shoulders squared, prepared for battle. "The cannons swivel, but not three hundred and sixty degrees."

"Meaning?" Colonel Willis snapped. She wore a black trench coat buttoned to her throat. Her dull blond hair was cut in a sharp bob to her chin. Deep lines scoured her pallid, sour face. With General Reaver gone, she and Colonel Reid were in charge.

Someone offered Cleo a cup. She waved it away. "If we can get the Phantom within the gates, we can take out the guns one by one."

"You'll still have to deal with the Sanctuary's security forces and armored drones," said a woman in a naval officer's uniform at the end of the table.

"I didn't say it would be easy. It will expose Theo and every one of our assets inside." She looked at each face. "But we're all in now."

"We cannot be hasty here!" Colonel Willis said. "We cannot risk it all for one person, even the General. Though we respect her years of service and leadership."

Cleo's face clouded. Her lips pulled back from her teeth, and her eyes slitted. Her body fairly vibrated with rage. Gabriel wouldn't have been surprised if she'd pulled out her gun and shot Willis then and there. Or leapt across the table and strangled the woman with her bare hands.

He understood her anger. After everything her mother had sacrificed, Colonel Willis was ready to abandon General Reaver, to leave her to the ravages of the Hydra virus. And from the look of sheer loathing contorting Cleo's features, Colonel Willis had just earned herself a life-long enemy.

But there was a hint of fear shining in Cleo's dark eyes. She needed to convince the people at this table to go to war now, or her mother was dead.

He understood her pain, but a war would put Amelia and Micah and Silas in danger. And that, he could not abide.

"Colonel Willis is right," he said, rising to his feet.

Cleo shot daggers at him.

"You're putting everything the New Patriots have fought and died for at risk," Gabriel said firmly. "You sent my people into the Sanctuary on a mission. Let them do their job. They need more time. If we go in now, we risk the cure."

"Who's to say Amelia won't turn traitor and keep the cure?" Cleo snarled.

Colonel Willis folded her hands neatly on the table. She tilted her head at Gabriel. "I thought he remained here to ensure that didn't happen."

Cleo looked about ready to explode. She glared straight at Willis, her eyes glittering onyx shards. "I—I may have overestimated her... connection to Rivera."

Gabriel winced. Cleo had. But Amelia would still come back. He was certain of it. "Amelia will not betray us."

"Who knows if this girl is even the cure?" said a balding man at the end of the table.

"It's reckless—if not downright stupidity—to risk so much on the word of an *elite*," spat an older Hispanic woman with short gray hair and glasses. "Even with the Phantom, we should wait until summer as planned, bide our time, and strike when we are ready."

"General Reaver will die," Cleo said between gritted teeth.

Colonel Willis leaned forward. She smelled blood in the water. "As we said, that is an unfortunate—"

The conference room door burst open. A low-level Patriot hurried in, his expression strained. He whispered something in Colonel Reid's ear. Gabriel recognized him—Bao Nguyen, the Patriot Cleo had nearly scalped in the garage bay.

Colonel Reid turned to Cleo, his expression tense. "I've just been informed that one of our all-terrain transports has been stolen. The back gate has been tampered with. Several members of the group you brought into our compound are unaccounted for. Captain Reaver, you were in charge of these people. Pray tell, what happened?"

Cleo's mouth tightened. Her gaze flitted to Gabriel. They were both thinking of the noise they'd heard in the garage bay. Someone had been listening. Willow and Finn and Benjie had disappeared, but he knew without a doubt that they would never warn the Sanctuary.

"Celeste," Gabriel said with a sinking feeling in the pit of his stomach. "Celeste betrayed us."

"Why would she do that?" Cleo asked, whirling on him.

He had believed Celeste had changed. She'd survived two days in Atlanta by herself. She'd survived Sweet Creek Farm, the Headhunters, the fire, the infected rats, the rabid dogs, the Pyros—everything they'd gone through, she'd been right by their side.

"She's an elite," he forced out. His words were ash on his tongue. "She's betting on the Sanctuary over us. She knows they'll take her in. She can return to her old life of comfort and decadence."

"It might not be her," Cleo said. "It could be Elise Black, Amelia's mother. She's an elite, too."

"Elise wouldn't do that," Gabriel snapped. But he felt like he was climbing an impossibly steep mountain, losing his grip on the slick rocks, about to fall. Nothing made sense.

The table erupted in a rumble of displeasure. "What are you saying?" Colonel Reid growled.

Cleo swallowed. "Presumably, one of the elites in our care fled to warn the Sanctuary."

"Warn them of what, exactly?" Colonel Willis asked, her tone deadly.

"Someone was spying on me during a private conversation." Cleo's nostrils flared. Her lips thinned in a bloodless line. Gabriel could tell she despised admitting to a mistake of any kind. "They overheard privileged information, which included my plans for an impending attack on the Sanctuary."

For a long, terrible moment, the conference room went completely silent. The Patriots leadership stared at them in shock and alarm.

"How long ago did they leave?" Colonel Reid asked Nguyen, who stood against the wall, twisting his hands nervously.

"Sometime between last watch and now," Nguyen said. "Could be up to seven hours."

"And how would they know how to reach the Sanctuary?" Colonel Reid asked.

Nguyen swallowed. "It's one of the GPS-programmed destinations in this particular vehicle. It wouldn't be difficult to find it in the system, if you knew what you were doing."

The hairs on the back of Gabriel's neck prickled. Could Celeste have figured that out on her own? Or did she have help?

Colonel Reid dismissed Nguyen with a flick of his wrist. "Send out a team. Stop them."

"Yes, sir." Nguyen turned and hurried from the room. The door closed with a loud thud behind him.

Whoever it was left hours ago. The action was likely futile.

Colonel Willis glared at Cleo, furious. "How could security be so lax as to allow—"

Cleo cut her off. "You refuse to allow security cameras and surveillance drones!" She shrugged helplessly. "Freedom is our bedrock, our foundation, but it has its downsides."

"I've had quite enough of your excuses—"

"It doesn't matter!" Cleo shouted. "If the Sanctuary thinks we're going to attack them, they'll strike first. We'll be devastated. They'll destroy us!"

The Hispanic woman scowled. "Now, wait just a minute—"

Cleo spoke loudly and quickly, trying to regain control of the room. "Which means we have no choice now. *We* must be the first to attack."

"We can evacuate," Gabriel said. A few people nodded. "We should run—"

Cleo whirled on him. "Leave everything and start over? Flee with our tails between our legs? That's worse than giving up! We're so close to victory! To changing everything!"

Gabriel leapt to his feet, knocking his chair back. "You're risking our people inside! You're risking Amelia, risking the cure—"

Cleo whipped her gun out and pointed it at his chest. Her finger wasn't on the trigger. It was a show of strength, of dominance, but she still needed him. And they both knew it.

Several Patriots soldiers lounging against the walls snapped to attention, their guns leveled at Gabriel.

Sweat broke out on his forehead. He remained standing, but raised his arms. "You can't do this."

"Stand down," Jamal ordered, his hand hovering over his holster. "Everyone, stand down!"

"We have to do this," Cleo said. "We're not risking the cure, we're ensuring *we're* the ones who get the cure! We know the schematics of the Sanctuary. We can protect the labs and the scientists. We can warn our people so they'll be ready."

The Hispanic woman adjusted her glasses. "You're suggesting that we take over now, and the scientists can keep working with the Black girl, even if they don't have the cure yet. But we'll have the Sanctuary."

"Yes. We can win this, we can—"

"Be quiet, girl," Colonel Willis said. "I will not risk a David-and-Goliath war here. You have no idea what a war entails."

"David won."

"What?" Willis snapped.

Cleo raised her chin with an imperious tilt. "David won, you idiot."

The room again fell into shocked silence. Then Jamal let out a loud bark of laughter. A few of the lower ranked Patriots smirked and nodded. They wanted a fight just as much as Cleo did.

Gabriel's heart sank.

Colonel Willis looked like she was sucking on lemons. Her mouth pinched, her eyes spitting fury. "This is insubordination—"

"Colonel Willis," Colonel Reid said sharply. He rose to his feet. "That is enough. I believe Captain Reaver is correct. The evidence she gave is compelling. And if this elite manages to warn the Sanctuary, then we have no choice. We have reached the point of no return. We must act. And we must act decisively." He nodded at Cleo. "Please continue. We are listening."

"It's time," Cleo said triumphantly, not even bothering to glance at Gabriel. He recognized that formidable proud jut of her jaw, that ferocity in her eyes, that cold and reckless disregard for anyone or anything.

It was terrifying.

"We're going to war. Not in six months or six years. Now." Cleo punched the table with both fists. "And we're going to win."

30

AMELIA

The cure.

Hope and elation and joy flared through Amelia. Even though this was what she came here for, it still seemed too good to be true. An impossible dream. "I—that's—I can't believe it!"

"Your blood was the key," Declan said. "I knew it would be."

Her mind snagged on his last words. "What do you mean? How could you know? I don't understand."

"We may not share DNA," he said, folding his hands behind his back, "but you are my daughter in every way that matters. I knew you would survive. I knew you would find your way back to me, where you belong."

He loves you now.

The thought stuck in her mind like barbed wire. She had managed to please him. She was the cure. She was finally something special, something worthy. He had finally looked at her with pride and adoration.

Do you really want to throw all that away?

She could still forget about the recording, could still choose to live

185

in this pretty fiction her father had created. A tapestry of beautiful lies.

But she couldn't do that. Could never do that. She lifted her chin. "You left me."

Her father stiffened. He turned his back and stared out the enormous window. She expected him to deny it, but he didn't.

"On the *Grand Voyager*. You left me to die."

"Do you think I wished to let you suffer?" His voice was raw, hoarse. "Do you think I wanted to abandon you? What do you think would have happened if I told them the cure did not yet exist? If I gave them any indication that I would sacrifice my dignity if they tortured my daughter further?"

"You could have done something. You let Kane take me—"

"I had no choice!" He whirled to face her. His mouth pressed into a thin, bloodless line. "If I did not find a way to survive, the entire world—humanity itself—would end. Do you understand the stakes? I could not choose you over the chance to fix BioGen's error."

She took a shuddering breath, willing herself to maintain control, to not lose it now. Too much depended on her. She couldn't let her emotions derail her from her mission. This was the moment. This was her chance.

"It wasn't an error," she said carefully, keeping her voice calm and even, though she felt anything but. "You and the Coalition designed the Hydra virus on purpose."

He didn't flinch. "I don't know what you're talking about."

All those years she'd lived walking on eggshells, studying his every facial expression, terrified of a shift in his mood came rushing back to her. She knew when he was lying. The tick beneath his left eye. That extra hitch to the swallow in his throat.

"I was there. I remember. Don't lie to me."

Declan's face darkened. He was losing patience. "It's in the past,

Amelia. Why rehash it now? All we can do is move forward. And we are moving forward. Why are you stuck in the past when we've just saved the future?"

She formed each word in her mouth before she spoke it, fragile and delicate as spun glass—and as easily shattered. "You may have found the cure, but you're also the one who created the virus in the first place."

He huffed an impatient, dismissive sigh. "Mistakes happen."

"You released it on purpose. BioGen and the Coalition worked together to intentionally infect a hundred thousand innocent citizens. You called it a moral imperative, remember?"

A line appeared between his brows, thick as a scar. "What is it that you want from me, Amelia? My position has not changed, despite the...unfortunate collateral damage. It is incumbent upon a government to restore order and protect the security of its people.

"Our government was feeble, weak. Our country's political leaders refused to see the danger lying in wait in their own backyard. The Coalition did what was required. We sacrificed a few to save the many, to ensure our national interests and survival as a nation. The people needed to see the true nature of their perilous situation."

"You mean you needed them to vote the Coalition into absolute power. To get that power, you murdered thousands of people."

His expression turned stony. "People die all the time, Amelia. It would have worked. The Coalition would have ushered in a new era of strength, peace, and prosperity. No one could have foreseen how the Hydra virus mutated. That is not my fault. I only did what I did so America could survive."

"How can you still defend yourself, after all this?"

"Enough!" he growled. "Your constant whining is tiring me. This is my moment of glory, my greatest achievement, one I wished to share with you first, believing you would understand and share my joy. But I see now that I was wrong."

He sniffed, his sharp gaze traveling over her face, her hair, her dress, his mouth twisting in all-too-familiar contempt. "I thought things would be different this time. Maybe you just have too much of your mother in you. Must you always ruin everything you touch?"

Every old feeling of shame, fear, and unworthiness surged through her. She had done her best for years, tried desperately to be perfect. But it hadn't mattered. None of it had ever mattered. She had never been enough to earn his approval, his love. Tears pricked the backs of her eyelids.

You aren't that girl anymore, a glimmer of a voice whispered deep inside her. She'd fought too hard, lost too much to go back. Her father's approval no longer determined her worth.

Only *she* decided that.

Amelia drew on every reserve of strength she had. She forced herself to lift her chin, refusing to cry in front of him.

His expression darkened. He smiled, but it was a dangerous, slippery thing, sharp-edged as a knife. "You, Amelia, are the pinnacle of my life's achievement. From working on you, I discovered the nanobots that I used to successfully manufacture BioGen's cancer cure. Then the universal flu vaccine. Now this, the cure for the world's most devastating plague."

It took a moment for the words to sink in. For their meaning to settle into her brain. "You've—you've been experimenting on me?"

"Safely, I assure you."

"You..." But there were no more words in her head. Shocked disbelief jarred through her body, her bones.

All these years, he could have been putting anything into her pills and auto-injectors. He had been willing to risk her brain, her very life, for his work, for yet another billion-dollar treatment, for more fame and more power. She hadn't expected this, not even from him.

Acid burned the back of her throat. She felt sick. "What if something went wrong? What if you poisoned me or—"

"Do not doubt me!" her father thundered. "I knew exactly what I was doing. I knew the nanos were the key to everything. And look, the entire scientific community was wrong. I was right! I did this!"

She stared at him, stunned into silence.

"Do you know what your mother was?" her father asked, abruptly changing topics. He was impassive, completely impervious to her pain. He seemed not to care that he'd just blown her world wide open. "Before I picked her out of the trash and set her at the table with kings?"

Amelia couldn't move. Dizziness wavered at the corners of her vision. She was dazed, shaken. Her brain couldn't process it all.

Declan stepped toward her. His voice was hard, sharp as steel. Every word cut in places she didn't expect, didn't have armor for. "Both her parents starved on that street drug Silk when she was twelve. She was a street rat until she hit puberty, and a scout from the syndicates noticed her."

"No," Amelia whispered.

Declan sneered. "Your mother was a whore. Did she neglect to tell you that part?"

Acid burned the back of her throat. He was upset with her. As punishment, he was trying to hurt her, to break her.

She wanted to say that she didn't care, that it didn't matter, to throw his insinuations back in his face. But how could she? She knew his words were the truth. Her mother never spoke of Amelia's biological father. She never spoke of her past.

Because of this. Because her biological father was nothing but a john. Amelia blinked back tears. Her fingers tightened around the neck of the violin, the case still lying open on the table in front of her. "That doesn't change who my mother is. That doesn't change anything."

Declan ignored her. "I once believed it was fate that brought us together. I found out later that she'd studied every research paper ever written on Dravet's syndrome. That's how she found me and my research trials. She worked the convention until she spotted me. She'd had a child by then, an infant only three months old. A baby already dying.

"When she told me about the infant and its prognosis, I confess that I was intrigued. She was desperate. I was smitten both by the scientific possibilities and by her charm and demure beauty. While I worked on developing a treatment protocol for you, we came to an understanding. She gave me her hand in marriage, and I saved her daughter.

"It was a business arrangement."

His intense gray-blue eyes held Amelia in his magnetic gaze. She couldn't look away. He saw that he had hurt her. He smiled. "You, my child, are my first great achievement, the one I could never tell a soul about. But the nanotech breakthroughs established by your treatment led to the breakthroughs with the BioGen cancer cure, using nanobots as vehicles to successfully target cancerous cells. And they enabled the Hydra virus.

"The medication I developed for you proved efficacious for epilepsy. I knew the nanoparticles would work the same way, only with viruses. Hemagglutinin is the surface protein embedded in the lipid membrane of the viral envelope, responsible for the attachment of the virus to specific receptors on a host cell surface. It facilitates the fusion of the viral envelope and the cell membrane. The virus injects its genetic material into the cell cytoplasm and unpackages its DNA, using the host cell to replicate its viral nucleic acids and proteins. The nanos I developed bind themselves to the hemagglutinin so the viral envelope can no longer fuse to the host cell receptors. Even with minor mutations, they remain effective.

"I introduced insignificant levels of our engineered virus into your system, training the nanos to recognize the Hydra virus signature to strengthen and multiply your white blood cell count.

"I wanted a vaccine before National Health Day, but the powers that be insisted on moving the date up. I was unable to finish my work with you. And then, of course, the virus underwent reassortment with the bat-flu and mutated into a highly virulent, highly contagious pathogen like nothing the world has ever seen. The *Grand Voyager* was hijacked, derailing my plans to formulate a cure. The rest of the story, you already know."

Her emotions warred within her, a tangle of fear and love, doubt and anger, and a dozen others she couldn't name. She leaned against the table, shaking.

"Do you feel all right?" Her father's brow furrowed in concern. "You are taking the medication I gave you in the correct dosage?"

"Yes," she whispered.

She wanted to hurl his medication back in his face, to scream at him, to pummel him with her rage and never stop. She reined in the anger, the shock and betrayal and hurt, forcing it all to some deep, dark place inside her.

He thought she was back under his control. He wanted a meek, malleable doll.

She had to make sure he continued to believe just that. "May I lie down, Father? I feel very tired."

"Of course. You must rest." He swiped his Smartflex. "I will call security to escort you to your room."

Harper and Quentin entered the penthouse, their faces impassive, their gazes staring straight ahead. Amelia picked up the violin and grabbed the bouquet of flowers, careful to cradle them to protect the recording device even as her fingers trembled.

He'll hate you forever if you do this.

She knew what she needed to do, had to do. Yet it still felt like some giant hand wringing out her insides, twisting her heart in its fist.

She thrust the flowers at Harper. "Will you please carry these?"

"Of course, ma'am," Harper said demurely. Her expression never changed. Quentin studied them both, his green eyes betraying no thought or feeling.

"I'm glad you're here, Amelia," Declan said from the doorway. "I have my daughter back."

31

MICAH

"What happened?" Micah asked eagerly as soon as Theo, Fiona, and Kadek had slipped inside the biodome. It was ten p.m. and dark outside, well past curfew. "Did anyone see you?"

"Of course not," Fiona scoffed, pulling off the black hood of her sweatshirt and shaking out her mass of red hair.

Kadek held out a sleek white thumb drive as he shrugged a duffle bag to the floor. One end featured a tiny camera lens with a speaker. "Amelia came through. We got it."

A thrill of hope—and fear—thrummed through Micah. "Is she okay?"

"Harper says she's fine," Fiona said, shoving her hair behind one ear. "They've done a butt-load of tests and scans on her and started injecting experimental serums into the infected. Preliminary results seem to be positive."

Theo thrust out an industrial-sized bag of gummy worms. "Hungry?"

Micah's stomach roiled with too much anxiety to eat anything. He and Silas had been stuck inside the biodome for four days, going stir-crazy and trying their best not to throttle each other. It was a losing battle. "What's the plan?"

Silas leaned against a glass wall, his arms folded across his chest, his expression sullen. "Please tell me it's happening tonight."

Kadek flopped down at a rusty table. "We've almost got it figured out."

"What exactly does that mean?" Silas asked.

"I can get us inside and through the first three security levels." Theo drummed his fingers against the arm of his wheelchair. "But to access the network requires security clearance level four."

"And that's going to stop you how?" Kadek said.

"Unfortunately, I don't have the skill set to override the biometric protocols...maybe with more time. I mean, I could upload a sophisticated Trojan horse virus into their system which runs by itself and will continually search for a shortcut into the network, but it'll take days to infiltrate the system's security protocols—"

Kadek sighed. "Theo. The easy way."

"Easy?" Fiona chuckled. "When do we ever do things the easy way?"

Kadek lifted one narrow shoulder. "Why do it the hard way when the easy way might work even better?"

"Operative word: might," Fiona shot back, but she was grinning.

"You're breaking my heart." Theo raised his hands in surrender. "Okay, okay. You win. Not sure if you'd call it easy, but I do know a faster way. You're not going to like it, though."

"What?" Micah asked, pushing down his anxiety. "We don't have much time, so fast is best."

"We have to kidnap someone who's a security level four."

Kadek's eyebrows shot up to his hairline. "No way. It's too dangerous."

"Not if we're adequately prepared," Fiona said from her perch on the edge of a faded armchair. She pulled up the building's schematics on her holopad. She bit her lip as she studied it. "And we nab the right mark."

Kadek frowned. "Who?"

"I have a guy in mind," Theo said around a bite of gummy worm. "Level four clearance. A real techy dork. His name's Herald Mather. He's got no family. He works long hours, way past everyone else. I hacked his schedule this morning. He's worked twelve-hour days five days a week for the last month, no exceptions. He'll still be in the building after eight p.m., with no one else but the security guards, a few drones, and the sani-bots. I'd bet my Marvel comic book collection on it." He gave a wistful sigh. "If I still had them."

"So we just grab him and put a gun to his head?" Micah asked dubiously.

"The biometric scanners detect increased heart rate and other stress indicators," Kadek explained. "Over a certain threshold, the door auto-locks. It won't open for anybody but the head of security. Trust me, we don't want to mess with that guy."

Silas let out a torrent of curses. "That's your big plan? Sounds like it's gonna crash and burn before it even gets off the ground."

"We can drug him," Fiona said.

Micah shoved his glasses up the bridge of his nose with his thumb. "How will we do that?"

Theo tossed a gummy worm into his mouth. "Fiona, our most talented thief, moonlights as a medical technician at Camp Quarantine, specifically the confirmed infected wing."

"The Sanctuary studies the infected for a vaccine or a cure or whatever," Fiona said as she stole one of Theo's gummy worms. "They take blood and tissue samples and inject them with potential serums. None of them have worked. But the scientists have tested other treatments, attempting to slow or eliminate symptoms. We've been dosing end-stage Hydra patients with a modified version of Serenaphin—more commonly known as Silk."

Micah's eyes widened. "The street drug?"

"It has its uses. You know how the virus releases a surge of adrenaline near the end? It makes people really aggressive, gets them up off their feet even though their bodies are literally eating themselves at that point. It's the virus's last-ditch effort to spread itself—spraying blood through coughing, et cetera."

"Like zombie Energizer bunnies," Theo chimed in.

Fiona frowned. "Not really."

"Silk calms them." Micah thought of his father, who'd starved to death from his addiction to Silk. It had stolen his appetite, his emotions, his motivation, even his will to live at the end.

"Right," Fiona said. "It slows their heart rate, impedes adrenaline and cortisol, essentially making them temporarily docile. Kind of like a mod."

Kadek whistled, drawing their attention. "We're getting off topic here."

"Bottom line," Fiona said with a surreptitious glance at Silas, "if we drug this Herald guy with Serenaphin, he'll be docile enough to pass the biometric scanners and get us through fourth-floor security."

"Perfect," Theo said.

"How long will it take for you to steal some?" Micah rose to his feet. He was anxious to get started.

These people seemed nice. They were funny, smart, and he could tell they genuinely liked each other. In another life, he'd like to be friends. But here, now, with Amelia in danger inside these walls and his brother in danger outside them, he only wanted one thing: to end this thing as swiftly as possible.

Fiona pulled a vial encased in protective foam out of her pocket.

She beamed at Silas, who only stared back at her, stone-faced. "Already two steps ahead of you."

Silas shifted, hunching his shoulders and plunging his fists deep into his pockets. He looked unimpressed. "Are we just going to waltz through the front door, then?"

"Maybe ten steps." Theo wheeled to the far corner and yanked back an old tarp Micah hadn't even noticed to reveal a neat stack of cobalt-blue uniforms. "Welcome to technical support, lady and gentlemen. It's mostly bots who do the labor, but they always send at least one human to supervise."

Micah studied the three of them. Kadek looked nervous, but Fiona and Theo seemed confident in their abilities to pull this off. Was there something about this whole thing that he was missing? It all seemed too easy. "What about the cameras? Surveillance drones? And your Vitalichip implants. Don't they track your every move?"

"Way to rain on our parade, man," Theo said good-naturedly. He tapped the side of his head. "Great questions. I can tell you're the thinker."

Sulking in his corner, Silas grunted in derision.

Theo wheeled over to the ancient desk. He pulled a small black bag from his jacket pocket and plopped it on the dust-strewn surface. He opened the bag and pulled out a dull, slate-gray cuff, thinner than a Smartflex, about an inch wide. He slipped it over his hand and clamped it tightly to his right wrist, just over the embedded microchip. He tossed identical cuffs to Kadek and Fiona.

"We can cloak them with lead," he said. "We could completely block the signal so we can't be tracked, but prolonged inactivity sends an automated alert ping to security, who immediately send their thugs to check things out. We've figured out that we can sneak out at night when the AI analyzing the incoming data assumes we're sleeping anyway. We've tested it up to sixty minutes. Any longer than that, and they release the goons. BioGen is already making a second gen upgrade that will nullify all of our hard work—"

"One day at a time, Theo," Fiona chided gently.

Theo sighed. "This girl thinks I talk too much."

"You *think* too much," Kadek retorted.

Theo just rolled his eyes. "So, we have to get there, do our thing, hoof it back on foot, and reactivate our chips within an hour. I can hack a transport for the way there, but the way back we'll need to go separate ways on foot."

He turned to Micah and Silas. "Now, you two are in the wind, so to speak. As long as we keep your faces out of sight of the facial recognition software on all the cams, you'll be okay. A hoodie and special digital-masking glasses will help for any we can't avoid. That's Fiona's expertise. Once we're in the building, Kadek will dub the footage and erase the building cameras." He gave them a self-satisfied grin. "See? Easy, right?"

"You guys think you're up to this?" Kadek asked, eyeing Micah and Silas skeptically, clearly uncertain whether to trust them.

The feeling was mutual. But neither party had a choice. The stakes were too high. The possible reward too great. Both sides had to risk it all.

"We are," Micah said.

Silas pushed himself off the wall. He cracked his knuckles, one by one. Everyone watched him. He looked up, his eyes glittering. "We sure as hell aren't here to shake hands and kiss babies, now are we?"

32

WILLOW

W illow woke with a start. She sat up fast, her sleeping bag bunched in her fists, her heart pounding. She blinked in the darkness, waiting for her eyes to adjust.

She was inside the tent. They were somewhere in the middle of the wilderness of the Blue Ridge Mountain foothills. The tent flap was unzipped. Finn was outside, keeping watch while she and Benjie slept. She'd been sleeping—dreaming about triple-decker burgers dripping with real melted cheese, not the soy crap—but now she was wide awake.

Benjie squirmed beside her. She could barely make out his shadowy form. He rubbed his eyes. "Lo Lo?"

She held her finger to her lips. He nodded, immediately falling silent, just like she'd taught him. She strained for sounds outside the tent. The wind in the trees. The creak and snap of the deep woods. Snow falling. Nothing unusual.

But something had caused adrenaline to spike through her veins, to set her heart jackhammering against her ribs.

She checked her Smartflex. 3:14 a.m. She crawled across her sleeping bag and peeked her head out the tent flap.

They were camped in a small clearing. A swirl of smoke drifted from the banked campfire ten feet directly in front of her, the coals still shimmering red. Her gaze tracked from the fire to the large log they'd used for seating, Finn's walking stick leaning against it.

Finn sat a few yards away, leaning against his backpack, facing the woods, a hunting knife gripped in his left hand, his right arm cradled uselessly in its sling.

The moon shone down from a circle of night sky directly above them. The stars were sharp crystal shards. The trees stood silent as sentinels all around them. Everything was still, everything was—

A branch cracked. The sound was loud as a gunshot in the stillness. A shuffling noise came from the woods to the west. Something large crashed through dense foliage.

Willow froze. "What is it?" she whispered. "What's out there?"

"I think," Finn said softly, "that we are being hunted."

The shuffling noises grew louder. Leaves and pine needles crackled. More twigs snapped. Something grunted.

Fear slid a blade between her ribs. Out here in the wild, they were no longer the apex predators. They were the prey.

"Get inside the tent!" she hissed.

Finn scrambled backward, as quietly as he could, but not quietly enough. Willow held the tent flap open while he scooted inside. His bulk nearly filled up the entire tent, especially with his pack still strapped to his back.

Carefully, Willow zipped up the tent, wincing at the scraping noise the zipper made, but it couldn't be helped. She and Finn crouched inside the tent, Benjie huddled between them.

She held her finger to her lips again. Benjie nodded mutely. The whites of his eyes gleamed.

Willow checked that her handgun was still in its holster. It was. She picked up the rifle she always kept beside her as she slept. Her pulse thundered so loud in her ears it was a wonder she could hear anything at all.

They waited in silence.

The creature shambled into the clearing. It was close. She could hear its huffing breath. A bear, from the sound of it. A big one.

She and Finn exchanged frightened glances. Hopefully, it would just shuffle on past, bypassing the tent for more intriguing pastures.

A large shadow fell across the tent wall. Dark and huge, with a heavy, thick torso and a massive head and jaws. The head turned toward them, its snout snuffling the tent.

Benjie let out a terrified gasp. Willow clapped her hand over his mouth. *Don't move. Don't breathe,* she commanded with her eyes, praying he would understand.

He was just a kid, but she needed him to be brave. He trembled beneath her fingers, but she didn't dare move her hand.

She couldn't get enough air. Her chest burned. She longed to suck in huge, ragged breaths, but that would make noise. She focused on barely breathing, on not making a sound.

The bear lifted one enormous paw and batted the tent. The sound of the bear's claws sliding across the nylon raised every hair on Willow's arms.

The tent wall pushed inward toward Finn. He eased back, barely breathing.

One claw punctured the fabric.

Willow didn't dare close her eyes, not even to blink. *Go away, go away, go away.* She chanted the words over and over in her mind, even as she scrambled for a plan, any plan her desperate, panic-stricken brain could come up with.

She longed to shoot the creature, but she couldn't. Not without the ability to see the thing and aim. Injuring the bear would just infuriate it. As long as there was the slimmest chance it would just amble away, she couldn't risk it.

For now, she could do nothing but hope, pray, and wait.

The bear jerked his paw free of the fabric with a bewildered snort. It took a few heavy steps and pawed the tent again lightly, batting at it the way a cat batted a toy.

If the bear attacked the tent, she'd unzip the door and tell Finn to take Benjie and make a run for it. A bear could outrun them easily. But she could stay and fight it, try to shoot it down before it got to her.

It was the only thing that might give Finn and Benjie a chance.

It wasn't a plan at all. But it was all she had.

How many shots would it take to kill it? Judging by its shadow and the noises it was making, it was massive. It would take more than one shot, she knew that for sure.

Unless she could hit it directly between the eyes. But for that, she'd have to see it.

Silently, she rose to her knees. She released Benjie's mouth with one finger to her lips. He nodded frantically. Finn wrapped an arm around him and pulled him close. She pointed to the small window flap a foot above her head and to the left.

Finn shook his head. He didn't want her to do anything dangerous. She shook her head back. The danger was already here.

Willow eased her handgun out of the holster. The rifle would be too hard to aim and shoot in such tight quarters. She barely had room to move an inch as it was.

Breathing shallowly through her nose, her lungs burning and her pulse a roar in her ears, she eased toward the window flap, the gun in front of her face. She peered through the mesh screen.

The beast was huge. Her gaze was level with its mid-back. She glimpsed thick black fur, could almost make out each individual hair. A sour, earthy scent filled her nostrils.

The bear lifted its great head, alerted by some noise deeper in the forest. She had to look up to see its eyes. They were small and dull, almost lifeless.

Her stomach unclenched, her tense shoulders relaxing. She exhaled slowly.

Other than their larger size and listless, docile behavior, it was their eyes that set them apart. Their eyes weren't alive with hunger or craving or anger or fear. They were alive. But at the same time, they were different, strange, unnatural.

The bear was a mod.

It was engineered not to kill for anything: not to eat, not to save its own life. Mods survived by scavenging. And now they had millions of corpses to choose from. No mod would attack a human. They were safe.

The creature huffed, shaking its great head, and ambled off into the forest in the opposite direction from which it had come.

Willow sank back on her heels, trembling in relief. She inhaled several deep, shuddering breaths. She was alive. They were alive.

She holstered her gun and wiped her sweaty palms on her thighs. "It's gone."

None of them wanted to stay inside the tent. They needed to stretch their cramped limbs. They needed air. Finn and Benjie scrambled out of the tent. Willow followed them with her rifle. There was no way she was leaving it behind, not after that scare.

"Did you see how huge he was?" Benjie gasped, stretching his arms as wide as they could go. "He could've squished us just by sitting on us!"

"No joke, Sir Benjie," Finn said, his voice shaky. "He could have squashed us flat."

"Like an ant!"

"Like a mosquito."

"Like a cockroach!"

"Speak for yourself," Finn said.

Willow was about to join in the conversation when she glimpsed movement in the trees behind Finn and Benjie.

Before she could react or even open her mouth to speak, something huge crashed through the underbrush, lunging into the clearing not twenty yards from their tent.

A second bear.

It swung its huge head from side to side, scenting its prey. Scenting *them*. It was massive but emaciated, ribs jutting from matted brown fur. Its eyes were black as carved onyx and glittering with malice.

A grizzly bear, and no mod. It was every inch a predator.

Two bears? It made no sense.

Understanding struck Willow like a sledgehammer. The grizzly had been hunting the modded bear.

Until it had scented them.

33

MICAH

"We're here," Theo said.

From the backseat, Micah watched as Theo inserted a thumbnail-sized electronic device into a tiny slot in their transport's interface. Electric blue gauge lights floated over the bottom and right side of the windshield—a destination code, GPS location, power and battery usage, environment controls, time.

Theo swiped in several passcodes before withdrawing the device. "Logs erased."

The transport had brought them within five blocks of BioGen headquarters. Theo, Micah, Silas, Fiona, and Kadek exited the transport into the cold, dark night. The transport powered down on the side of the street, waiting for its next passenger.

This part of the Sanctuary was deserted. It wasn't yet curfew, but it might as well have been. Everyone was ensconced safely inside their homes, the warm light of electricity glowing from the windows. The street lamps were dark until their sensors detected movement within a specified radius, then they flickered on.

Three blocks to the east, two patrolling soldiers turned onto a perpendicular side street. Fiona gestured to Micah and Silas. They moved off the sidewalks and slipped into the shadows between apartments.

They crossed several empty back alleys in the darkness, following Theo. It was snowing softly, fat wet flakes drifting down from the sky. The cloud cover was so thick that no stars were visible. Even the moon only let off a glimmer, edging the buildings they passed in hues of faintest silver. The snow gave everything a quiet, muted feeling, like they were the only people left in the world.

A drone whirred almost silently behind them.

Micah flinched, ducking instinctively. It was a surveillance drone, small and H-shaped, not like the large nighthawks bristling with gun turrets. But still.

Fiona laughed softly. She bent and punched Micah's shoulder. "Relax. It's on our side."

Micah hardly dared to straighten. "What? How?"

Theo wheeled to face him, his eyes dancing with pride. "We've managed to snare and hack a bunch of them. We entered our own ghost protocol and released them back into the wild. Even a few nighthawks, too. How do you catch a drone, you may be wondering? The answer? With another drone. Kadek constructed a drone of our own, with a built-in net propulsion feature. It shoots out a twelve-foot-by-twelve-foot carbon-nanotube fiber net. The fibers are stronger than steel; they're unbreakable. And coupled with the propulsion force of—"

"Theo," Fiona chided gently. "Let's not get carried away."

Theo shrugged. "You can see the results for yourself."

Micah watched the surveillance drone whir along above them, both wary and impressed.

Silas looked equally skeptical. "So, you can control these hijacked drones whenever you want to? It's not going to suddenly spazz out and alert every drone within the Sanctuary of our presence?"

Theo grinned. "Of course not. They're completely under our control for as long as we desire. We've commandeered one for tonight to stay with us. The surveillance drones aren't too bright. They're basically programmed to collect and send data and roam pre-gridded zones. They automatically remain a certain distance from other drones to minimize overlapped territory. Which works in our favor. They'll detect our drone and stay away."

"Camera twenty yards to the northeast," Kadek warned as the six-inch long wand-like object he held blinked red. It was a wireless camera finder. "On both eaves of that condo's entrance. Turn your heads forty-five degrees right to avoid the facial-recognition detectors."

Micah's heart rate spiked. He wiped his damp palms on the pants of the blue technician uniforms Kadek had stolen for them.

"But don't look too suspicious," Fiona added. She struck a nonchalant pose and grinned impishly at him. She was dressed like a boy again, her mass of fiery curls stuffed into a gray knit cap. One tiny curl, damp from the falling snow, clung to her cheek.

"As long as we aren't flagged by the surveillance network's system and elevated to a live agent for a risk assessment response, we'll be fine," Theo said. "Don't hunch your shoulders. Don't look at or away from the cameras. For those of us who are chipped, maintain your vital stats at normal levels—heart rate, breathing, perspiration, cortisol levels."

"Easy-peasy," Kadek mumbled.

Micah straightened his shoulders, tried to look normal while still avoiding the cameras, tried to look like his pulse wasn't thudding in his throat, like every muscle in his body wasn't knotted with tension.

Several alleys later, they finally reached their destination—city hall, a tall, gleaming white spire less than a hundred yards from BioGen's headquarters and the capitol. LED security lights bathed the area in crisscrossing patterns of harsh white light and deep shadows. The enormous Unity Square stretched before them—an enormous rectangle of engineered grass rimmed with sidewalks, topiary bushes, and the fanciest residential buildings Micah had seen yet.

Kadek and Fiona took cover behind a chest-high row of manicured hedges across from city hall. A dusting of snow filmed the too-green, perfectly pruned leaves. Theo rolled in after them, with Micah and Silas taking up the rear.

"What happens if we trip an alarm?" Silas asked quietly.

"In case of a security breach, all external doors immediately lock," Theo explained. "The level three security and higher doors require two independent biometric scans to get inside. That's not one but two people. Twice the work, quadruple the danger. Plus, the alarm will alert at least twenty human guards and a few dozen of the nearest drones."

"Not a pretty picture," Kadek said. "So don't trip an alarm."

Micah and Silas exchanged cautious, wary glances. Micah gave a helpless shrug. He fought down his own anxiety. He didn't like it either, but they had to trust that these people knew what they were doing.

They had to trust, period.

They crouched behind the hedges as two guards crossed the grounds in front of the entrance. They strolled around the west corner.

Kadek swiped a timer on his Smartflex. He to his feet and gestured for them to follow. "Now."

Micah and the others strode quickly to the front entrance. He noted the heated concrete with relief. They wouldn't leave snowy footprints.

Theo stretched and pressed his hand against the biometric scanner installed to the left of the revolving glass doors. The scanner beeped and released the lock with a hiss.

They entered the building. The lobby was decorated in shades of peach and cream, with luxurious dove-gray velvet lounge chairs and gilded sconces affixed to the walls. The balconied walls rose several stories on all sides. A hint of moonlight shimmered through a transparent roof at least five stories above them.

"Wait," Fiona hissed. She pulled several items out of her duffle bag and passed them around. They looked like pairs of socks until Micah realized they were microfiber foot covers made to cover the soles of their shoes and muffle their footsteps. Micah yanked them over his wet boots and drew the gun that Theo had given him earlier. Silas did the same.

Kadek eyed the guns warily. "You won't need those."

"We'll see," Silas said. "But I'm bringing it anyway."

They strode silently through the empty lobby, paused at the security checkpoint where Theo passed them through with another biometric read of his palm. They entered the elevator.

Fiona selected the third floor. "Our dear Harold has fourth floor access but works on the third level in Logistics and Supplies. He should be in his office."

Micah bit the inside of his cheek. His mouth was dry. It felt like his tongue was caked with sand. He could have drunk an entire bucket of water and still been thirsty. He'd engaged in his fair share of gun battles, but never a sneaky, covert operation like this.

His stomach twisted in knots. Every hair on his neck stood on end.

"There's an emergency button beneath his desk," Fiona said. "He can also alert the room's AI. We have to stick him before that happens."

They crept along a wide hallway, a balcony overlooking the lobby atrium to their left, a bunch of offices, doors all closed, on their right.

Three offices down, a light shone beneath the door. Micah tensed and tightened his grip on his gun. Fiona angled her chin, indicating that this was the guy they were seeking.

Kadek and Theo hung back out of the doorway's line of sight. Micah and Silas pressed against the wall on either side of the door. Fiona dropped her duffle bag in Theo's lap, removed her knit cap, and shook out her hair. She took a small tube of gloss out of her pocket and daubed it across her lips.

She grinned at Silas as she knocked gently on the door. "Technical support," she said sweetly, pitching her voice higher to sound both more feminine and unthreatening.

"Uh..." came the confused reply from behind the door. "I didn't put in a request for—"

"It's right here on my holopad." Fiona turned the handle and burst through the door with a radiant smile. "My report says your network connection is corrupted. That's why your Net speed has been so slow."

"Oh, well, that makes sense. I have been thinking it hasn't been as efficient lately."

"We'll take care of that for you right now. Just let me have a look at your desk terminal."

"Okay, um, sure thing."

"Great! Thanks so much."

There was a shuffling noise. "Hey!" Herald said in pained surprise. She must have pricked him as she moved to his side of the desk. "What did you just do to me?"

"Nothing to worry yourself about," Fiona purred. "Looks like I can't do anything from here. But I can fix it from the Network Command Center. We can go take care of this right now, if you'd like. I heard you've just been promoted. Congratulations! I always knew you deserved it. You work harder than anyone around here."

There was a pause. Several seconds passed. Micah exchanged a tense look with Silas. Would this actually work? Would the guy buy it? What were they going to do if he didn't?

Finally, Harold Mather said, "Thank...you," in a slow, drawling voice. "Sure...I can take you up there."

"Fantastic. You literally don't know how much this means to me." Fiona appeared, grinning slyly, a sloppily dressed, middle-aged man leaning heavily on her arm. He was a puffy-faced white guy, balding, wearing a suit that looked slightly too small for his bulging gut. "Guys, meet Herald. Herald, these are friends of mine. They're going to hang out with us for a bit."

"Cool..." Herald murmured. His eyes were unfocused, like he was trying unsuccessfully to wake from a deep slumber.

Herald allowed Fiona to tug him along to the elevator, which refused to move until Fiona lifted Herald's palm, pressed it to the biometric scanner, and simultaneously pushed him to the iris scanner. "Look here, please."

The elevator rose to the fourth floor. They hurried down the hallway to a steel-reinforced door marked "Network Terminal." Theo pointed at the last door, "Aerial Security" emblazoned on the front. "They manage the drones in there. I can hack them individually, once we've captured one by hand—"

"Not an easy feat, by the way," Fiona interrupted.

"—but from there, you could control them all through the cloud." Theo's eyes gleamed with the possibilities. "Sadly, not even Herald can help us get in there. Only those with top-secret clearance get inside that room. But think of what we could do with a battalion of drones. Think of how we could—"

"One thing at a time," Fiona said, gently redirecting Theo to the task at hand.

Theo gave her a tense grin. "Right."

Fiona helped Herald press his hand and eye to the security panel. The door hissed and swung open. They slipped into a large white room filled with banks and banks of computer consoles.

They were in.

34

WILLOW

W illow wasn't wearing her boots. They were still in the tent, nestled next to Benjie's smaller pair. The dampness of the snowy ground seeped through her wool socks. She wore her coat, no scarf, the wind slipping icy fingers down the back of her neck.

She inhaled sharply. The cold seared her throat.

Sticks and rocks poked the tender undersides of her feet. She didn't feel the sting. She didn't dare feel it.

There wasn't time or space for anything but the bear.

Hulking and monstrous. Hot breath steaming through its jaws. Bone-crushing jaws. Jaws that could rip Benjie's head from the stalk of his neck, could tear out Finn's spine.

The thought seared her to the core.

Willow could smell the sour stink of it, foul and rancid. It reared up on its hind legs and gave a loud, rumbling growl. Its teeth gleamed white in the moonlight. Darkened saliva smeared the fur below its jaws.

She knew what that meant.

It was infected.

Panic surged in her chest, followed by a crushing, nameless fear. She didn't know what to do. She'd never been in the wild. She didn't know bear behavior. All she could think of was how to get between the people she loved and the thing trying to kill them.

There was no time to think of a plan. She had to act.

Willow raised the rifle. "Run to me, Benjie. *Now!*"

Benjie obeyed. He raced toward her, arms flailing, his face etched in terror.

The bear lurched after him, drawn by his movement.

"HEY!" Finn shouted at the top of his lungs, waving his good arm. He hurled his hunting knife at the grizzly bear's flank. It fell uselessly to the ground.

But the grizzly hesitated, swinging its great head between Finn and Benjie. It turned sideways as if it wasn't sure which direction to charge. It made loud, angry whuffing sounds. Bloody drool soaked its jaws.

This was her chance. Maybe the only one she was going to get.

Time slowed. Every second hammering through her. She aimed, willing her hands to stop shaking, for her shot to strike true. She pulled the trigger.

The bullet punched a pine tree behind the grizzly, spraying it with bark.

Her sweaty fingers nearly slipped off the trigger. She huffed her bangs out of her eyes. *Focus. Focus.* She fought to quiet her thumping heart, to still her ragged breathing. She couldn't hear through the blood roaring in her ears.

Her second shot went wide of the target, merely grazing the grizzly's humped back. Blood streaked an arc across its tangled fur. But it wasn't enough. It wasn't nearly enough.

The grizzly turned on her with a bellow of rage. It squared its massive shoulders, ears pressed back against its skull, and roared. Dark spittle flew from its gaping jaws.

She'd only served to enrage it, to make it even more dangerous. Damn it all to hell.

The bear lunged. It charged her so swiftly, her brain barely had the time to process that the beast had even moved.

She staggered back, heart in her throat, half-turning to run. But it was too late. The grizzly swung a massive paw and struck a glancing blow across her ribs. The impact lifted her off her feet and slammed her against the trunk of an oak tree.

The rifle spun out of her grip. Her head cracked against the hard, unforgiving wood. Her breath rushed from her lungs.

The world spun above her, glittering stars in the sky a swirling, sparkling vortex. Sounds blurred in and out of focus.

She managed to lift her head. Dizziness washed over her, every-thing spinning, spinning. She blinked, forcing her brain to think, her eyes to focus.

Across the clearing, Finn lay on the ground beneath the grizzly. He was on his stomach, his legs tucked beneath him, his hands clenched over his neck, the elbow of his left arm tucked in to protect his side. His right arm hung limp, exposing his ribs.

For a terrible second, she thought he was dead.

Then she heard him. His breathing was heavy and labored. But he was breathing.

The grizzly swiped at him with a roar, biting at the backpack he still wore—the backpack now protecting his spine.

But for how long?

From a great distance, someone was shouting. Indecipherable words. Words that didn't compute. That couldn't compute. Because their meaning was too horrifying to comprehend.

I am Sir Benjie! I am a knight! If you don't leave my friend alone, I will be forced to slay you!

Her brother, impossibly small, impossibly brave, a fierce streak of movement hurtling toward the huge bear, the tiny knife of Finn's multi-tool grasped in one hand.

Her scream shattered the air.

35

MICAH

"Through here," Theo said. "We need the server software access."

The room was much larger than Micah expected, filled with sleek, integrated computer modules and giant wallscreens. The far wall was lined with rows of servers stacked vertically. Thousands of tiny lights blinked like eyes. Thick bundles of cables snaked along the floor and ceiling.

"This is the Sanctuary's command and control center," Theo said with a loving pat on an integrated computer desk. The giant wallscreen in front of him was subdivided into a dozen smaller squares, each displaying individual data feeds. "Security. Communications. Transportation. Dedicated asset management and control. The network. It's all here."

Micah left the door cracked so they could hear anyone approaching. He and Silas stood guard on either side of the door while Theo went to work.

"Now that we're in, we have—" Kadek checked his Smartflex "—nineteen minutes and twelve seconds before the next patrol."

"You neglected to mention that part!" Silas spat furiously.

Kadek shrugged his narrow shoulders. "Oops."

Fiona gestured to Herald, who was swaying on his feet. "Sit over here, Herald. Why don't you take a little nap?"

"I am feeling rather tired," Herald mumbled.

Theo rummaged through Fiona's duffle bag and pulled out something he called a "relay hub" along with a tangle of cables and connectors.

Micah winced at the mess. "Let me untangle these for you."

Theo frowned. "No thanks. I've got it under control."

"No one touches Theo's stuff," Fiona explained. "No one."

"He's kind of uptight about that," Kadek said from the other side of the room, where he was jacking into the building's security footage and redubbing it, erasing their existence.

Theo connected the relay hub's adapter to a power source, then hooked up some sort of satellite antenna to the window. He disconnected the cables from the crypto relays and plugged them into his own with a bit of colorful cursing as he worked to find the correct connections.

Kadek edged a peek around the doorway. "Patrol due in less than ten. Less bragging, more accomplishing tasks, please."

"Well, since you asked nicely." Theo tapped a bunch of codes into the wallscreen, swiping like mad, his tongue protruding slightly in concentration. "I'm disabling the tracking systems, making us ghosts, essentially. There won't be any record of our presence."

He pulled a small oblong object out of his pocket—the thumb drive recorder Harper had passed them from Amelia— and jacked it into a port in the command terminal. The display keyboard pulsed to life on the sleek desk.

Theo let out a breath. "Excellent."

"I wanna go home..." came a muffled voice.

"Herald's waking up," Fiona warned.

"Five minutes!" Kadek said.

Micah's heart rate accelerated. He edged around the doorway, nudged the door open a few inches, and leaned out. His glasses slid down his nose. He jammed them back into place. Empty hallway. Silence. No movement.

Theo grunted. "Just let me splice this footage, synchronize the sound feeds, and I'm good to go."

Kadek wiped a bead of sweat from his brow. "A little faster."

Thirty seconds later, Theo unhooked his relay hub, tangle of cables, and the thumb drive, and pushed away from the bank of servers. "It's scheduled to break into the daily news report at six p.m. tomorrow. That's prime time. Everyone will be watching. Let's go."

They cleaned up, leaving no trace, then descended to the third floor. They left Herald in his office, dumped unceremoniously on his leather sofa. Fiona rumpled his shirt, loosened his tie, and removed his shoes before pulling a half-full bottle of bourbon out of her duffle bag and setting it on the coffee table next to him.

"Smart," Micah said, watching her.

She shrugged like it was nothing, but her cheeks bloomed crimson. "He'll come to think he's waking up after a bender. Anything he thinks he remembers will be sketchy as heck."

"Time to go!" Kadek hissed.

They raced down the hallway, Micah and Silas taking point, clearing each opened door in the hallway. The passing seconds ticked inside Micah's head like a bomb just waiting to go off.

They reached the elevator and ducked inside. Theo activated the biometric scanner. He stuck a thumb drive into the port, swiped in a bunch of code, and deleted the elevator's records for the last hour.

"Don't look now, but two guards are approaching one floor down."

Silas pointed toward a flashlight bobbing along the polished tile below them.

The elevator walls were glass. They offered zero protection. Micah and Silas pressed against the far wall, but it wouldn't make a bit of difference if either of the guards looked up. They were like fish in a transparent barrel.

The elevator descended, achingly slow.

"If they see us, this is all for nothing." Micah bit the inside of his cheeks so hard he tasted blood.

"Whatever you do, don't move," Fiona said out of the corner of her mouth. "They're on the second floor. As soon as we fall below the next floor, they won't see us as long as they don't look over the balcony. We'll be home free."

"Don't count your chickens before they're hatched," Kadek muttered.

"Chickens don't come from eggs anymore, dummy," Fiona said, her body stiff, her lips barely moving.

As the elevator descended, the guards came into view. Micah whispered a silent prayer as the first guard paused to check an opened door, his body half-turned away from the elevators.

The second guard was leaning against the wall, arms crossed, smoking a faux cigarette. He only had to look up to see them, only ten yards away, sliding right past him.

Micah held his breath.

The guard didn't look up.

The elevator crept lower, lower. Finally, it slid below the guards' line of sight.

Silas inhaled a ragged breath. Micah whispered a relieved prayer of thanks. Fiona and Theo gave each other silent fist bumps, grinning like kids. Fiona turned to Silas, fist out, but he just gave her an awkward glare. She shrugged and punched his shoulder instead.

Silas jerked away like she'd stabbed him.

Micah stifled a tense laugh. Someone had a little crush, and Silas had no clue what to do about it.

The elevator continued to the lobby. Before the elevator doors slid open, Fiona put her finger to her lips. They still needed to be absolutely silent to slip out the entrance doors without attracting the notice of the guards upstairs.

Kadek checked his SmartFlex. His eyes widened as he signaled them. One minute before the exterior guards strolled around the front corner.

They strode as quickly as they could to the front entrance, Micah's adrenaline-fueled muscles begging him to run. Fiona reached the glass door first and held it open for Theo. He rolled through, his muscles bulging as he maneuvered the wheelchair with skill and speed.

And then they were all racing across the manicured lawn to the cover of the hedges across the street, where the surveillance drone waited for them like an obedient pet.

The chill in the air was a welcome relief against Micah's hot skin. Breathing hard, he risked a peek over the top of the bushes. Like clockwork, the two exterior guards marched around the corner.

"Time to separate," Theo whispered. "We'll meet at a location still to be determined at ten before six to watch it all go down. I'll message you. Good night and good luck."

Micah and Silas followed Fiona as she slipped off into the darkness, heading for the agricultural sector, the drone drifted along behind them.

The adrenaline slowly seeped from his veins. He shivered, suddenly cold, slightly stunned at how well they'd pulled it off.

A tiny prick of doubt niggled the back of his mind. It had almost seemed easy.

When had anything they'd ever done been easy?

36

WILLOW

Willow's scream ripped from her throat, a primal thing full of love and terror and dread. "Benjie!"

She would switch places with him in a heartbeat, lay herself down to die for him, to bleed every drop from her body if it could save him.

But her body wouldn't move. Her legs and arms were strangely numb. Her head rang with terrible sounds. Her lungs burned from every breath she couldn't take.

She was forced to watch, horrified and helpless, as her eight-year-old brother fearlessly took on a grizzly bear.

Benjie ran straight at the bear. It was still crouched over Finn, clawing at his backpack, growling and snarling. Benjie thrust the small blade into the bear's haunches.

The bear rose with a ferocious roar. It twisted and lunged for Benjie.

Benjie fell, scrambling back on his elbows.

No! Willow screamed. But she didn't know if she'd even made a sound, or if the scream was trapped inside her own head.

"NO!" came again, but it wasn't her voice this time, but a deep, booming shout.

Finn pulled himself to his knees, scrabbling in the snow and leaves and dirt. He whirled, Willow's gun in his left hand. He didn't hesitate a second. He pulled the trigger.

The first shot struck the bear in the right shoulder. It roared and reared onto its hind legs. It swung its head, searching with wild, murderous eyes for the source of its pain. Its massive paws dangled over Benjie's body, deadly claws glinting.

Benjie cowered. He curled his arms over his head. It wasn't enough. All seven hundred pounds of the grizzly would slam down, crushing Benjie's bones to dust, shredding muscle and skin and flesh.

Run! Willow screamed. *Move!* But maybe that was a mistake. Maybe if he ran, he would only draw the bear's attention.

Maybe he was doomed either way.

Her breath slammed back into her lungs. She inhaled a single, shuddering breath. "FINN!"

Finn stumbled toward the bear. He lifted the gun again and fired. The bullet went wide, smashing against the branches somewhere above their heads. The bear bellowed, still on his hind legs. He took a step away from Benjie, his head swiveling toward Finn.

Finn fired another shot. Missed. His arm shook.

He shot again. The bullet struck the grizzly in the gut. Dark blood gleamed black, matting the creature's fur. It still didn't retreat. It didn't fall. It didn't leave.

How many bullets did it take? How many were left?

Her head cleared, painfully slow.

One. One bullet left.

"Leave. Him. Alone!" Finn screamed. He ran toward Benjie, toward the bear, close enough that he wouldn't miss. Couldn't miss, even if it killed him. A single lunge, one strike of that powerful paw, and it would be over.

Bloody saliva glistened from the grizzly's jaws. It lumbered toward Finn, still towering on its hind legs. Finn aimed for the creature's skull. He pulled the trigger.

The bear's head snapped back. It moaned, staggered, and fell with an earth-shaking thud.

It moaned again, eyes rolling wildly in their sockets, jaw working, paws scraping at the snow like it could climb right back to its feet again.

But it didn't. It couldn't.

With a final, wounded groan, the great bear shuddered and died.

"Benjie!" Willow scrambled over rocks and hard-packed snow, crawling on her hands and knees, oblivious to the cold and scratches. She reached Benjie and yanked him into her arms. He was warm and soft and alive, so damn alive.

"I'm okay, Lo Lo," he said in a shaky voice.

She choked back a sob. "I thought you were dead. I thought I'd lost you!"

"I'm right here."

She checked him all over for blood, for punctures, for bite marks. She patted his arms, legs, head, chest. His right cheek was scratched. A huge bruise already swelled an ugly purplish yellow on his forehead. His coat was torn in several places, including five gashes slashing across his left arm.

She tugged off his coat, her gut clenching, expecting tattered flesh, severed tendons, damage beyond hope of repair.

But only three of the bear's claws had pierced Benjie's skin. The cuts were bleeding, but she didn't see bone or muscle. The blow had been a shallow, glancing one.

The grizzly had been too distracted by Finn and Willow. It hadn't had the chance to focus its attack on any of them individually—which was why they were alive.

"I had to save Finn." Benjie endured her ministrations without moving. Tears mingled with dirt streaked his face. "I had to do my brave thing."

"You did, Sir Benjie." Finn stood in the center of the clearing, half-bent, his hand on his leg. He was breathing hard, white breath puffing from his mouth. His whole body was trembling. "You saved me."

Benjie managed a tremulous grin. "And then you saved me."

"Shall we just agree that we all saved each other?" Willow helped Benjie to his feet. She took her own unsteady steps—her ribs screaming, her head splitting. But now that Benjie was safe, she wouldn't let anything stop her from reaching Finn.

She went to him, her heart surging in her chest, relief and hope and love pumping through every vein in her body. She didn't hesitate. She wrapped her arms around his huge chest. "Are you okay?"

He sucked in a tremulous breath, dropped the gun, and pulled her into an embrace with his good arm. "That thing just took 'mean as a bear with a toothache' to a whole new level."

"That's not an answer, you big oaf." Her tears were cold as ice on her cheeks. She bit back another sob. If she started now, she'd never stop.

"I didn't think I could do it. I didn't want to kill it. But I did," he said unsteadily. "I did what I had to do."

He squeezed her tighter. She never wanted to leave the warmth of his arms. "You saved us."

37

AMELIA

"Aren't you having the best time?" Vera leaned against an elegant marble column and fingered the pearl necklace at her throat. "These galas are simply fabulous!"

"Immensely," Amelia lied. She touched the voluminous folds of her gown, which radiated shades of sapphire, lapis, and cobalt, the luxuriant fabric soft as cashmere. President Sloane's stylists had spun a French braid around the crown of her head, the lower half of her hair cascading down her back in glossy waves.

She held a crystal goblet of wine in one hand, but she hadn't taken a single sip. Her stomach was too knotted with anxiety to enjoy anything.

She was attending a gala full of officials, advisers, and scientists as everyone gathered for a grand celebration. The twenty test subjects' fevers had broken the night before. The twelve-year-old boy was weak but on his feet.

Serum 341 worked. They'd found a cure.

The gala was held inside the capitol, in a grand hall of marble, black granite, and crystal. The room swirled with silk and perfume. Crystal chandeliers hung from the vaulted ceiling.

Amelia wasn't sure what she had expected of the Sanctuary, but it wasn't this. She'd thought it would resemble the government's underground bunkers, modest and practical, with an emphasis on security, safety, and survival, not extravagance. But when had the elites ever been anything but extravagant?

She glanced across the room at President Sloane. Sloane's gown was a soft lemon-yellow chiffon, draping over her svelte form in undulating waves. Her long fingers were adorned with a half-dozen winking garnet, ruby, and sapphire rings. She was surrounded by advisers, generals, and the other members of the Coalition, along with her retinue of staff. Amelia recognized her chief of staff, Selma Perez, as well as Senator Steelman and General Daugherty.

The president's head of security, Angelo Bale, stood like an imposing mountain behind her. Bale was statue-still. Only those beady eyes roved intently, taking in every detail.

At President Sloane's left hand, Declan Black beguiled the crowd with his magnetic presence. He plucked an hors d'oeuvre from a passing silver tray laden with slivered meats, gourmet cheeses, and other delicacies. He popped it in his mouth and said something charming, letting out a booming chuckle. The group turned to him with eager, upturned faces, laughing appreciatively at whatever he'd just said.

Amelia dragged her gaze away and scanned the rest of the grand hall. At least thirty soldiers were stationed between the pillars throughout the room, dressed in sharp gray uniforms and white gloves.

Both Harper and Quentin were here, never straying too far from her side. She'd met Harper's gaze earlier in the evening. Harper had given her the slightest nod before averting her eyes. Quentin ignored her, as always.

But it seemed he was the only one. All evening, she'd felt eyes on her, scrabbling like spiders. President Sloane's aids and advisers. The scientists and doctors she'd passed in the hallways of BioGen's lab, never learning anyone's name. Senator Steelman's shrewd gaze, following her every movement as if waiting for her to trip, to make a mistake.

So Amelia drank wine and champagne. She laughed and she danced with Vera and her father and she ate caviar and tried not to feel sick. She was every inch the charming daughter her father desired, the sweetly innocent but oh-so-brave survivor President Sloane wished to show off.

She knew what they wanted. And she gave it to them.

The wallscreen flickered to life, and the crowd turned to watch the daily update. The same message was echoed on every Smartflex and holoscreen throughout the city. Amelia's breath quickened, her skin hot and clammy. The Patriots had received the recording. It was up to them now. When would it happen? Tonight? Right now?

She barely heard the droning voice-over as she took in the images of disease and destruction. A drone captured footage of a FEMA holding facility for the infected somewhere in the Midwest. It was nothing more than a fifty-acre field inside a reinforced electrified fence. Lining the barbed wire fence were steel-girded watchtowers equipped with machine guns turned inward, aimed at the dirty, terri-fied faces of hundreds of men, women, and children. Some of them coughing heavily, others pale with fever, many curled up in make-shift beds, too sick to stand. A secondary fence contained the bodies, stacked chest-high against the barrier.

Amelia's stomach lurched. Acid burned the back of her throat. So many sick, dying, and dead. How quickly could the Sanctuary manu-facture and distribute the vaccine? How many millions—billions were already dead? Was it already too late to make a difference?

She glanced at Vera out of the corner of her eye. She was facing the screen, but her eyes were vacant, unfocused. She wasn't really watching. She didn't want to see.

Vera pinched the bridge of her nose and gave a world-weary sigh. "It's just so damn depressing."

A sharp edge of anger sliced through Amelia. Like Vera would know. Like she had any idea what it was like out there, how so many had suffered and died, what it took to survive. They were just images on a screen to her. They weren't real. They weren't a part of the world Vera knew. Not before, and not now, safe behind the walls of the Sanctuary.

Guilt pricked her. This was why Willow and Gabriel had despised her when they'd first met. Her old self would have reacted the same way. She had deserved their derision for this, at least.

She reigned in her anger, swallowing a sharp retort that would've made Willow proud. She managed a gracious nod instead. "Now, with the cure, we can really help them. We can open our gates and save everyone."

"That's just what I was thinking." Vera pasted a tight smile on her face and gestured for a hover tray filled with fresh champagne. "Another glass? I'm parched."

"Thank goodness we don't have to worry about that anymore," President Sloane said as the newsfeed wound down. She turned away from the screen with an elegant swirl of her skirts and raised her goblet.

Her staff lifted their glasses. "Here, here," they chorused.

Abruptly, the newsfeed cut out. There was a moment of static. Then the head and shoulders of a digital avatar appeared: a bald, vaguely human, bluish figure with a shimmer like a hologram. His deep, baritone voice was modulated to imitate a computerized AI. "Citizens of Sanctuary, you have been deceived. The government you've trusted to keep you safe from the Hydra virus is the same government who knowingly and intentionally unleashed it upon you, their own people."

Gasps echoed throughout the grand hall. Guests glanced at each other, eyebrows raised in alarm. Others just stared at the screen, mouths hanging open, shocked.

Vera set her glass on a passing tray and swiped at her Smartflex with a frown. "How in the world..."

"What is this?" Selma Perez asked in confusion.

"Get it off the screen!" Senator Steelman barked, jabbing her finger uselessly at the wallscreen.

"We bring you evidence that Declan Black, chairman of the Coalition, not only had knowledge of the bioweapon attack, but orchestrated it," the avatar continued.

"It's on the entire network!" Vera stared aghast at the incoming data streaming to her Smartflex.

"Shut down the network!" Declan shouted. "It's a hoax! Take it down!"

General Daugherty put his finger to his earpiece, either taking or giving orders as he strode hurriedly from the room, flanked by eight soldiers.

"It'll take a minute," Perez said. "We're working on it."

"We don't have a minute!" Declan roared.

But it was too late.

The screen filled with a view of Declan Black's penthouse, the quartz table and the gently undulating jellyfish in the wall aquarium. Declan himself turned toward the hidden camera, admitting everything in his own words: "*I did what was required...We sacrificed a few to save the many, to ensure our national interests and survival as a nation...No one could have foreseen how the Hydra virus mutated...*"

"Citizens, you have the truth," the avatar said. "Now, you must act. Overthrow your corrupt government and start again. We can work together to build a new world, a new society based on freedom and choice, not fear and tyranny."

The wallscreen went dark. The grand hall fell into a deafening silence. The scientists and staff gaped. Amelia stood frozen, the wine glass still in her hand, her blood rushing in her ears.

She'd done this. It really happened. Now her father would know how she'd betrayed him...

"Is this real?" Perez asked incredulously. "Tell me this isn't real."

Everyone stared at Declan Black in confusion and suspicion. Several people moved away from him, as if he'd just contracted the Hydra virus himself. The soldiers manning the outskirts of the gala rushed toward Declan but didn't touch him. Their hands hovered over their pulse guns, just waiting for the president's orders.

"Of course not," Declan spat. His fists were clenched, his shoulders stiff, his eyes flashing with rage. "It's a joke. A ridiculous charade—"

"It's real." President Sloane stepped back, shock and fury contorting her features. "Security, take Declan Black into custody immediately."

Two dozen guards swarmed Declan. He tried to wrench free, his face purpling with outrage, but the guards were already forcing him to his knees, yanking his hands behind his back.

"You did this!" he shouted.

Amelia shrank back against a pillar. But he wasn't looking at her. He was looking at someone else, someone she couldn't see in the crowd—

"How dare you do this to me!" he cried. "If you think you're going to get away with—"

"Stun him!" President Sloane ordered. "I will not listen to one more word from this traitor's mouth!"

Bale pulled a stun gun and shot Declan before President Sloane had even finished speaking. Declan's body juddered. A second later, he slumped to the floor, unconscious. The guards hauled him up and dragged his limp body from the grand hall.

"No wonder he found the cure," Vera sniffed. "He was the one who created the virus in the first place." She turned and stared at Amelia, her expression going hard and suspicious. "Did you know? Were you a part of this?"

Suddenly, everyone's eyes were on her. Senator Steelman was staring at her with open hostility and suspicion. "Her timing is a bit too perfect, don't you think, Madam President? The daughter of a terrorist shows up and just happens to have the cure in her blood? And you're going to stand here and tell us you're innocent?"

"I am," she forced out. She didn't know how to defend herself. Anything she said would make her look like she was concealing the truth behind a veil of unconvincing lies.

The room echoed with the buzz of dozens of confused, angry voices. This is what her mother was afraid of. She believed the people would blame Amelia, simply for being her father's daughter.

Sweat broke out on her forehead. "What he did was—I would never—"

"Of course not!" President Sloane strode across the black polished floor. She wrapped a comforting arm around Amelia's shoulder, steadying her, and raised her voice so everyone in the room could hear. "Amelia Black is an innocent bystander. She has already proven her loyalty by submitting to test after invasive test to help our scientists develop a way to stop the insidious Hydra virus. She is not a suspect. No one here should treat her as anything but an honored citizen."

Relief flooded through Amelia. She glanced up at President Sloane gratefully, sorry she'd ever suspected this woman of foul play. She was clearly incensed at Declan's behavior, willing to bring him to justice while also trusting and protecting Amelia. It was more than she'd expected. "Thank you."

Sloane smiled warmly at Amelia before turning to the rest of the crowd. Her expression hardened. "I suspected someone in the government must have colluded with the terrorists, but I was never sure who without proof. I don't know how you accomplished that little feat with the recording, but I thank you. Everyone here thanks you profusely.

"Declan Black may have just found us the cure, but he is also a terrorist. And he will pay for his crimes. Every single citizen must know how the Sanctuary deals with terrorism—swiftly and decisively." President Sloane's lips tightened in a thin, bloodless line. "For his crimes against humanity, Declan Black will be executed by firing squad."

Amelia felt sharp and brittle, dangerously close to shattering into a thousand pieces. What had she expected? Not this, not so soon. She was prepared for imprisonment, a trial—but this?

Shaking, she touched the charm bracelet dangling from the leather thong around her neck. It offered no comfort.

She took in a shuddering breath but still couldn't get enough oxygen into her lungs. Everything went blurry and distant. She swayed on her feet.

"Amelia, darling," said a voice from far away.

"I want to go home," she whispered.

"You are home," the voice said.

Her legs felt like water. She slumped against the nearest pillar. "I want Micah. I want to see my brother."

Strong arms gripped her shoulders, keeping her up.

"We'll find them soon, don't worry," President Sloane said.

"Take her to her quarters," someone murmured.

She blinked, trying to focus. "I don't want to stay here."

"Oh, darling," Vera said sweetly, "there's nowhere else to go."

"Get a doctor," President Sloane ordered. "She's distraught. Not in her right mind, poor child."

Amelia wanted to argue, to scream, to run. She could do none of those things.

She couldn't do anything at all.

38

WILLOW

Willow couldn't sleep, not with the adrenaline still spiking through her veins. Benjie was safely snuggled in the tent next to her, curled up like a puppy in Finn's sleeping bag. After the attack, Benjie had clutched her hand with white-knuckled ferocity, refusing to let go or loosen his grasp. An hour later, he'd finally collapsed into exhausted sleep.

After checking to make sure Benjie was still sleeping, she climbed out of the tent, wincing from the shot of pain in her side. The world was silvered in moonlight. Finn sat on the overturned log, hunched over the dying campfire.

"You okay?" she whispered.

He looked up at her, his face strained, his eyes huge. "Benjie almost died. You almost died."

"We're alive," she said. "We're okay, Finn."

They were all bruised and battered. Willow was pretty sure one of her ribs was bruised, maybe fractured. The back of her head throbbed from where she'd cracked it against the tree trunk. Blood still trickled down her scalp.

But they were alive. Safe.

Finn's gaze dropped back to his hands. His shoulders were tense, his lips pressed together in a thin, bloodless line.

"What's a bear mauling between friends?" she quipped. But when he didn't flash his usual crooked grin or even look up, she knew something wasn't right.

This wasn't like Finn. Something was bothering him.

She hobbled over to the campfire and sank down on the log next to him, adjusting herself gingerly to keep the pain in her side to a minimum. The bottoms of her socks were soaked from the snow and tinted red. The soles of her feet stung and burned. She would fix them up with the antiseptic spray from her pack later. But right now, Finn needed her more.

The warmth of his body pressed against hers. She breathed in his familiar scent. "What's wrong?"

He flexed his left hand. His right remained stubbornly limp. He inhaled sharply. "I thought I'd lost you."

"I'm right here."

"I was wrong," he said, still not looking at her. "I thought I could never use a knife or a gun to hurt a living thing. But I can. I did. I had to.

"When that second bear came crashing into the clearing—I thought it was over. That was it. We'd survived so much, and it was all going to end in the middle of nowhere, for no reason. I couldn't let that happen. I didn't even think about my own life, Willow." He cleared his throat, his voice gritty. "All I thought about was protecting you and Benjie."

"The man protecting the woman is so last century." But it sounded lame and stupid. She *had* needed help. Benjie would be dead without Finn. Probably she would be, too.

They were a family. Families protected each other.

She rubbed her hands together in front of the fire, suddenly very aware of how close they were sitting, how his leg was only an inch from hers. "I felt the same way."

He said the words so softly she barely heard them. "I don't know what I would do without you."

The wind picked up, scraping through the trees. Somewhere, icicles tinkled against each other. Her whole body stiffened. "What?"

"I mean," he stammered, "I know your heart belongs to someone else. I'm not the kind of guy who'd try to get in the way of that, so don't worry—"

"Wait. Back the heck up. What?"

He poked at the frozen ground with a stick. "You and Silas..."

Her heart stuttered. She gaped at him.

He sighed. "You're going to make me say it, aren't you? I know you love Silas."

"I do love Silas," she said, amazed at the words coming out of her own mouth. She'd never thought of it that way, but as soon as she'd spoken, she knew it was true. She cared deeply for Silas, loved him even—the prickly bastard.

Finn's face fell. He gave a pained smile that didn't reach his eyes. "He's got a hard shell, but I'm sure there's some humanity deep inside him...somewhere."

Willow snorted. She tried to imagine Silas in a romantic situation, with a girlfriend or boyfriend he'd have to actually be nice to—but it was impossible. "Finn. Silas and I are friends."

"Yeah, I know."

"We're *only* friends."

"Oh." He sounded surprised, slightly confused, possibly hopeful. Her heart leapt. "All this time, you've thought...?"

"Yeah, I did." He shook his head, rolled his shoulders, sucked in a breath. Like he was preparing for something. "I guess you might think I'm an idiot for this, but I need to tell you something—"

Willow put her finger to his lips. His breath warmed her hand. She'd had enough of words. She'd almost lost the two people that meant the most in the entire world. They were her everything.

Life was too short not to take risks. Not to take the leap. Hadn't they learned that these last desperate months? Hadn't they learned it again tonight?

She was tired of being scared, of feeling weak, of giving in to her own doubts. She was the girl who'd scaled the outside of a cruise ship in the middle of a hurricane to save her brother. She was the girl who'd killed a Headhunter to protect her own, who blew up a thousand rats in a sewer to save everyone she cared about.

What the hell was she so scared of now?

Here he was, big goofy beautiful Finn, smelling like wood smoke with his huge brown eyes, and an uncertain crooked grin and that adorable gap between his front teeth that always made her blood fizz, that made her stomach flutter, that made her want to do so many things she never thought she would—

And then his hand was on hers, tentative, questioning, so light it felt like the brush of a bird's wing. She exhaled softly. She couldn't tear her gaze away from the earnest warmth of his brown eyes.

Finn leaned in and kissed her.

Her lips opened, startled. But she didn't pull away.

He kissed her again, his lips barely brushing hers, soft and gentle, still hesitant, asking the question her heart was screaming at her to answer.

She kissed him back. Harder, more insistent, leaning into him. Her heart was soaring, her palms damp, her stomach a flutter of thrilled panic.

The world around them was a dark, frozen wonderland, but right here was heat, flame, fireworks.

Life.

Dizziness flushed through her. Willow leaned back with a heady gasp, catching her breath. She lost her balance, her arms flailing. She nearly fell off the log like an idiot, rendered immobile by the sparks sizzling through her veins and exploding in her stomach.

"Sorry." Her face burned. Pain seared her ribs. She ignored it, waved her hand sheepishly. "I'm not exactly used to this."

"I don't exactly mind." Finn flashed her favorite lopsided grin. He tugged her hand and she went to him. She settled into his lap as he wrapped his strong arm around her. She leaned into him and pressed her face into his broad chest, closing her eyes.

She loved the sound of his heartbeat, so steady and safe, so reassuring.

She had to be strong all the time. Out in the wild, she could never let her guard down. But here, with Finn, she knew she could. She wanted to.

"I really like you, Willow Bahaghari."

"I—I like you, too."

"How'd I do? I was going for sexy and suave and smooth."

"Smooth as gravel, you big oaf," she said into his chest, smiling.

They kissed again—longer, deeper, hungrier.

They were so focused on each other that they didn't see the pair of yellow eyes or sense the dark shape slinking through the trees until it was right on top of them.

Finn gasped. Willow leapt up, tuning out her body's aching protest. Whipping her handgun from its holster, she spun around, aiming at shadows.

Or, more specifically, one shadow.

"Took you long enough," came a voice from the woods. A figure eased into the clearing and stepped off her hoverboard. She flung back her hood, revealing glossy black hair and a small, tough face, her mouth twisted in a wry smile.

Shadow and Raven had found them.

The End

ACKNOWLEDGMENTS

Thank you to my awesome beta readers. Your thoughtful critiques and enthusiasm are invaluable, as always: Lauren Nikkel, Kimberley Trembley, Michelle Browne, Leslie Spurrier, Jazmin Cybulski, Jeremy Steinkraus, and Barry and Derise Marden.

To Michelle Browne for being a great developmental and line editor. And to Eliza Enriquez for catching those last little proofreading errors.

To my husband, who always helps with deadlines and plot holes and listens patiently to problems about imaginary people.

And to my kids, who are my everything.

ABOUT THE AUTHOR

Kyla Stone is an emerging author of contemporary young adult fiction and apocalyptic dystopian novels. She lives in Atlanta, Georgia with her husband, two children, and two spoiled cats. When she's not writing or spending time with her family, she loves to read, hike, draw, travel, and play games. Her favorite food is dark chocolate.

Kyla loves to hear from her readers. For news and new releases, visit her at:

www.FaceBook.com/KylaStoneBooks

www.Amazon.com/author/KylaStone

Email her at KylaStone@yahoo.com

PART I

SNEAK PEEK OF RAGING LIGHT: THE LAST SANCTUARY BOOK FIVE

1

MICAH

"They're not doing anything," Nineteen-year-old Micah Ramos Rivera said. "Why aren't they doing anything?"

He stood with Silas, Theo, Fiona, and Kadek outside a bot-repair center in sector three. They leaned against the wall, Smartflexes and holopads in hand, pretending to be engrossed in the latest vlogger feed while surreptitiously scanning the crowds.

Dozens of Sanctuary citizens were out and about, hurrying to jobs or home for lunch or strolling with small children, all hunched inside their coats. Their faces were more tense, the shadows under their eyes deeper perhaps, but they were still going about their daily business.

There was no uprising. No protests. No revolt.

Four nights ago, President Sloane had put out an emergency broadcast, a mere twenty minutes after they had hijacked the network. She'd sat calmly in her presidential suite, modeled to resemble the Oval Office in the White House, and informed the people she would do everything in her power to determine the truth.

"I've been listening to my co-workers, my family, anyone I could get close enough to overhear," Fiona said, twirling a bright-red curl between her fingers. "They're angry, sure, but they feel helpless. Two elite women were going on and on about how Declan Black's confession must have been coerced or faked. How easy it was to manipulate pixels."

Silas shoved his hands deep in his pockets. His gray eyes were cold, hard. Micah wasn't sure what he was thinking. How did he really feel about all of this? Declan Black was his father, after all. But Silas was an enigma. His face revealed nothing.

"Or they say it was Declan Black acting on his own, a rogue agent, that there was no way our government would ever kill their own citizens," Kadek said. He spat in disgust.

"They don't want to believe," Micah said, still watching Silas.

"Or they'd have to do something about it." Kadek's narrow face darkened. "If they believe the government intentionally harmed their own citizens, how could they stay here and continue to trust that same government? They couldn't. But this is the only place they're safe. So it's better to disbelieve evidence they've seen with their own eyes than to risk their safety and the people they love, the few who are still alive."

"I understand it," Theo said, his voice cracking. He held an unopened bag of gummy worms in his hands. He twisted the bag over and over, crumpling it between his fingers. He had been uncharacteristically subdued since the broadcast. Micah didn't know him well, but he'd been full of optimism and enthusiasm all the time Micah spent with him. He truly was nothing like his sister. "I don't agree with it, but I understand."

Fiona glanced at the time on her SmartFlex. "Thirty seconds until President Sloane's broadcast."

They stared up at the huge holoscreen affixed to the five-story building across the street. All over the city, ads, vlogs, and video feeds cut out on every screen and holoport and SmartFlex. A tiny version popped up in glowing 3D over Theo's, Fiona's, and Kadek's wrists.

"Citizens of the Sanctuary," President Sloan announced. She was standing on a raised platform before the marble steps of the capitol, the grand, ornate building gleaming white behind her. She was surrounded by a retinue of secret service agents, soldiers, advisers, and generals.

Micah sucked in a startled breath. Amelia stood beside President Sloane, dressed in slate-colored silk dress and a chinchilla-gray fur shrug. Her hair was long again, blowing like a white-blonde ribbon in the frigid wind.

President Sloane's hands gripped the narrow, transparent podium. A hovercam floated a foot from her face. Her jaw was set, her eyes grim. She projected power and authority, someone fully capable of enacting justice and keeping her people in line. "After seriously investigating the accusations made against former BioGen CEO Declan Black," she announced, "the Coalition has determined the validity of the televised confession and Declan Black's guilt."

Everyone within sight stopped whatever they were doing. They craned their necks to stare up at the closest holoscreen or peered down at their Smartflexes.

"The investigation found that Declan Black acted as a lone wolf, manipulating the government and deceiving those who most trusted him. He is a terrorist and traitor of the worst caliber, his every intent and motive to destroy the very fabric of this great nation and the world."

"She's still lying," Micah whispered. There was no way Declan Black acted alone. "The Coalition was involved. They had to be."

"This will not stand," President Sloane continued, her strong voice carrying over the wind and the American and Coalition flags whipping behind her. "For his crimes, he will be sentenced to die by firing squad at six p.m. on January thirtieth, in two days, right here in Unity Square in front of the capitol. Attendance is mandatory. We will eradicate this threat to our safety, to the well-being of our children, I promise you that.

"If any among you would plot against that safety and attempt to take it from us, we will retaliate with the full force of our power. We will find you, and you will pay for your crimes against humanity, just as Declan Black will do." She leaned over the podium, her eyes glittering intently. "Hold your children close tonight and sleep in peace. Tomorrow is a new day."

Her gaze slanted at Amelia, hovering there for a moment longer than necessary. Then she turned back to the cameras and lifted her right arm, punching the air with her fist. "Unity through might. Freedom through strength. Peace through safety!"

The Coalition's symbol appeared—a white triangle with the American flag flying behind a menacing sword—hovering over thousands of Smartflexes and holo ports before winking out.

The regular ads returned, a buzz of nonsense that Micah instantly tuned out. He spun to face Theo. "What now? Why is Amelia there and not here? What's going on?"

Theo sighed heavily. "I don't know."

Silas glared at him. "That's unacceptable!"

Theo didn't answer. He tilted his head back and gazed up at the darkening sky. From the west, a bank of black, billowing clouds was rolling in. "Storm's coming."

"What are you thinking?" Fiona asked Theo quietly.

"We have no choice now." Theo balled up his bag of gummy worms and shoved it in his pocket. "If Amelia can't get us the cure, and the people just accept President Sloane's word that Black is the only mastermind, then Cleo's plan wins." He sounded tired. Angry and defeated. "We have no choice but to take the Sanctuary by force."

"Amelia promised to smuggle out the cure!" Micah said. "She's going to do it. She just needs more time."

Theo shook his head sadly. "We're out of time."

"Sloane and all the Coalition minions will be on the stage for the execution," Fiona said. "That's the time to take them out. We can get a message to General Reaver and coordinate the attack."

Silas surged toward her, his expression ferocious. "Amelia might be on that stage."

Fiona threw up her hands and retreated a step, her back against the white quartz wall of an apartment building. "I'm just saying. It's an idea."

"Amelia can't be hurt." Micah knew he should stop Silas, step between him and Fiona and the others, but the sickening, wrenching sensation in the pit of his stomach prevented him. All he could think of was the danger threatening Amelia from every side. "Do you hear me?"

"You should leave," Kadek said as he forced himself between Fiona and Silas. His narrow features sharpened, his gaze bristling with hostility. "Now."

Theo spread his hands. "Everyone back up ten paces and take a breath."

"This isn't helping anyone," Micah said. "Not Amelia, not us, not the cause."

Kadek and Silas glared at each other for a long, tense moment.

"Fine." Silas unclenched his fists. He stepped back, palms up, standing down.

Micah took a relieved breath. Fighting among themselves helped nothing.

Fiona crossed her arms over her chest. "He's still right. It's not safe for you here anymore. You heard Sloane's announcement. Anyone she finds, she'll just lump them in with Declan Black. And she's definitely still looking for you. They've increased patrols threefold since our network hack."

"It's going to be incredibly dangerous for you here," Theo said heavily. "War is coming. My mother and Cleo will attack in only a few days' time. I don't know how much longer we can assure your safety."

"We can sneak you out tonight," Kadek said. "The Sanctuary is more concerned with what's coming in than what's going out. We can get you out the service entrance. We'll hijack a few of the nighthawks to give us cover just in case."

Micah and Silas exchanged glances. Silas shook his head. Micah gave a small jerk of his chin in agreement. They were in this together.

"We aren't leaving without Amelia," Silas said.

Theo rubbed his forehead. "Did you see the guards surrounding her? There were dozens. There's no way we can reach her."

Silas whirled and pointed a shaking finger at Theo's chest. "You let her go into the lion's den, *unprotected*, and now you're not going to get her out?"

"What about Harper?" Micah asked. "She can help us."

"Harper is only one person," Fiona said.

Micah shoved his glasses up the bridge of his nose with his thumb. Anxiety roiled in his stomach. He felt sick. "I thought you said you had more soldiers on your side."

"Not ones with that kind of access," Kadek said. "Look, Cleo anticipated this. That's why she went ahead with the plans for attack."

"Anticipated what?" Silas asked in a low, dangerous voice.

"Amelia is an elite. She's one of them. It makes sense that she'd want to stay here, in comfort and decadence—"

"No!" Micah said too loudly. Several people glanced their way. He lowered his voice. "No. You don't know what you're saying. You don't know her."

"Amelia would never do that," Silas said.

Micah glanced at Silas. Only a few short weeks ago, Silas had expressed his own doubts. But now his jaw was set, his body rigid, his eyes flashing with anger at Kadek's insinuation. "If you won't help us, we'll go get her on our own."

"And get yourselves killed," Kadek snapped.

Fiona put a soothing hand on Silas's arm. He jerked his arm back like she was infected. A shadow of hurt passed across her face. "We underestimated her security. I'm sorry. I imagine even if she wanted to leave—"

"She does!" Silas hissed.

"She looked pretty happy next to the president in her fancy dress," Kadek snapped.

Silas stared daggers at Kadek. "She did the same thing for my father. I guarantee you she wasn't happy then. And she's not happy now. So why don't you shut your mouth before I make you—"

Kadek strode forward until he was inches from Silas's face. "Are you threatening me?"

A two-guard patrol rounded the corner down the street. A nighthawk glided above them.

"Keep your voices down!" Micah moved beside Silas. He turned to Theo, Kadek, and Fiona with steely determination. "We're not leaving. No matter what's coming. We're not leaving Amelia behind."

Grab your copy of *Raging Light* for the epic conclusion
to *The Last Sanctuary* series.